Wadhurst Ghost Stories

James Ward

COOL MILLENNIUM BOOKS

1

This is a work of fiction. All names, characters, and events are the product of the author's imagination, or used fictitiously. All resemblance to actual events, places, events or persons, living or dead, is entirely coincidental.

First paperback edition 2022

A CIP catalogue record for this book is available from the British Library.

ISBN: 978-1-913851-54-5

Cover picture shows a view from Primmers Green towards St Peter and St Paul Church.

This novel was produced in the UK and uses British-English language conventions ('authorise' instead of 'authorize', 'The government are' instead of 'the government is', etc.)

To Arthur
who always loved Wadhurst

"The ghost should be malevolent or odious. Amiable or helpful apparitions are all very well in fairy tales or local legends, but I have no use for them in a fictitious ghost story."
MR James, *More Ghost Stories of an Antiquary* (1911)

"Literature is either essential or it is useless. I believe that the Evil - an intense form of the Evil - which literature expresses, has an absolute value for us. But it does not exclude morality. Quite the reverse: it requires a 'hypermorality'."
Georges Bataille, *La Littérature et La Mal* (1957)

Contents

The Ancient Serpent	7
The Strange Birth of the Oilman	51
The Wealden Excelsior	87
The Wadhurst Obelisk	123
The Never House	157
Dr Jenkinson's Machine	188
Roddy Samhain	238

The Ancient Serpent

I.

As a junior lecturer, Ijeoma, my girlfriend, always had her hands full. Giving lectures to undergraduates – the thing that, given her job title, you'd think would be her bread and butter - was less than a quarter of it. Above all, she spent her time writing or researching. As she told it, everyone at her professional level was similarly overloaded, mainly because they felt insecure. There were too few tenured posts. There was too much pressure to write and publish papers for which 'enough' research could never be undertaken. In fact, outside sleep, I'd say research took up most of her life; it certainly extended well into her leisure time, sometimes hijacking it for weeks, even months at a time.

Superficially, it wasn't a recipe for a happy relationship. I had what I'd call a 'normal' job; by which I mean, it began every day at nine and ended at five, excluding weekends. We lived in a small flat above a shop on the edge of a housing estate in Oxford. We were hoping to get married sometime within the next twelve months.

Yet, maybe because of the deeper things, we *were* happy. For a start, we shared the same interests. Yes, we'd grown up in different parts of the country (she was from Bristol, I hailed from Betws-y-Coed), but since she was only two years younger than me, our early years had been defined by the same social and political milestones. Maybe those particular events, coming on top of our similar upbringings in terms of values –

work hard, be kind, show good manners, etc. – gave us topics of conversation we could always fall back on and even agree about. It's just a theory.

I don't know when I first noticed something was 'wrong' with her. I think it was one Thursday evening late in December. I remember glancing at the clock as I heard her coming up the communal staircase outside. More unpaid overtime, I thought: she'll be dispirited and shattered. I'd made a carbonara bake, and I couldn't see her eating more than half of it. She'd have 'snacked' on the way home.

But she came through the door with a spring in her step, and a hint of a mischievous smile. She deposited her two bags carefully in the cupboard next to the bedroom, put her arms round me and kissed my neck; she asked if she could help in the kitchen; she said something about the lovely smell; she poured herself a glass of wine that somehow looked, in the controlled relish of her gestures, more celebratory than compensatory; she talked cheerfully about four or five articles she'd read in the free newspaper on the bus ride home.

We ate the meal I'd prepared, sitting up in bed, watching something forgettable on TV. Afterwards, she sang Jorja Smith songs in the shower.

"Good day at the office?" I asked when she got back in bed.

"I feel rejuvenated," she replied. "And no, I haven't 'met someone'."

"I never suggested you had."

"It's going to sound really weird when I tell you. Okay, here goes. I've struck gold. Not real gold, obviously. Research gold. I know I'm always going on about how much I hate work. Don't get me wrong; the subject's my passion. I love Late Medieval and Early Renaissance European History. But no, I don't love the seven account books of a monastery in Wiltshire for the year 1356, and I'm not so keen on the agricultural produce of the village of Dumbhurst in 1531, and I definitely don't like the fourteenth century annals of the incumbency of the Bishop of Dumbchester."

"I take it those aren't real place names."

"They ought to be."

"What counts as 'research gold', then?"

"A map."

I laughed again. "Of Dumb*hurst* or Dumb*chester?"*

"I'm working on the assumption that it's not the only copy," she continued, either ignoring or not hearing me. "That there *are* copies. There must be. There's definitely something missing in the manuscript."

"Okay."

She sat bolt upright, suddenly tense. She put her fingertips on her forehead. "Bloody hell."

"What?" Sometimes, she was like this. When she was sufficiently excited by Late Medieval and Early Renaissance European History, she talked to herself, and it was like I was outside the building. "What's wrong?" I asked again.

"Professor Sir Dimbleby Manfred," she said darkly.

I considered, and immediately rejected, the idea of asking facetiously whether this was another made up name. The truth is, it wasn't the first time she'd mentioned Dimbleby Manfred, nor the first time he'd threatened to wreck her mood. Nor even the tenth. She'd mentioned him so often, I'd actually gone to the trouble of Googling him two months ago.

An aside, then. In some ways, Dimbleby Manfred was her nemesis. In others, her ideal. Seventy years old, clean shaven, gaunt, regulation upper class tweed jacket and brogues, the universally acknowledged king of Late Medieval and Early Renaissance European History. Not that the average Waterstone's reader or BBC4 watcher would know: he didn't do 'popular' histories, nor did he do TV. 'An elderly white guy with an elderly white guy's privilege' was how Ijeoma once described him. But that was after he'd given her the brush-off at a conference, and I knew it was only hurt feelings on her part. The truth was, so I learned, he didn't like conferences, and he didn't like his peers. 'Despised' might be a better word. And of course, all that simply increased his prestige. Nothing enlivens the crowds like a *bona fide* misanthrope. Meanwhile, he was the academic's academic, author of four or five books with titles like, *Concepts of Reprieve and Release in the Fourteenth Century English Medical Treatise* and *The Influence of the* Benedictus Deus *on the Papacies of Clement VI and Innocent VI.*

"What about him?" I said. "I thought you said earlier you hadn't met anyone."

It took her a few seconds to realise I was joking. Once again, she talked past me. "He's got a whole crowd of assistant researchers," she said. "No one knows how many. If they get wind of what I've discovered, they'll pull the rug out from under my feet without a second thought. I'll get no credit at all. But if I succeed, I'll be able to get any job I want, anywhere in the world. Maybe. I'll certainly be a lot better off than I am now. We both will."

I waved my hand in front of her eyes. "Er, hello, Earth calling Ijeoma. What are you talking about?"

She turned to face me as if she'd emerged from a trance. "This is important to me, Peter. I need you to get time off work. I want you to come with me."

"Come with you where?"

"Wadhurst. It's a village in East Sussex, before you ask. I don't want to do this on my own. I know it's short notice, but I've never asked anything of you before. I mean, yes, I have, obviously. But not like this. I've got to act, and act quickly. Before Manfred's minions put the heat on me."

"You make them sound like *mafioso*."

She shrugged. "I don't know what lengths they'll go to. Nor do you. I grant you, they probably won't resort to violence, but I wouldn't put theft past them."

"I take it you've come across them before."

"No."

"What?"

She laughed. "I said, no. Look, I'm making them up, okay? But they *could* exist. I'm hyper, I know that. I've had a shock. A good shock. A brilliant one. The map's in my bag, by the way, in the cupboard, and it's staying there, under lock and key, until Monday. I've won the lottery, feels like. It just fell out of a book in the library in Elfeston Manor. Just like that. Just *dropped*. Another story, sorry. Anyhow, tomorrow, I'm calling into work ill, and the day after too. In order to guard it, obviously. I've already booked a cottage in Wadhurst. Self-catering, washer-dryer, wood burning stove, fridge-freezer, king-size bed. Done and dusted. After day one, we needn't leave. Until our time runs out, of course. All I need you to do, is get a few days off. If necessary, take a cue from me and pretend to be ill. Either way, you're coming with me."

I'd never seen her like this before. Naturally, I said yes, I'd move heaven and earth to get the necessary holiday. If the boss said no, I'd take unpaid leave, even if it put my future at risk. Call me romantic, but girlfriend over job every time, in my book.

"We'll go to sleep now," she told me, as if it was an order. "We'll need all our energy."

"Yes, ma'am."

She put her arms round me. "Peter, it could be a *treasure map!"*

I nodded, obligingly. 'A treasure map' was the sort of thing she thought I'd understand. I knew it wasn't remotely what she believed, but I found it touching that she thought I still needed bolstering. When it turned out not to be a treasure map, she'd be in my debt. She already knew that too.

Stupid, the games couples play.

II.

As I just pointed out, the fact that she'd so breathlessly told me it was a treasure map suggested she already knew it wasn't. But she must have *some* theory about it. Something she wasn't telling me.

Procuring the map from her bag wouldn't tell me anything. I had no knowledge of how to interpret that sort of document. Which probably meant I just had to trust her.

I decided against a conversation about leave with Marsha, my line manager. She'd definitely say no. *Who's going to cover you at this short notice? All holidays have to be booked at least two weeks in advance, Peter, you know that. I'm sorry, really I am, but December's a very busy time of year,* etcetera, etcetera. A million reasons to say nix, none to say yes, except seasonal goodwill maybe, and realistically, who's got *that?*

So, I decided I'd throw a sickie; call Marsha on Sunday, pretend I had stomach cramps.

The good thing about Wadhurst was it meant I could lounge about the flat a little over the weekend. Normally, I went grocery shopping on Saturday – never a happy experience - while Ijeoma worked on her latest paper. But this time, we'd probably be better off stocking up later, when we got to the cottage. Nevertheless, I bought a few essentials in the corner shop on my way home on Friday, just to be on the safe side.

As I was putting everything away, I told her I was probably going to be staying in tomorrow. I thought she'd be pleased – I could bring her tea and snacks - but she tensed. Obviously not what she expected or wanted.

A few moments later, when I went into the bedroom to get changed, I heard her quietly go into the cupboard outside the door. Retrieving her map from one of the bags she'd brought in the previous evening? If so, she clearly didn't want me to catch her in the act. I guessed she didn't trust me.

I didn't challenge her, though. As I think I've already indicated, she definitely has her quirks and neuroses, and I suppose I've got mine. We've learned to live with each other.

That evening, and throughout the next morning, I noticed how much praying she was doing. She comes from what I would call an aggressively evangelical background, and over the years, I've got used to her churchgoing and her periodic bouts of pious enthusiasm. I'm not saying I'm anti-Christian – I'm much more agnostic than atheist – but the whole charismatic thing leaves me cold. Midnight mass on Christmas eve, that's about the limit of my commitment.

However, live and let live.

On the other hand, there was suddenly an awful *lot* of praying, to the point where she began to make me feel uncomfortable. 'Spooked' might be a better term. I couldn't help drawing the obvious conclusion that it was something to do with the map. At this point, I wasn't so much concerned with what it *was* – I'm not sufficiently superstitious for anything like that – but more with what *she thought* it was. In my view, superstition and religion are never that far apart, and I worried she might be whipping herself up into some sort of mental disturbance. She'd already admitted she was 'hyper', and, as far as I could tell, she had yet to calm down. On the contrary, she seemed to be getting worse.

There were prayers in bed, prayers on her knees in the living room, mumblings from *The Book of Common Prayer*, prayers in the kitchen while we were cooking, hymns, recitations, Bible readings, retrievals of memorised passages, long meditative silences, snatches of ancient liturgies in languages I didn't recognise, under-the-breath entreaties to Christ. All of a sudden, I was living with a different woman. I admit, I was worried. I began to wonder what my, 'yes, I'll accompany you to Wadhurst' had got us both into.

Obviously, I asked her about it. Her answer? She was getting into 'the spirit' of a vastly more religious, more superstitious (yes, she did use that word) age: the age of Late Medieval and Early Renaissance English History. Somehow, the prayers were necessary to what she wanted to achieve. But she resented me noticing, and was embarrassed by my asking. Of course, her 'explanation' was no explanation at all. I didn't want a row, so I let it drop.

We were due to leave for Wadhurst on Monday morning. It couldn't come soon enough for me. At ten am, on Saturday, Ijeoma told me she was going to church. And then once more, that afternoon, at three, and later again, at eight. I didn't even know that the building – a nineteenth century Anglican pile called Saint John's – opened that frequently. Or that her brand of Christianity even had much in common with theirs. She must have been in a singular frame of mind to risk leaving me alone in the flat with her precious map. Wherever she'd hidden it (or maybe she took it with her).

On Sunday, it struck me that maybe I'd better keep an eye on her. She definitely wasn't telling me everything, and, for all I knew, she might not be telling me anything. What if she'd fallen into debt somehow, and she'd become mixed up with extortionists? What if she really was 'seeing someone else'? After all, the best way to inoculate your partner against suspicion of unfaithfulness might well be to introduce the notion yourself at the earliest possible stage, then make fun of it.

On Sunday evening, I decided to follow her to church. I gave her a five-minute start, then set off for Saint John's.

When I got there, it was closed. No lights on inside, the double doors locked. I did a circuit of the building, just to be sure there wasn't some little 'informal' entrance. Absurd, I know. Then I went into the porch and used the torch on my phone to check the times of services. Today's sole item: Morning Communion 10am. Nothing at all yesterday.

Maybe she'd gone home. That wouldn't necessarily explain anything, but at least she'd be safe. We could have it out. We'd have to. Oh, God.

I took my phone out and texted her: *where are you?*

Thirty seconds later, I got an answer: *I told you, I'm in church.*

My stomach turned over. Saint John's was set back about ten metres from the street and its porch had a built-in bench on each side, in more or less complete darkness. I sat down and put my head in my hands.

It suddenly hit me that Saint John's wasn't the only church around here. And she'd never actually mentioned it by name; I'd just assumed this was where she'd be coming. I actually laughed out loud. Not out of the woods yet, but at least I had a lifeline.

Then I got a nasty shock. A disembodied voice said, "I expect you want to know where she actually is."

Whoa! someone was sitting opposite me, as deep in shadow as I was, and barely a metre away. I stood up. I didn't have time to get properly scared: it all happened too quickly, and the voice wasn't hostile, and I wasn't too frightened to grasp the words' sense.

"Where *who* is?" I said idiotically.

The speaker got to his feet. A tall, thin, clean-shaven man of about seventy, with a widow's peak of grey curly hair and penetrating brown eyes. He dusted down his dark overcoat and regarded me superciliously. I guess he must have detected recognition in my features.

Professor Sir Dimbleby Manfred. What the *hell - ?*

A dream? It had to be! I felt light headed enough. I needed to sit down again. Or no, I didn't. I didn't know what I wanted. To wake up.

"Let's walk," he said.

I followed him as mindlessly as the sleepwalker I'd become half-convinced I was. When we got onto the street, he turned to face me under a yellow sodium lamp. He didn't look happy.

"If you want to find her," he said, "you need to try the Roman Catholic church, two streets from here. That's all I'll say on the subject and I hope you'll take it as evidence of my essential goodwill. I'll come straight to the point. She's got something I want. A map, or that's what I suppose she's told you."

"How did you know where to find me?"

"I've been watching your flat. I want to make you an offer. Fifty thousand pounds for the 'map'."

I laughed. "Why aren't you talking to Ijeoma?"

"Because I happen to know she's as passionate about the subject as I am. She won't give it up."

"You could at least *try* her."

"I find the thought of making a fool of myself... abhorrent."

"Fifty thousand pounds is quite a lot of abhorrence."

"Her map's missing a lot of information. Without that, it's relatively worthless. Okay, forget the fifty thousand. I need you to talk to her for me. Tell her, we can work together on it, co-author a paper. I've got the other half."

"What 'other half'?"

"She must have told you it's incomplete. She's very talented. I'd be surprised if that had passed her by. I've got the missing portion."

"Wait a minute, you've just offered me fifty thousand."

"I thought you might be open to bribery. I was hoping to turn you into a thief. It's surprising how one can entertain such ideas when sitting completely alone in the darkness of a church porch, and how completely they evaporate when, two minutes later, one comes face to face with the intended dupe, and discovers a gentle, empty-headed soul who's quite obviously besotted."

"Thanks."

"That's my offer, then. We co-author a paper, she and I. Good night and thank you for hearing me out."

He turned to walk away, but seemed to change his mind at the last second and swivelled back. "You don't have to answer this question if you'd rather not, but believe me, I'm not being flippant. Are you frightened of snakes?"

I half-grinned. I suppose I must have looked as puzzled, and possibly suspicious, as he expected. "Er, well, yes. Who isn't?"

"If she declines my offer then, you might do well to reconsider your long-term future with her. Sorry, but it would be morally remiss of me not to warn you."

I suddenly wasn't in the mood for humouring him anymore, but I suppose he must have anticipated that too. He walked away so briskly it was clear he'd spoken his final word on the subject. I didn't attempt to follow him.

III.

When I told Ijeoma what had happened, she didn't take it as badly as I expected. I half-envisaged her exploding. Instead, she sat on the sofa, leaning forward with her elbows on her knees, regarding me with a terrifyingly neutral expression. When I told her about the snake bit, she giggled slightly. I let it pass: her prerogative. Maybe Manfred had a reputation for cryptic asides designed solely to bamboozle.

"Obviously, I *have* been behaving oddly," she said calmly, when I'd finished. "Even *I* can see that, and you wouldn't be much of a boyfriend-stroke-future-husband if you weren't concerned. Yes, you followed me, but I'd probably have done the same had our positions been reversed. Forget about the snakes: that's just the sort of thing he says: 'eccentric with a hint of creepy' doesn't begin to cover it. The important thing is that the actual Professor Dimbleby Manfred said – what were the words you used? 'I happen to know she's as passionate about the subject as I am'? My God, Peter, *he knows my name!*"

"I'm not sure that's the central point," I said.

"I'm pretty damn sure it *is!* Dimbleby Manfred's so confident of my academic potential that he actually *goes to the trouble of staking out my house!* And that he wants to work with me, *co-authoring a paper!*"

"Are you going to accept?"

She chuckled. "Maybe. But not right away. If I look too desperate, he'll take advantage. I mean, his name will be in big, bold, size fourteen font, and mine will be ten metres underneath it, in size eight. No, we're going to Wadhurst first. I'm going to do all the research half a document permits – and don't forget, we've only got his word it's half: it could be three-quarters, or seven-eighths - "

"Have you considered that you going it alone might turn him from a potentially influential friend into a powerful enemy, capable of snuffing your entire career out? Especially given how weird he apparently is?"

"Of course, yes," she said, in a tone which suggested she hadn't. "Yes, you're right. Obviously, I suppose ultimately, I will have to collaborate with him. But let's see what I can dig up on my own first. He'll respect that. Did he give you a phone number, or any way of getting back in touch with him?"

"No, he just walked off."

"That's good. It means he's not in a hurry. But obviously, he *will* expect an answer. Anything else would be rude. My point is, intentionally or not, he's made it unnecessarily difficult for us to get back in touch with him, and we can use that to our advantage."

"I appreciate you using the word 'our', but - "

She jumped. "You didn't tell him where we were *going*, did you?"

"Obviously not. In any case, he didn't ask."

She gave a relieved sigh. "Look, Peter, when this is all over, I'll buy you a car, okay?"

I laughed. We both did. It wasn't until the next morning that it struck me just how odd it was that Manfred had staked out our house, or that Ijeoma had just accepted it. But then, maybe that sort of thing happens a lot in academia. Arcane artefacts become matters of life and death. A consequence of all those ivory towers, perhaps. In any case, it's perhaps a measure of how far my outlook on life had rapidly become assimilated to hers that I didn't think about it anymore. I called into work, sick, and told myself that, whatever happened, we'd get through it.

IV.

We caught the train to London at seven the next morning. I kept my head down until we were well and truly out of Oxford, and raised it only after thrice checking that none of my work colleagues was on board. Ijeoma was similarly jumpy, but it was Manfred she was on the lookout for. Once she'd reassured herself on that count, it was his 'minions'.

We disembarked at Paddington, nervously crossed London, and got on the train to Wadhurst at Charing Cross. I think it's fair to say Ijeoma didn't relax until we were halfway there.

Outside the carriage window, the landscape seemed to grow increasingly bleaker. Skeletal hedges dangling the remnants of climbers, bare, dead-looking trees, the earth seemingly hammered down and devoid of livestock, the light insipid, the sky pale. Clouds hung in thin bands of livid grey, and over and above all this, I had a depressing sense that the whole world was agonisingly freezing to death. The sun, on the few occasions it appeared, looked as desolate as everything else.

It took us three and a half hours, all told, from Oxford. We arrived in Wadhurst just after ten-thirty and stepped onto an old-fashioned platform surrounded on all sides by tall, thin trees. There was no taxi rank. A bus took us up a gentle incline to the village, about a mile away. From what I could tell, Wadhurst consisted of a short high street, lined on both sides with shops and parked cars. A church steeple was just visible to the east, and partly screening it, what looked like the crown of an aged cedar. It was still too early for lunch. We shopped in a mini-supermarket, then sat on a bench beside a car park and ate a sausage roll each.

Our holiday cottage was about four miles away, reachable by car, bike or on foot, but not by public transport. Ijeoma had brought an Ordnance Survey map, and we purchased a more detailed guide to the area in a bookshop called Barnett's. We hadn't brought much luggage with us – we weren't expecting to stay beyond two days – and we'd come half-expecting to walk at least part of the way. By that, I mean we'd set off that morning in hiking boots and cagoules. It wasn't raining, so we held a brief conference over the maps and set off.

In retrospect, that was probably a mistake. We were couple of young ramblers with little real familiarity with rambling, and each secretly looking for opportunities to make the experience more memorable. Pretty soon, Ijeoma discovered a 'short cut', partly I think because she noticed me quietly looking to discover the same thing on the Ordnance Survey.

"There's a public footpath here," she said. "It should cut about twenty minutes off our journey. Look." She showed me her map.

I shrugged. "On your head be it."

We seemed to be walking a long time, and I couldn't help noticing her increasing perplexity. An hour later, we emerged from the screen of a long privet hedge onto a view of what looked like an almighty lake.

"Oh, my God," she said angrily. "That must be *Bewl Water!*"

I didn't know exactly where our cottage was, but I knew it was nowhere near the local reservoir.

"We're totally and utterly lost!" she added.

"We've still got the maps."

"But we could be looking at *any part* of Bewl Water! It's got something like a thirteen mile perimeter! We've no idea where on the map we're standing right now!"

"Maybe if we just try to retrace our steps."

"Brilliant! Mrs Forsythe will be waiting for us! I told her we'd be there no later than midday! And before you say, 'phone her', I haven't got a signal!"

"Nor me. Nor Google Maps. Let's go back."

"Why the hell didn't we bring a compass?"

"Because we - "

She stomped off.

Two hours later, we were still lost – if anything, even more so: we'd given up on the roads and footpaths and we were tramping across an open field with the remains of a scarecrow at its centre. Our extremities were frozen, but because we were going at a brisk pace, and because our luggage, although light, was far from weightless, we weren't particularly cold more generally. I think we were both more depressed than exhausted. Looking repeatedly at the map, I wasn't sure how it was possible to get so lost in such a seemingly small area.

I say 'lost', but of course no one is ever truly lost in today's England (the Scottish Highlands and parts of Wales and Northern Ireland are probably different). There's always a minor road nearby, and they all quickly lead to bigger roads, which all lead in no time at all to towns and villages. So, yes, maybe we could have gone back to Wadhurst, or even to Ticehurst, the next village along, but that would have been a defeat. Or so Ijeoma said.

Eventually, I realised we were - at least partly - going in circles. After three hours, Ijeoma began to cry with frustration. The light was leaving the day. The map, tantalising as ever, suggested we might be on the verge of a breakthrough, but we'd long since stopped believing in it. We'd just emerged from another wood, and we were walking uphill at a tortoise's pace, probably to nowhere at all. We needed to keep to the roads now, so I was surprised to see Ijeoma suddenly pick up speed and climb onto a stile which, as far as I could tell, led into yet another endless muddy field.

"What are you - " I began, only coming to a halt in response to her raised hand. Best not to antagonise her, though none of this was my idea; paradoxically, *because* of that.

I sat down on the wet grass verge a few feet downhill from her. She opened her travel bag and took out a large notebook with a few loose sheets of paper inside. I didn't look at her. I don't know whether she was still crying. I felt like crying myself.

We sat without speaking for about five minutes. I could feel the cold beginning to creep into my bones.

Then I had a kind of dark epiphany. Strange as it may sound, for the first time, I saw with total clarity the senselessness of what we were doing. It was time to stop hoping for … well, what *were* we hoping for? For our holiday cottage to appear? Even if it materialised on the horizon in thirty seconds' time, how the hell were we going to recognise it? Why, really (despite Ijeoma's crazy claim about it being defeatist), weren't we trying to get back to Wadhurst?

"We're nearby," she said quietly. "We're almost on top of it."

"We need to stop looking for the cottage," I said. "I don't know why we didn't see that two hours ago. We need to call in at the next house and ask to use their phone."

"We're very nearby now, Peter," she said again.

"What we've been doing is literally insane. What have we been thinking?"

"I'm sorry."

"It's not *your* fault," I said. "We've *both* suffered an intellect crash."

"This was always going to be part of it. Part of the looking process. I know where it is now. We've got to go there."

It took a moment to sink in. She was subtly trying to tell me that she'd planned all this; that it had been central to her agenda from the start.

I didn't believe her. She was delirious.

"Follow me," she said.

"No, *you* follow *me*," I replied. "You're confused. I don't even know what you're trying to say, except, I think – and I'm partly guessing – that all this apparently aimless tramping is connected to your so-called treasure map, and that you now think that, as a result of the last few hours of misery, you're now in a position to identify the precise spot marked by an X."

"Something like that," she said smugly.

"It's getting dark. Another hour and we won't be able to see two feet in front of us!"

"I know exactly where the cottage is, Peter. From where the 'treasure' is, it's about half an hour's walk. The two things are in the same direction, so we wouldn't even be going out of our way!"

"Listen to yourself. You're not making any sense!"

"I'm better than I've ever been. You'll just have to trust me. If this comes off, everything will change. It could be wonderful."

"If there's buried treasure, neither of us has even brought a spade!"

"It's not that sort of treasure."

I was getting nowhere. Disconcerting though it sounded, perhaps the best way forward was to let the whole thing play itself out. Maybe I was exaggerating the risk of hypothermia. We were both young; we'd had a hard day, but we were probably more dispirited than physically depleted. A quick walk to where she thought the 'treasure' was, a few minutes' going through the motions of an investigation, then leave for the cottage. Don't get me wrong: I didn't believe for a moment she actually knew where the cottage was. That was just another delusion. But once she'd got this mad fallacy out of her system, we could definitely locate a house with a phone, and thence, a Tunbridge Wells taxi. We'd laugh about it later. A bit.

So, I followed her. We walked across another wet, boggy field. Darkness was definitely falling now, and in the only dwelling I could see - a lone white bungalow with smoke rising vertically from its chimney - a light went on. The sky above was completely clear. The sun was virtually on the horizon, but screened by a long line of firs in the far distance. The whole scene looked sombre and somehow eerie. A succession of hedges and tall trees and empty spaces, all completely still, like they were watching us, waiting for something ominous to happen. I'd like to say a rook called, just to complete the image, but there was total silence. Not even the distant sound of vehicles.

After about fifty yards, we left the footpath; or rather she did, and I followed her. We ascended a little hillock planted with a copse of ordinary-looking semi-mature trees, where we found ourselves in a slightly deeper darkness.

She'd increased her pace to pull ahead of me, but then she came to an abrupt halt. "It's here."

I looked at the ground, although I didn't need to. I couldn't see us excavating it: not now, possibly not ever. Unless the weather changed, there was going to be a hard frost tonight, and the earth would turn to iron.

"Right," I said. "So, we've found it. Yahoo: mission accomplished. I'm really cold now, and I'm sure you're frozen. You said the cottage - "

"My God, it's *lovely* here, Peter!" She put both arms in the air and span around. "It's absolutely *beautiful!"*

I made a show of looking around me. "It's, er, not bad, but I think we'd better get moving."

She threw her arms round me and burst into tears. "No, it's *gorgeous!* It's utterly – utterly" – she laughed frenziedly - *"I can't even find any words good enough for it!"*

Okay, I was worried now. At the very least, an almighty argument was on the cards. Us both dying of exposure suddenly didn't look so unlikely, after all. And if she refused to budge, I was in no condition to make her. I certainly couldn't carry her, and she definitely wouldn't let me.

"Please, Ijeoma," I said, trying to put all my anxiety into my tone, "we need to go!"

"Just ten minutes!" She released me from her embrace, walked five paces away and unzipped her travel bag with her back to me. I saw her take out the notebook and the pieces of paper, then she turned back. "Just ten minutes, I swear! Honestly, Peter," she went on, in a more measured, but also more artificial, tone, presumably designed to reassure me, "I can see you're worried, and I understand that. We might die of

the cold, or get frostbite, I know, I know, I know. But we can't postpone this. The date may have escaped you, my love, but it's December the twenty-first. It'll be too late tomorrow!"

I groaned inwardly. The winter bloody solstice. So now it was supernatural treasure we were hunting! What the hell had got into her? Junior university lecturers weren't supposed to be like this: all the ones I'd ever met before were sniffy secularists.

"Do what?" I said, weakly. "You said, 'We can't do this tomorrow'. Do what?"

"*You* don't have to do anything. All I need you to do is sit on the ground and close your eyes. Try to forget about the cold. In an hour's time, we'll be inside our cottage, and we'll order a pizza, and get a warm fire going, and it'll be as if none of this ever happened. Sit on the ground. Close your eyes. Please. Ten minutes."

"What are you going to do?"

"What do you mean?"

"I mean, what will you be doing while I'm sitting on the ground with my eyes closed?" The horrible thought had occurred to me – it'd have been mad in normal circumstances, but it seemed entirely appropriate now – that she might be going to sacrifice me to some sort of pagan deity.

"You've just got to trust me," she replied. She obviously intuited my fears, because she said, "I promise I'm not going to slit your jugular, invoke the Moon Goddess, and thrust your face into the soil as your life force drains away. Happy?"

"Delirious."

"Do you trust me? Yes or no? Because if you don't, we might as well call it a day. I mean, on our relationship."

I ran my hands through my hair. She wasn't right; she was speaking out of light headedness. How to respond?

Suddenly she was on her knees in front of me, her hands clasped. "*Please,* Peter! Ten minutes. Literally! Sixty seconds in a minute, six hundred seconds in ten minutes, so count up to six hundred! One Mississippi, two Mississippi, three Mississippi, like that. When you get to six hundred, stand up. I swear to God I'll go with you. We'll go straight to the cottage."

"Why do I have to close my eyes?"

"Because if you see what I'm doing, you'll think I'm insane. And I'll see myself through your eyes, and so will I! And, well" – she stopped for a giggle – "a snake might appear."

"A snake?"

Then I remembered: Manfred. She was trying to introduce a pretext for complicity. *Us against the crazy old man.* Well, it was too late.

She tittered again. "I shouldn't have said that. Just ignore me. Ten minutes, that's all I ask. Ten minutes to save our entire future together. Our love. I love you, Peter. Please don't send me away. I love you. I always will. Just ten minutes."

I sighed and something inside me caved in. "Okay, then," I said wretchedly. "Ten minutes. No more."

"Start counting."

I wasn't in the least sure whether she'd keep her promise, but at this point I'd have tried anything, and ten more minutes didn't seem exorbitant. Quite the contrary: it might be just long enough for me to come up with a workable exit plan. Because right now, I had nothing. I started to count, but although I kept the succession of Mississippis going, my mind was on other things. Weird things. How old the earth was – billions of years – and what this spot must have looked like in previous geological eras. Sometimes under the sea, sometimes part of a mountaintop. And then, sometime recently – within the last three thousand years – someone, some antediluvian group had decided it was sacred, and how that had come down through the generations...

Behind me, I could just about make out Ijeoma. She seemed to be pacing up and down. Occasionally, she uttered some word or phrase I didn't catch.

I realised she'd duped me slightly when I got to a hundred-and-twenty-one Mississippi, which seemed to take much longer to say than the required temporal second. I sped up to compensate. When I reached five hundred and ninety-nine Mississippi, I felt something slide across my hand. I opened my eyes, startled, to see a tiny snake, or possibly slow worm, slither away into the loam. I stood up.

"Finished!" she declared happily. "I'm ready to go!"

In my eagerness to get going, I forgot all about the snake. She'd already packed the travel bag. She linked arms with me.

"To the cottage!" she exclaimed.

V.

She set off as if she knew exactly where we were going. We entered another wood, took a downhill footpath between closely packed trees – the darkness was nearly total now, and we could hardly see where we were going – crossed another stile, then a grassy field, until we found a gate set into a long, tall stone wall. We unlatched it and found ourselves on a tarmac drive with neatly mown grass edges, and a row of potted conifers draped with Christmas lights. Beyond that, three or four brick houses. Meanwhile, a wind seemed to have arrived, so far perpetually at our backs, bearing us forward, but hissing unpleasantly across the grass and through the trees. Neither of us spoke, but I could feel Ijeoma becoming nervous. I assumed her confidence about the cottage had evaporated. We were lost again. I wasn't annoyed; I'd never expected anything else. At least here were houses of some description. I just hoped one of the occupiers was feeling charitable enough to let us use a landline.

A crescent moon had appeared in the sky. We closed the gate behind us. Ijeoma stopped. I blinked slowly, sensing she was about to fall prey to some sort of new fixation. Fine. In that case, I was finally prepared for a real, good old-fashioned argument. I'd been accommodating. I'd indulged her more than was reasonable. I deserved some reward, if only to take the lead for the rest of the evening.

"Can you hear that?" she said. "Or is it just me?"

"Hear what?"

"That hissing sound!"

"You mean, the wind?"

"There *isn't* any wind, Peter! Look at the grass! Look at the trees!"

She was right. Everything was as motionless as it had been earlier in the evening, before the sun set. But it could have been anything. A jet of water somewhere, a wind from which we were shielded by the trees.

She looked panicked, though, as if something sinister had arrived. She began to deep breathe.

I suddenly remembered Manfred and his 'snake'. Of course. Somehow, the whole exhaustion and cold thing had affected her more deeply than I'd imagined.

Which didn't seem explanation enough. Being pursued by snakes was the sort of thing full blown mental collapses are made of. We had to get out of here as quickly as possible. We needed to get her home.

"Come on!" she said. "This is *it!* This is *the cottage!* We've got to get inside!"

It took me a second to process her announcement. We were here!

We ran to the front door of the detached house at the end of the row. She knelt down to access a little security box. She keyed in a code, the lid flipped open, and she took out a key. Her hand shook as she unlocked the front door.

"Get inside!" she yelled.

I did as she commanded, and she slammed the door behind us and switched on the lights. We were in a narrow hallway with woodchip wallpaper and landscapes in gilt frames. A staircase to one side led into the gloom upstairs. A corridor led to what looked like a kitchen, with a living room halfway down on the left.

For the second time that day, she got down on her knees before me, and for the second time, she was crying. But these were tears of terror, not frustration.

"Oh, my *God*, Peter, I'm so *sorry!* I promise I knew nothing whatsoever about the snakes until Digby Manfred mentioned them! I had no idea! I didn't even know he was being serious! What have I got you into? I don't care about me anymore, I – " She stood up. Her mood changed. "What am I saying?" she said harshly. "It's academic now. Go round the house. Switch all the lights on, check there are no gaps in the window frames or under the doors. Look *everywhere*: inside and behind the wardrobes, under the bed, in the cupboards, on top of them, under the fridge and the washing machine, *everywhere*." She stopped. Her face, already pale, turned even paler. "Peter, you know when we were on the hill together, and I made you close your eyes?"

"Well, it was only about three-quarters of an hour ago, so yes."

"You didn't – you didn't actually *see* a snake, did you? I made a joke, I don't know whether you remember, I was being flippant, that's all, but - "

"I didn't see anything at all," I lied.

She came down a notch. "Okay, okay, that's – that's good. *Where are you going?"*

"You just told me to switch on the lights and check the rooms."

"Not without me! Don't leave me alone! We've got to check the external doors first. Don't open any. If it's not in here, we might still be able to keep it out."

She was losing her sanity. In the morning – if we made it that far – I might need to take her to a mental health professional of some description. I had only the vaguest idea whether that was the right course. The local hospital, maybe. What *do* you do with someone who's had a catastrophic nervous breakdown?

As we searched the rooms and checked the doors for gaps, I got to thinking about what could have brought her to this point. Overwork, obviously. That second-hand meeting with Dimbleby Manfred had probably tipped her over the edge. I wondered if he'd foreseen the possibility somehow and provoked it, so as to get his hands on Ijeoma's precious document?

No, it had started before that. When she came home with her two bags, and I'd cooked that pasta bake. No Dimbleby Manfred in the mix at that stage.

Pointless speculating. She needed to sleep. We'd had nothing to eat since those sausage rolls at midday, but we hadn't brought any food, and there was none in the house. We finished the security check to her half-satisfaction and showered together. Not, I should add, for erotic reasons, but simply because she was afraid to be on her own. And she was becoming more petrified by the minute. We towelled ourselves dry, locked ourselves in the bedroom at her insistence, and got straight into bed. She ordered me not to switch the lights off under any circumstances, not just in here, but anywhere in the whole house.

Nevertheless, she fell asleep more quickly than I expected. She was as physically exhausted as me, probably, but I think all the high-pitched dread had finished her. Her brain couldn't take any more, and it had flicked the off switch for her own safety and possibly survival.

I was in the opposite predicament. 'Safety's sake' gave me *too much* to think about, and made sleep an undesirable luxury. How to get her out of here and how to look after her once I had? I should probably call her parents in the morning, they'd be able to help. Or perhaps she'd be back to normal when the sun rose, after she'd had a good night's sleep.

I didn't think so. Why had I agreed to any of this? I ought to have seen the warning signs at the start. I loved her so much. I couldn't bear anything to happen to her. I'd be nothing at all without her, a life not worth living!

My thoughts were going along in this vein when she suddenly jerked awake. It took her a second to realise where she was, then her eyes fixed on mine, and she grabbed me as if her life depended on it, and burst into tears again.

"I've been *stupid,* Peter! I don't want *any* of this! I thought I *did,* but I *don't!"* She swallowed, and seemed to constrain her emotion. "Listen, I'm not going to make it through tonight," she said weakly. "It'll start to kick in soon, and then we might be separated for ever. Our only chance lies in Dimbleby Manfred. I won't be here in the morning, Peter. Or rather I will, but it won't be me. Take the map to him and give him it. I'm so *sorry,* Peter! I'm really, *really sorry!* I love you! I'll love you forever! *I don't want this!* Oh God, what was I thinking? God *help me!* Please, *Jesus,* remember all those prayers! Please *help me survive!* Jesus, Son of God, *please!"*

I told her I loved her, it'd all be okay in the morning whatever she thought, and listened to her ramble on a bit more. She kept telling me this would probably be the last time I saw her. After ten minutes, thank God, she fell asleep again.

The silence should have been absolute, but once she'd stopped whispering, the hiss returned. For a moment, I thought it must be the wind, rushing across the eaves or whatever it does. Even so, it unnerved me.

Then suddenly – I have no idea what caused it – I got the distinct impression it wasn't outside at all. On the contrary, it was *right here, in the bedroom.*

The horror took a while to establish itself. I kept asking myself whether my hearing was functioning properly, and how it *could* be, and why the million and one possible rational explanations weren't pushing aggressively forwards, and what was happening to my mind, and whether it was possible for delusion to spread from one person to another like a contagion.

But to no effect. I really could hear a hissing. It wasn't coming from outside. That only left one alternative.

In the same horrible manner in which the conviction that it wasn't outside took hold of me, I acquired a new certainty. It was actually beneath the bed.

Of course, we'd both looked there when we'd done our search and found nothing. We'd searched the entire house.

Then it struck me. There must be some sort of gaps in the floorboards. The wind was getting in from the outside somehow – possibly through the air bricks – and it was coming up here. If it was under any sort of pressure, and the gaps were small enough, it would make a faint noise as it squeezed through. Combining all those tiny soundwaves into one – which is what would occur – would probably result in a hissing sound.

Okay, now I simply had to exorcise the metaphorical demon by scientifically confirming its non-existence. I disengaged myself gently from Ijeoma and got up.

The bed was an imitation old-fashioned model, made of brass, on four legs, with the mattress on a raised frame a foot or so above the floor. I got on my knees, lifted the edge of the duvet and looked. Nothing.

But my surmise seemed correct. The hiss was definitely coming from down here.

No, I couldn't see any gaps in the floorboards, but then the light was subdued, and they were probably small enough to be visually indiscernible. I'd have another look in the morning. In the meantime, it was something reassuring to tell Ijeoma.

I don't know why, but instead of continuing to examine the floor, I looked up at the underside of the bed. What I saw there paralysed me for a moment, then made me jump with sufficient force to smash my neck violently on the metal frame above.

Even now, trying to describe it fills me with a visceral revulsion. An enormous snake, coiled up malignantly, ready to strike, with a body as thick as a tyre, as long as a room, and covered with markings that looked curiously like script. What distinguished it even above all this however, was that its eyes were horribly human.

I only saw it for a flash. After hitting my neck, I turned groggily to face it again.

Instead of attacking me, however, it darted upwards, and *through the bed*. The mattress bounced violently and I heard Ijeoma emit a loud groan.

I scrambled backwards into the room, got frenziedly to my feet and looked around for something, anything to use as a weapon. It was the work of a split second to discover nothing. We were defenceless. I'd have to use my bare hands.

But when I looked about, gasping, I couldn't see any sign of a snake. I was full of adrenalin now. I rived the duvet completely off the bed. Nothing. Then I looked under the mattress again. Nothing. Then in the wardrobe, under it, behind it, on top of it. Nothing. I drew the curtains. Nothing. And the door was shut and locked.

Ijeoma lay on her back, naked. I'd expected all this to wake her up. Put it another way: that was the very least I expected. But no, she was sleeping soundly.

Then I noticed she was smiling. Part of the skin beneath her ribcage rose and fell, as if something tubular and flexible had just passed beneath it.

VI.

Obviously, I tried to wake her up. I exhausted the usual means, then I gave her a gentle shake, then a rougher one. I soaked a towel in cold water and put it over her. I tried ice cubes. I did all this very quickly, because I already knew something was very wrong. Her skin kept – I don't know if there's a word for it – rising and sinking like there was something beneath it.

I knew that wasn't physically possible. Anything moving about inside her like that would have torn the inside of the skin from the fascia beneath, probably causing massive internal haemorrhaging. But she definitely wasn't bleeding. She continued to smile, and every three or four minutes, she emitted a contented sigh in her sleep.

And the snake. Whatever was beneath her skin couldn't be what I'd seen under the bed, not unless it had drastically shrunk. I recalled the snake I'd seen outside, in the copse. It had been minute.

All these considerations passed through my mind almost simultaneously. The bottom line was, I couldn't wake her up. That was sufficient grounds for calling an ambulance.

Her breathing was becoming noticeably shallower. She was no longer smiling. I rang 999, then rifled through her travel bag to find her precious 'map'. It was a photocopy: presumably, the original was too delicate to handle. It was probably in some safety deposit box somewhere.

I looked at it for a long time, stupidly trying to discover a cure. It consisted of a large title, then an ovular drawing with squares on, surrounded at irregular distances by tiny Christian crosses, and then, half a page of diminutive writing in a script I'd never seen before. The same script I'd seen on the snake, I think, but my brain was overheating, and I may have been mistaken, fervently creating pointless connections where none existed.

I had to get this map to Dimbleby Manfred, didn't I? That's what Ijeoma had told me. For all I knew, it might end up being her dying wish. *Our only chance lies in Dimbleby Manfred*, that's what she'd said. 'Our'. A cure. Oh God, please.

The ambulance arrived twenty minutes later. The paramedics – a man and a woman in their forties - quizzed me on the way to the hospital. I told them about what I called the 'lumps' rapidly appearing and disappearing under Ijeoma's skin. I didn't tell them about the whatever-it-was under the bed, because I was beginning to have doubts about the reliability of my senses. It had been night, the tag-end of a long day; it hadn't felt like a hallucination, but then it probably wouldn't. In the meantime, the arrival of the ambulance had restored the primacy of the twenty-first century, throwing everything since our arrival in Wadhurst into relief. The last fifteen hours began to feel increasingly unreal. I told them only what I considered consistent with science and sanity. Which was, I'm sure, as much as they wanted to hear.

I called Ijeoma's parents when we got to the hospital. They arrived two hours later in a furious mood which, in the end, played to my considerable advantage. They asked if we'd been using drugs. I said absolutely not. They called me a liar. It went on like this for about five minutes, then a doctor came over and quietly announced they'd done blood tests, and there was no trace of anything 'unexpected' in her body. Her parents apologised. I pretended to be much more offended than I really was: in reality, drugs weren't an outrageous assumption. When I told them I was going home to Oxford to get the necessary gear to maintain a bedside vigil, they didn't argue. I sensed Ijeoma didn't have long, which meant I had to act quickly and decisively.

Yet as I left the hospital, I wondered how on earth I was going to find Manfred. The academic term had ended weeks ago. Data protection meant no one would tell me where to find him, even if they knew. He might be anywhere in the world.

VII.

On the train back to Oxford, I slept for the first time in nearly twenty-four hours. I dreamed Ijeoma and I were still in that copse. I sat on the ground with my eyes closed, she quietly paced and muttered behind me. She gave a yelp. I stood up. She pointed. Way in the distance, that enormous snake – five hundred yards long now - making its way over the fields towards us at speed. Again, those horribly human eyes. We ran. But we knew it was hopeless. I jerked awake.

I must have fallen asleep five or six times across the course of nearly three hours, and each time, it was like I'd pressed re-set. When I disembarked at Oxford, I felt queasy. I wondered if I should get some Nytol from the pharmacist in town. I'd probably function twice as effectively after a proper rest.

But no. Sleep was out of the question. I needed to find Manfred. How, I still didn't know.

Then I realised. I wouldn't need to find him. He would find me.

Which probably involved walking about a lot outside the flat in an effort to ensure that, wherever he was lurking, he'd catch sight of me. Perhaps I should wear bright clothes. No hat: he had to see my face. If it was going to work at all, it'd work quickly. My hypothesis assumed that he'd be in the immediate vicinity and actively on the lookout.

With all that in mind, I decided to give him twenty-four hours. If the whole thing failed, I'd have to get back to Pembury Hospital and Ijeoma. I could explain the delay to her parents with a claim that there had been lots of loose ends to tie up at work.

In fact, I'd forgotten all about work. I wasn't sure how I was going to account for any of this to Marsha, my manager. I was supposed to be laid up in bed, ill. How to explain I'd been in a holiday cottage in bloody Wadhurst?

And, if Ijeoma died, the police would almost certainly want to talk to me. They'd have a hard time construing her death as murder, but they might decide to give it a go. Even if I escaped a prison sentence, I could well end up becoming a pariah.

Relatively speaking, though, that was a minor worry. The only thing that really seemed to matter was that I might never see her again. It only fully struck me when I'd got back inside the flat and closed the front door. I lay on the bed and wept uncontrollably.

I finally pulled myself together with the knowledge that every moment indoors was time wasted. I showered and changed into my duffle coat. I grabbed Ijeoma's yellow scarf from the cupboard. I picked up the clutch of Christmas cards from behind the front door. I could open them as I walked.

Where to go? The porch of Saint John's was a stupid choice, I knew that. But it was as good as anywhere. After that, the local supermarket. I badly needed food, drink and two Paracetamol.

It was when I opened the third of the six cards that the breakthrough occurred.

To Ijeoma and Peter,

Happy Christmas from Dimbleby Manfred.

PS. If you need to contact me for any reason, I will be staying at the Beaufort Madrigal Hotel in Mayfair until the 28th of this month.

VIII.

I called The Beaufort Madrigal, grabbed my credit card, a Cornish pasty and a can of dandelion and burdock, and set off. After I'd eaten, I slept all the way to Paddington, then I ran across London to the Beaufort, dodging the last-minute Christmas shoppers.

Manfred was waiting for me outside the hotel. He held a briefcase. "Did you bring the map?" were his first words.

I wasn't going to hand it over without securing significant concessions. "I need you to help Ijeoma," I said.

"Where is she?"

"In hospital. In Pembury. Tunbridge Wells."

"You're going to have to tell me everything if I'm to assist you. But rest assured, I *can* do so. Shall we leave for the station?"

He looked delighted at the way things had turned out, but trying hard to conceal it. I waited till we were on board the 14.53 to Hastings before I handed the map over. We sat opposite each other in a virtually empty first-class carriage, with two vacant seats either side of us. He studied the document for a few moments, then looked quizzically at it upside-down and sideways.

"It's stating the obvious to say this is a photocopy," he remarked eventually. "I don't suppose you know what she did with the original?"

"No, but she might be able to tell you when she recovers."

"Never mind. It's of solely antiquarian value. What happened, exactly?"

I told him everything, down to the smallest detail, beginning with Ijeoma's reaction to his offer of co-authorship and finishing with me opening his Christmas card.

"I suppose you've realised by now that was no 'snake' you saw," he said. "Or rather, yes it *was*, but not in the biological sense." He held his hand up. "Don't talk, just listen. Wadhurst's only an hour away. We haven't much time."

"Wadhurst? But aren't we...? I mean, the hospital's in Tunbridge Wells."

"We can't do anything there. Have you ever heard of an old Muslim remark about camels? God has one hundred names. Humans know ninety-nine of them. Camels know the hundredth, but not the other ninety-nine. I'll explain its relevance in a moment.

"Meanwhile, you may have been wondering what the 'missing half' of Ijeoma's document is. Well, it's a short description of some goings-on in Wadhurst in the seventeenth century. Rather later, historically speaking, than falls within my specialism - or Ijeoma's, for that matter. It reports that, between 1625 and 1657, a clutch of villagers reported seeing a huge glowing 'snake', only grotesquely bigger and with human eyes. The story gets vague at that point: it's partly obscured by time, but also, I think by a kind of wilful forgetting. The various clues to the snake's lair led to a local hillock, under which the 'demonic thing' was deemed to live. Another, independent line of the investigation uncovered evidence to suggest the hillock itself was the favoured site for regular meetings of 'witches', although no specific individual 'witches' were ever named. My own researches have uncovered why. 'Witches', then, as nearly always, tended to be defenceless old women, slightly aloof from the wider community, possessing a certain degree of coveted wealth, dealing perhaps in herbal remedies, charms and diverse innocuous 'spells', and easy to scapegoat. The 'witches' of the

Wadhurst hillock however, were of a different stripe: they were all influential men from London. Warlocks, I suppose you could call them, or simply occultists. They came from a variety of walks of life, all professional. Esoteric 'science' was highly fashionable in those days: intellectuals of all persuasions got aboard: Isaac Newton himself was a fan. In any case, these men had the power to make ruinous accusations rebound on the accuser, with possibly fatal consequences for the latter.

"Even so, they must have been nervous. They gave the authorities today's equivalent of half a million pounds to 'forget' what had been discovered. The villagers weren't so easily bought off. They staked out that particular hillock on a nightly basis for over twenty years." He laughed humourlessly. "Imagine that! Twenty years!

"Anyway, the occultists apparently dispersed and the sightings of snakes petered out. It wasn't until a hundred and fifty years later that the whole thing came to anyone's notice again. The sect associated with the Wadhurst hillock had produced a limited edition quarto – eight pages, in Latin, entitled *Clavicula Serpentis* – of which a copy was discovered in the Bodleian Library. Its central contention was that something went wrong in the Garden of Eden, but it could be put right: the human that finds a way of doing so will find a way of becoming like God. Snakes know what it was, but they don't know anything else. You can probably see the relevance of the Islamic camel now. The difference is that *one snake in particular* holds the key.

"Of course, the Garden of Eden story's a myth, you're probably thinking. No one believes it nowadays, not even Christians or Jews." He chuckled. "Well, that depends on what you think a 'myth' is. Myths can contain a lot of truth, in their way. In fact, sometimes they can be truer than modern methodological history. After all, the past doesn't exist. It literally *doesn't exist*. All we have are converging documents from which we construct something that we agree to call 'the past'. It's a very, very deeply established convention. But it *is* still a convention, nevertheless.

"All of which brings me to Ijeoma's map. An incredible find. Once in a lifetime, and that only if you're lucky. What it conclusively proves is that our seventeenth century Wadhurst occultists were no innovators; that the central claim of the *Clavicula Serpentis* didn't originate with them. My educated guess is that it was already ancient when they discovered it. By ancient, I mean, far older than either of us can imagine. The original of this photocopy, even if Ijeoma can produce it, will still be a copy of a copy of a copy of something now irretrievably lost. You've probably guessed by now that I never had any intention co-authoring an expository paper with her. Had she accepted my offer, I'd have taken the thing and burned it. For her own good.

"Which is all very interesting and curious, of course, but how will any of this help her? The truth is, this isn't the first time I've ever seen the document you've just handed me. I first encountered a copy when I was in my early twenties, the equivalent of a junior lecturer, just as she is today. I was researching the background to a book called the *Picatrix*, I don't know whether you've ever heard of it? A long dissertation on astrology and magic, translated from Arabic into Latin in the thirteenth century, and circulated initially in Spain. I'd gained scholarly access to a library in a mansion house in Córdoba. It was late evening. I was sitting beside a large landscape window, gazing out at one of the great Moorish gardens of the Al-Andalus era, by the last rays of sunlight. I'd just decided to wind up my labours for the day, and I began gathering piles of textbooks to re-shelve them, and it just fell out from between the pages of a volume on Alfonso the Wise.

"It took me a few days to realise what I'd got, but when I did, I managed to decipher it – just as Ijeoma must have done, although she probably didn't tell you. Unlike her, however, I put it together with the *Clavicula,* about which I'd already heard a little at a weekend conference in Warwick. And then, of course, I travelled – just as you did – to Wadhurst. I stood on that little hillock, just as she did. I pronounced the words, made the gestures, and walked the specified paces in the stipulated directions.

"And of course, the snake appeared. Well, one can hardly call it a snake, can one? A monstrous thing. The ghost of a snake, really: the original, the blueprint, of which all others are fallen parodies. And it bit me, as I meant it to. And then it slithered away.

"And then… well, my whole world changed."

He looked out of the window, as if not sure how to continue. Then he looked directly at me. Something about his gaze told me he'd been so absorbed in his own story, he'd not really noticed my reaction. He was looking to see how far, if at all, he'd left me behind.

But after all I'd seen recently, I'd have believed more or less anything. "In what way, 'changed'?" I asked.

"I now know what went wrong in the world, and what humans can do to put it right. Only, it's a kind of trivial knowledge: nothing we don't all know already. Meanwhile, I can see things others can't. And that's the worst of it. I've learned to live with it because I have to, but believe me, it's no exaggeration when I say I wish I'd never been born."

"Hang on, let's go back a bit. You say the snake *bit* you? So, is – is that what happened to Ijeoma then?"

"I'm afraid not. I'm pretty sure she hadn't accessed the *Clavicula,* so she almost certainly didn't perform the whole thing correctly. There's virtually zero margin for error, you see. No, the snake's invaded her body, and, left to her own devices, she'll die in a day or two. Asphyxiation, probably. Just an ordinary, run of the mill death, though. And she'll likely be sedated at the time, so she won't feel anything. As for the afterlife, well, she did do a lot of praying beforehand, so she's probably still in credit. Just."

I looked at his expression for any indication that he was joking. He wasn't.

"Look at the seat next to you," he said. "Tell me what you see."

I did as he asked. "You mean - ? What do you mean? Synthetic velvet…? Variegated shades of blue…?"

"I mean, do you see the *figure?*"

There *was* no figure. But I didn't want to offend him: he was probably Ijeoma's last hope. "Sorry, what are you talking about?"

"Believe me, I'm not making fun of you, Peter. It's accompanied me everywhere for nearly fifty years now. As big as a hyena, covered in bristles, huge, bulbous, inhuman eyes. 'Knowledge': I've almost got used to it. Oh, it won't hurt me. It *can't*, not yet. It's waiting for me to die."

The train slowed down for Tunbridge Wells. Only another two stops to Wadhurst. My head span. But I still hadn't heard anything about what he intended to do.

"We're getting off," he said, suddenly. "We'll get a taxi to our destination. There isn't time to walk."

"What's – what's your plan?"

"Hopefully, reverse everything. I haven't seen a copy of the document you've just given me since the last time I followed its instructions, fifty years ago. I don't know what happened to my original. I half-suspect Ijeoma found it. And that, even if she destroys it - which for pity's sake I hope she will - it'll keep reappearing to selected individuals, on selected occasions, in perpetuity. Selected by what means, by who or what, I don't pretend to know. God help those individuals." He picked up his briefcase and got to his feet. "Come on."

IX.

It was more or less dark when Manfred ordered the taxi driver to stop. The final twenty minutes had felt like a re-run of two days earlier. An endless succession of country lanes, most of them apparently impassable in two directions at once, terminated by the seemingly arbitrary declaration of a destination reached. There were no other vehicles about, so no risk of causing an obstruction, and we came leisurely to a halt in the middle of the road. I don't know what Manfred thought he recognised – it all looked identical to me – or even whether he was clinically insane. I hadn't the luxury of indulging the last possibility. Neither of us had spoken since getting off the train. The sky was sprinkled with stars. It was freezing cold.

"You're probably wondering why I brought you along," he said, as the taxi disappeared over the crest of the incline before us. "We need to cross this stile, then just follow me." He handed me the briefcase. "Carry this. It contains everything we require, apart from the map, which I need to keep. Forces will try to take it off us."

"'Forces'."

"Things, forces, powers. An energy of some sort that doesn't want Ijeoma to live, and wants to guarantee my eternal damnation. Is that specific enough for you?"

"I didn't mean to sound sceptical."

He laughed. "Why not? In your shoes, I'd be beyond incredulous."

"I've seen what happened to Ijeoma."

"Even so, this must have stretched your powers of credulity to the limit. A magical ceremony, a primeval document, a group of seventeenth century warlocks, a foul fiend crouched invisibly on the synthetic velvet chair of a modern-day railway carriage?"

We crossed the stile and he set off at a brisk pace.

"I'm past scepticism," I said. "I just want to save Ijeoma. If we can do that, I'll believe anything you tell me."

"Very touching. And if true, my salvation, so I'm not knocking it."

"What exactly do I have to do?"

A wind came out of nowhere. But this wasn't a preternatural hiss masquerading as wind. It was a genuine movement of air, seemingly growing in intensity. On the horizon, even in the dark, I could see huge clouds massing.

"When we get to the hillock, in about three minutes," he said, "I need you to hand me the briefcase, then sit on the floor with your back to me. I want you to pray. I don't know whether or not you're a believer, and it doesn't particularly matter. Don't make it complicated: just say the same words over and over again. If things go as I expect them to, you'll be too frightened to deploy your imagination. 'Jesus Christ, Son of God, have mercy on us sinners' ought to do it. The 'us' is very important, of course."

"And you'll tell me when to stop?"

"If I do, it'll mean I've failed. Otherwise, you can stop when the storm's passed. It'll be up to you to judge that, but better too late than too early."

"Where will you be?"

"I'll be dead. I hope."

"Dead?"

"I stayed at the Beaufort under a false name. You might not have noticed, but on the train, and in the taxi, I took great care to conceal my face. There's nothing to connect us, Peter, and don't worry: no one will ever find my corpse."

I threw my hands up. "Okay."

He laughed. "'Okay'? You must love your girlfriend an awful lot!"

We left the footpath and ascended what I recognised as Ijeoma's hillock. The clouds were overhead now. I felt the first drops of rain. The wind shook the trees.

We stopped. He turned to face me.

"The creature I spoke of on the train, it *will* materialise. If you open your eyes, which I sincerely hope you won't, you'll probably see it. I'm going to set things up in such a way that you become a protective barrier: only by stopping you can it stop me. If you see it, the shock will probably paralyse you, at least momentarily. That'll be sufficient time for it to break in. This is my one shot at salvation, Peter. It isn't enough for me to rescind the covenant I stupidly entered into here. I need to save another person. Greater love hath no man, etcetera. This is an opportunity that won't return. If you succeed tonight, you'll have saved two individuals. Ready?"

I nodded. He wished me 'good luck'. He patted my shoulder. I sat down with my back to him and started to pray in the way he'd suggested. Just a fairly mechanical recitation of words in a specific fixed order.

Over the course of about five minutes, the wind grew until it screeched. Rain fell like little missiles. Thunder boomed nearby, then shattered overhead.

Then seemed to die down. Something grabbed my shoulder. I closed my eyes tighter and tried to ignore it.

"Peter, it's me. I'm okay now!"

My God, Ijeoma!

But no, it couldn't be. I almost skipped a beat, but in contrast to earlier, when my sceptical faculties were entirely in abeyance, now they were working overtime.

"Peter, turn round, for God's sake! I'm getting *wet!* Don't you even care? Please, Peter, look at me. What's the matter with you? *Look at me!*"

More pulling and pushing. She started to cry. "Peter, don't listen to Manfred! He hasn't told you the truth all night! He's brought you here to sacrifice you! Please, don't let us *both* die!"

Her last sentence faded away, as if the sound of her voice was being sucked backwards along a tunnel. I felt a blade on my neck. Then it penetrated the flesh and sank deep.

Manfred's voice. "Sorry I lied to you, Peter. And thank you for being so gullible."

I felt a deluge of blood run down my front. The pain was so intense, I wanted to faint, but I kept the words going.

Had it not been for the phoney Ijeoma, I'm sure I'd have believed this really was Manfred. But the creature had played its cards in the wrong order. My eyes filled with tears of agony. Nevertheless, I kept from blinking them open.

Another crash of thunder. I seemed to see a sudden burst of light through my closed eyelids, and I heard a tree fall nearby. Manfred screamed. I kept the words going. Manfred kept screaming. I kept going.

The screaming died away. Eventually, the rain died away too. The wind dropped and then expired. Finally, everything became still.

But this might just be another illusion. I kept going until I sensed I was entering that state of deadly euphoria that they say sometimes precedes death by exposure. I opened my eyes and stood up. I shivered violently.

There was no fallen tree, no blood anywhere on me, no incision in my neck, no pain. The moon was sufficiently large, and my eyes acclimatised enough to the darkness, for me to be able to discern my surroundings. Manfred lay on his back. I tried his pulse, but as I expected: nothing. I felt a weird sense of relief, and a dawning hope. He looked a lot older than when he'd been alive. More than that: I got the weird sense that he was actually decomposing before my eyes.

A victory, albeit a Pyrrhic one. I mentally prepared myself to die out here. I couldn't call in at a house and ask for a phone. When Manfred's corpse was discovered, there would be an inquest, and someone would recall the stranger who'd coming knocking that night. Somehow, I had to get to Wadhurst, or Ticehurst, find a pub and call from there. Even that might be risky, but I had to compromise with what was practical now.

It took me an hour. I was half dead when I walked into the village and The White Hart. Being nearly Christmas, it was fairly full. I don't think anyone noticed me in any meaningful way.

I called Pembury hospital. The receptionist kept me waiting a long time.

Then Ijeoma's mother. "Peter, where *on earth* have you been?"

"I – I'm sorry. I got held up."

Her tone changed. "Well, I've got unbelievable news!" She laughed. "*Good* news. You're never going to believe this. I hope you're sitting down! You missed the main event, about an hour ago: she just – sat up in bed! She's talking! She's sitting up! She's eaten some food! She even walked around the ward a bit! It's early days, and the doctors say don't take anything for granted – and we're not, oh God, we're not! But at the moment, it actually looks like she's made a full recovery!"

I chuckled. A few seconds ago, I'd felt half dead. That hadn't changed, but it was thrown into irrelevance by the recognition that it had all been worth it. "I've been praying," I said.

A short silence as she considered whether I was being ironic, and probably a further beat for her to realise it didn't matter. "Good boy," she said.

X.

We married later that month. Ijeoma burned the original of her map and left academia to set up her own business making authentic-looking medieval artefacts for display in people's homes (which quickly morphed into a bespoke art gallery). Dimbleby Manfred's 'disappearance' was reported in the national press, but no one ever came after me. I reckoned he must have been better than I thought at disguising his identity and appearance.

I didn't realise *how* good until I later saw a list of items being sold off from his estate. Ijeoma went to the auction house for the public viewing. She tells me that, among the objects on display was a document comprising a long, anonymous account of an evening spent in a library in a mansion house in Córdoba. And how, one evening, as the sun set, the author had reclined in a chair, beside a large window, gazing out at one of the great Moorish gardens of the Al-Andalus era, before carefully re-shelving his reading books. The auctioneers' expert analysts confidently assigned the entire description to 'sometime in the early eighteenth century.' It contained no mention of the slip of paper containing the map.

I later discovered there never *had* been a finding in the Bodleian library of a '*Clavicula Serpentis*'. However, a document of that name *did* appear for sale in London in 1873, in the catalogue of an antiquarian merchant called Borlick and Wood. It was immediately snapped up by an anonymous private buyer. Needless to say, that was the last anyone ever heard of it.

Reports of snake sightings in Wadhurst, and rumours of London warlocks – those things were true.

What to think?

I really don't know. 'The past'. It's a very, very deeply established convention.

The Strange Birth of the Oilman

I.

My name is not important, only that I am a ninety-three-year-old retired GP, and, as far as I'm aware, the only person still alive with any connection at all to the events I am about to describe (and even that is merely indirect). For reasons of confidentiality, I've always kept the entire story to myself, but the woman at its epicentre passed away three months ago, and, in our last meeting, she revoked her lifelong policy of reticence. She specifically asked me to air it, partly because she'd discovered, in old age, that one of the principal actors wasn't remotely who he claimed to be. She never found out who he was - or *is*. There's a very slim possibility he's still alive, and although I always maintained the statistical inconceivability of that, I couldn't convince her to share my assessment.

I came to know the story in two parts: the major portion when I first became acquainted with her in my professional capacity, in the nineteen-fifties; the rest later, after we became friends. I warn you, it begins rather like a pantomime, specifically Sleeping Beauty.

Cecily Welldringham, she was called. She's buried in the graveyard of Saint Peter and Saint Paul now. In late October, 1953, however, she was twenty-one, and she'd just become engaged to a worthy middle-class local called Trevor Stangson. Stangson was twelve years her senior, tall, dark haired, slightly melancholy - both his parents had been killed on a single night in the Blitz, and he'd never quite got over it - a committed Christian and a keen geologist. He'd seen action in North Africa and France and won a couple of medals for gallantry. After VE Day, he worked in Austria and Italy providing aid to refugees, then, in 1950, he returned to England and retrained as a surveyor. When he met Cecily, the following year, he was already a rising star in Whiteway's, the construction firm, in Crowborough. She was, by all accounts, his first girlfriend: 'sweetheart', as we would probably have said then.

Cecily's was one of the wealthier families in Wadhurst - they owned a big house called Headingly Grove on the long road between Durgates and Mark Cross - and since she was an only child, her parents wanted an engagement party that pushed the boat out. They hired a hotel on Mount Ephraim in Tunbridge Wells and invited all the local and not-so-local notables. According to *The Courier*, they got an excellent turn-out: Cecily and her fiancé were both attractive and well-liked, and of course it was free food; this was six months before rationing ended, and wealthy people especially (as always) were keen to save even tiny amounts of money wherever they feasibly could. Despite the plaudits, however, I doubt it was *that* extravagant an occasion. While it's true that the Welldringhams were well off, they certainly weren't rich. Relatively speaking, property was much, much cheaper then, so even their big house doesn't signify as much as you might imagine.

All of which might explain why, when Cecily's great-great-uncle Ian (on her mother's side) turned up at the party uninvited, although a certain number of feathers were ruffled, Mr and Mrs Welldringham were loath to turn him away. And – you'll have to indulge me here - this is where the story assumes rather a 'Grimm Brothers' flavour.

Great-great-uncle Ian – let's just call him 'Uncle Ian' for the sake of brevity – was a tall, brawny man with a lantern jaw, grey eyes and a habitually supercilious expression. No one knew exactly how old he was: estimates ranged between seventy and a hundred, even though in 1953 – I've seen photos of him – he didn't look frail enough for a centenarian. He always dressed expensively, and gave a plausible impression of having hoards of cash. And I mean very plausible. Although, for some reason, he wasn't well-liked by his kith and kin, he was unfailingly generous. He'd saved at least one member of the family from bankruptcy, and another from destitution after that individual had returned from Monte Cassino with a leg missing, only to discover his house had been obliterated by the Luftwaffe.

Cecily's mother, Viola, a thin, confident woman in her late forties with a clipped upper-class accent, claimed the reason Uncle Ian hadn't been invited had primarily to do with his age – "it was a young person's bash," she said – and, in addition, the fact that he lived several hundred miles away in the Lake District. But I'm not so certain. Surely, it would have been polite to go through the motions of inviting him, even – no, *especially* - if they thought he'd decline. They'd have ensured his goodwill for the mere price of a postage stamp.

On the other hand, maybe she knew more than she was letting on. You see, it later transpired that 'Uncle Ian' wasn't a member of the Welldringham family at all. Just before she died, Cecily had a search done on one of those genealogy websites you're always coming across on the internet: there was no trace of an 'Ian' anywhere in her ancestry, near or distant, and no individual who could conceivably fit his description. Who he really was – or *is*; I'll come to that later – remains, and must probably continue to remain, a complete mystery.

In any case, he'd come to her party bearing a present. Or rather, presents. Before I tell you precisely what they were, it'll help if you realise that, together, they supposedly comprised the undisputed ownership of an oilfield, and thus the possibility of great wealth – even if all the lucky recipient did was sell them on to the highest bidder. The first part of the 'gift' was the title deed to three-quarters of an acre of fenced grassland within the civil parish of Wadhurst. Superficially, the other part of the 'gift' was even more singular: a seventeenth century parchment describing a small field in a geographical depression – presumably, the same patch of land as in the title deed - fouled from beneath by 'a coloured substance which defileth all things which do attempt to live or grow therein'. It had an addendum in Latin, predicting that one day, a virgin would come into possession of the field, and magically become rich.

Stangson, Cecily's fiancé, strongly suspected that Uncle Ian had added that part himself. As for Cecily, she was slow on the uptake that night: she wasn't sure whether it was meant to be a joke, or whether the *whole thing* was meant to be a joke, or really *what* it was meant to be. It certainly wasn't a conventional present: a nice piece of jewellery, or a silk dress, or a pair of West End theatre tickets. It was a literal… field.

Good manners prevented her showing her bemusement. She danced with the giver, and tried her utmost to compensate, as well as hide her discomfiture, for not inviting him to her party. She still had no notion what to make of him. He was an old man, and he wasn't married, so he'd probably lived a peculiar life. For all she knew, he might even have been one of those 'shell shock' victims of the First War, one who'd never quite recovered. There were probably lots of them still about. And, given that she hadn't expected any gift at all from him, she couldn't feel disappointed.

At eleven o'clock, as Joe Phelps's Big Band was into its penultimate number, Uncle Ian made for the exit. Cecily followed him out, probably intending to apologise yet again for not sending an invite. She was like that. The foyer was full of people in the heartiest of moods, most probably slightly inebriated, all getting hats and coats and promising they must meet up for lunch in this, that or the other town sometime soon.

Uncle Ian stood in the doorway, putting a silk scarf on. He looked to be in a hurry. She ran up to him.

"Thank you again," she said. "I'm really glad you came tonight."

He discreetly took her arm, moved her bodily to one side and whispered in her ear. "Don't look lightly on what I've given you. There's oil beneath Wadhurst, and you can lay claim to it. You could become one of the richest women in the world!"

She suddenly realised what he'd given her. What he *thought* he'd given her.

Taking advantage of her speechlessness, he kissed her hand, hailed a cab and gave her a final, grim wave from the rear seat.

As he pulled away, she sighed with relief. He hadn't quite ruined the party. The fact that he hadn't been invited: *that* had ruined it. She should send him a big thank you card, and invite him over to stay at her house for a night or two, regardless of what her parents might think. And, of course, yes, he might be slightly bonkers, but she was at least obliged to go through the motions of investigating his claims. She couldn't add negligence to injury.

All of which was horribly bothersome.

II.

In bed that night, Mr and Mrs Welldringham had a private *tête-à-tête* about Uncle Ian's bombshell appearance at the ball. They quizzed Cecily the next day. The three sat in the drawing room, Cecily in the centre of a large sofa with her hands clasped in her lap and her toes together, her mother and father on separate armchairs, facing her. Cecily recounted in detail what she'd already told them in outline before going to bed last night. She showed them the two documents.

When the account was complete, her mother laughed unconvincingly. "I'm afraid it would be hilarious if it wasn't so sad."

"I'm not sure I like this bit about a 'virgin'," her father said, frowning as he examined the writing. "I think it's in rather bad taste. What is it? Some kind of pagan allusion?"

"'Virgin' simply meant young woman in those days," her mother said. "There need be nothing prurient about it."

Her father hmm-ed. "I'd be a lot more inclined to believe it was the deeds to an oil well if he'd actually had a few soundings done; consulted one or two experts. A seventeenth century scrap of paper talking about 'a coloured substance' proves nothing at all. There are lots of things it might be and lots of reasons plants might not grow there. Besides, oil's black, it's not coloured."

Cecily raised her index finger. "When the light shines on a thin enough film - "

"Don't let's split hairs," her father snapped. "What he's actually given you, my dear, is a useless, infertile piece of land, suitable for neither crops nor livestock. I'm prepared to give him the benefit of the doubt and assume he meant well, but I strongly suspect he's a bit of a simpleton."

"Why didn't we invite him?" Cecily asked. "It was quite embarrassing when he just turned up!"

"We don't necessarily invite *all* our relatives to *every*thing," her mother replied indulgently. "We don't consider ourselves to be that interesting or important."

"We didn't invite your uncle William or your great-aunt Grace," her father said. "Should we have? It was *your* day, or meant to be; yours and Trevor's. Would you really have wanted a clutch of old biddies loitering about, sniping, and devouring all the cheese and ham sandwiches?"

Her mother nodded. "Now the *wedding:* that will be a different matter. Weddings *are* for families." She took the parchment her husband had passed her and held it up to the light from the garden. "I'm going to London tomorrow morning, to do some shopping. Your father knows a firm of experts who can pronounce authoritatively on the supposed 'seventeenth century' provenance of this… whatever-it-is. Would you like me to take it in, to see them? I can guarantee a quick verdict, but obviously, I warn you, Cess: prepare to be mightily disappointed."

"Yes, of course," Cecily said. She suspected a trap, though an amateurish one. The truth was, she didn't need that particular document any more. If her mother accidentally 'lost' it on her way to or from 'town' (as she usually called the capital), it wouldn't make the slightest difference. She knew the location. Even better, she *owned* the location, at which there either was or wasn't subterranean oil. She was personally convinced there wasn't, but determined to keep an open mind for Uncle Ian's sake.

The following morning, Mrs Welldringham left for London at nine with the parchment in her handbag. Half an hour earlier, Mr Welldringham had gone into work in Tunbridge Wells (I believe he worked for a firm of solicitors). At 10.30, Trevor Stangson appeared at the house. Cecily let him in, although she hadn't expected him. She poured him a scotch and they sat side by side on the sofa like a pair of lovers. She squeezed his arm. He kissed her fingernails. They talked about the party, what a perfect blast it had been, and how they couldn't wait to get married. Then they discussed fixtures and furnishings for their new home, and what all the latest kitchen implements could do. They'd already decided to set up house in Wadhurst.

Yet all the while, Cecily kept wondering what had made him drop in unannounced, and so early in the day. He wasn't necessarily expected to make an *appointment* to call, of course - this was *nineteen* fifty-three, not *eighteen* fifty-three! - and she was genuinely happy to see him. Even so, it was unlike him to simply *turn up*.

She became convinced he had news. There was something he wanted to tell her, something portentous. He was merely looking for the right opportunity.

Eventually, she couldn't bear it any longer. "Please don't take this the wrong way, darling. I love you, yet I can see there's something on your mind. Have I done something to upset you?"

"Absolutely not, my precious!"

"Then what?"

He stood up, put his hands in his pockets and went to stand in front of the empty grate. "Your great-great-uncle," he said. "I saw him today, at ten, just before I came here. He's in Wadhurst."

She looked at him dumbly, as if to say, what of it? "He's probably just staying on a few nights," she said, "before getting the train - "

"I've seen him twice before in the last few weeks. The first time, nearly a month ago. When he turned up at our party, I recognised him by sight, though initially, I couldn't quite place him. It was only afterwards that the penny dropped. It therefore came as rather a surprise to discover that he's supposed to be living in The Lake District!"

Cecily drew her eyebrows together. "You're absolutely sure it was him?"

"I'm certain."

He sat down on the armchair, facing her. They endured a short silence.

"Well, it explains how he got to know about the party," she said at last, "but it certainly isn't evidence of duplicity. He didn't *claim* to be living in The Lake District, after all – that was my parents' idea. True, it seems odd that he should be living somewhere right on our doorstep. But not overly. He might just know he isn't welcome here, and so be keeping a low profile."

"I suppose it's not impossible," Trevor said.

"Which simply makes it all the more pitiable, of course. My parents have obviously 'cut him off', as the phrase has it. If it reflects badly on anyone, it's them. I need to have a stern word with them when they get in. This is the twentieth century. There's no longer any room for black sheep in a family."

"Hear, hear." He chuckled. "Although I never officially used that expression. It's not for me to come between you and your parents."

"My mother's gone to London, to get Uncle Ian's document assessed."

"'Assessed'?"

"Dated. To see if it's genuine sixteen-hundreds."

"Oh, dear. I wonder what the verdict will be."

"'I'm afraid it's a complete forgery,'" Cecily said, imitating her mother. "'Oh my, what a terrible shame!'" She added, in her own voice: "I feel really sorry for Uncle Ian now."

"Why do you think he didn't tell you he was living in Wadhurst, when you met him at the party?"

"Does it matter? Oh, Trevor, what if it's all *true?*"

"If it is, you'll need to buy up the surrounding land pronto. And I'll tell you something else. These 'authenticators' your mother's taken it to: if she tells them the whole story, as she very well might, they could get ideas. They might dishonestly declare it a forgery so they can steal a march on you. You might end up owning nothing more than a tiny corner of a gargantuan oilfield. And, of course, then they'll elbow you out pretty sharpish."

"I think you're getting ahead of yourself, darling," she said. "I'm much more concerned that my mother will return with 'proof' that it's a fake document, and that any further investigation on my part will look like I'm questioning her honesty. Once she gets home tonight, it'll be *subject closed* for ever. And of course, there really *might* be oil down there! If Uncle Ian lives locally, maybe he knows a thing or two about the lie of the land; a thing or two more than he let on!"

"I suppose that's possible, yes."

"So, we've got to act right *now*, Trevor, before my parents get home! There really isn't a moment to lose! You know all about oil, don't you? I mean, geology's your hobby?"

"I'm no expert. But yes, if there really is oil in your little three-quarters of an acre, I'll probably be able to detect it. It's an incredibly long shot, but Uncle Ian's gift might yet end up making us rich."

Cecily got changed into a pair of riding boots, a worsted jacket and jodhpurs. Luckily, the weather was fine, and the forecast said it would stay so. Her field was about two miles away, over open countryside. They set off like zealots on a mission.

III.

Their sense of adventure, as they left Headingly Grove and struck out southwest across the fields for Tidebrook, diminished as they increasingly got the impression they were being followed. Neither could explain it, nor could they find any supporting evidence, so they agreed not to talk about it. But since they couldn't stop thinking about it, they fell to walking in silence. They arrived at their destination just over an hour later.

Trevor had a map and compass, but even he found the location difficult to pinpoint. Once they got there, however, the recognition was eerily instant: this was the spot. A fenced-off dip in the ground, like a collapsed mineshaft, surrounded on all sides, at a distance, by tall fir trees which seemed to be leaning in, lugubriously, as if curious to see something. The fence was an old-fashioned chestnut pale, and broken or decayed in several places. It had probably been put there to prevent livestock straying in, rather than to stop anything getting out. The declivity was shallow; even so, the lowest point, in the middle, was a whole ten feet or so below the level of the fence, and partly overgrown with reeds. Perhaps because the entire place was in perpetual shade, it felt gloomy. But there was also a distinct ambiance of something not wholly congenial to life.

"Spooky," was Trevor's first comment.

"Can you see any oil down there?" Cecily asked, "or should we climb over the fence?"

"Probably safer to walk through one of the gaps. There's so little light I'll need to get a lot closer to the bottom, I'm afraid. And of course, those reeds aren't helping."

"Can reeds grow in oil?"

"It wouldn't be pure oil. When it rains, water must collect down here. I'm surprised it's not a lake, frankly, or at the very least, a pond. I'll go down and have a look. You stay here."

"I want to come with you. We're going to be married soon, and I want us to do things *together*."

"I don't want you to have an accident."

"I'm not a child, darling. I know I haven't been in the army or anything, but I'm still capable of walking up and down a gentle gradient without breaking my neck. What do you think we've been doing for the last two miles?"

"I'd hardly call this a 'gentle gradient'."

"It's not a mountainside."

"I'll go down first, then when I'm at the bottom, you can follow. That way, if you fall, I can catch you."

She shrugged. She didn't want a tiff, and he was only being nice, and he had been in the army.

He edged his way through the fence where it had decayed and walked slowly down the slope, watching his footing and holding his arms out slightly for balance. Then his feet slipped from under him. He fell on his back with a slap, tried to sit up, and slid down the hill as if he was on a sledge. When he came to a stop, near the bottom, he looked at his muddy palms as if he couldn't quite believe it. He didn't look pleased.

Cecily had a choice. She could either go after him and probably suffer the same fate, and then die laughing, or she could stay where she was and die laughing. Either way, she'd die laughing. Reasoning that it's always better to laugh with someone than appear to be laughing at them, she chose the former.

"I'm coming!" she called.

"No, *don't!*" he replied.

She pushed the fence out of the way, charged forward, slipped and fell on her bottom – it wasn't even deliberate! – skidded ignominiously, and came to rest beside him, equally muddy.

"Ow," she said.

"Quite," he remarked.

For some reason, she didn't feel like laughing any more. As she put it later, it was almost as if, in breaching the fence, she'd crossed some kind of boundary, and things weren't, and couldn't be, funny down here. On top of which, it smelt overpoweringly of decay and stagnation. Almost instantly, she wanted to get out and go home.

The next thing she noticed though, was that the 'gentle gradient' didn't appear so gentle from here. It looked formidable. A shiver ran through her entire body, and it had nothing to do with the increased cold. She thought: *what have I just done?*

She turned round and tried to clamber up to the fence. But she slipped onto her front and slid back to where she'd started.

"We're trapped," she said.

"I think that's probably a bit premature," he told her. "Since we're down here and caked in mud, I suppose we might as well check for oil. It is, after all, what we came here for. Are you all right, darling?"

"Never been better!" she quipped.

Now that they were almost at the base of the depression, they could see clearly where the reeds were growing. A shallow-looking pond coated with a thin film of what could be petroleum, but could equally be any kind of oil at all.

Trevor stood up and walked towards it.

"What are you doing?" she said anxiously.

"I'm going to test the waters."

"But what if it's a swamp? What if you get sucked in, and we can't get you out? We could be miles from help, depending on whether there's anyone out for a walk in this part of the woods! You might just sink slowly without a trace!"

"I'll tell you precisely what we're dealing with here," he said calmly, "and then I want you to stop worrying. It's a collapsed tunnel, that's all. From what I remember, they used to mine clay, in Wadhurst, for making iron. Or it may have been iron ore they were after. And that would be before the seventeenth century. Either way, I know there are disused mineshafts round here. What we're sitting in is a collapsed one. In other words, it's sunk down as far as it'll go. We're probably safer here than at the top of the slope, because that part might be yet to collapse."

"Yes, I see," she said.

"You're shivering." He removed his jacket. "Here, put this on."

She didn't complain. She felt like crying. She suddenly wondered whether Uncle Ian had planned all this. Maybe there was a reason her parents had 'cut him off'. And hadn't she and Trevor had the distinct impression of being shadowed all the way here? True, it might be paranoia, but if not, who *else* would be following them? Who else would anticipate their impetuously setting off, full of the desire to investigate the source of their newly-acquired future wealth, and their subsequent entrapment? Deserved entrapment, because they'd been greedy. Or he might see it that way.

Trevor had waded into the pond without taking his shoes off. He crouched down and pressed his hand onto the bottom.

"What are you doing?" she asked, trying to show an interest.

"There is a little oil on the surface," he said, "although I'm not sure what kind: we'd need to test it in a laboratory. However, there might be more. If I can get my hand down far enough, I might be able to identify a particular type of rock, if there is any, although I would imagine it's entirely clay. So, I'm just checking to see how far the whole thing goes down. Now we're here, we might as well be as thorough as possible." He chuckled. "Save us coming back."

"I never want to see this place again," she said.

Suddenly, he lost his balance as his arm seemed to be swallowed up. He fell side-down in the water with a yelp. Cecily gasped.

Then he righted himself. He grinned, awkwardly. "There's a – there's a cavity down there!"

"Come away!"

He ignored her and put his arm right down, so that he was on his side again, but in a controlled way. "I can feel something," he said. "Something… unusual."

He stayed in the same position for a few more seconds, probing. His face gradually changed. He sat up suddenly, with an expression of intense shock.

But Cecily wasn't looking at him. She'd caught sight of something way above the perimeter of the fence, where the acclivity met the skyline. In between the trunks of two huge fir trees, the small black outline of a tall man, obviously watching them.

It looked like Uncle Ian.

"We need to leave," Trevor said. "Come on. If we try the other side, it'll probably be drier. There has to be at least *one* relatively dry slope. Rainwater can't run down every side."

"Uncle Ian!" she shouted. *"We need help!"*

The figure didn't move.

Trevor followed her sight-line. His expression became incredulous, then indignant. *"You've had your fun, you blighter!"* he yelled. *"Now do the decent thing, and help us get out of here!"*

The figure didn't move.

IV.

It took them three-quarters of an hour to get out. When they finally crawled through the fence, 'Uncle Ian' had gone. They sat side by side, gasping for a few moments, then Cecily said: "What was it?"

"What was what?"

"You felt something down there. When you were putting your hand in. That was why I turned away. I could see how scared you were, and that made me doubly frightened. To take my mind off it, I looked for Uncle Ian, since I was thinking about him."

"What were you thinking about *Uncle Ian* for?"

"Because he led us into this! He *must* have known! He must *hate* us! No wonder Mummy and Daddy were suspicious at the party! If anything, they were too nice about the whole thing! Oh, I can't believe I've been so *stupid!*"

"Don't blame yourself. I've been a pretty useless fiancé."

She burst into tears again. "You've been a *perfect* fiancé! Don't ever say that! If you hadn't been there, I'd probably have come down here on my own, then I'd *never* have got out!"

"We need to get moving, my beauty. The weather's looking as if it might change, and we need to get back to your house and get you cleaned up before your parents get home. They'll call me all the names under the sun if they find out I've got you into this state!"

He got to his feet and offered her his hand. They walked northeast for a few seconds, then he stopped.

"I've dropped my watch," he said. "Stay here."

She looked at him as if he was insane. But he was already on his way back. Before she could follow him, however, he picked up his wristwatch from just beside the fence and announced, "Got it!" in an unconvincingly chirpy voice. Instead of rushing immediately back to her, however, he glanced down into the crater.

It was then that she realised the watch was just a pretext. He wanted to check something at the bottom of the depression. Her suspicions were confirmed when his face filled with a new level of alarm.

He ran back to her, put his right arm firmly round her waist, and propelled her forcefully in their original direction.

She didn't ask what he'd seen. She didn't want to know, not yet anyway. Not until they were out of the wood and in bright sunlight. Perhaps not even then.

They walked briskly rather than ran, because the ground was uneven and they were exhausted. Just as they reached the last of the trees and the beginning of open farmland, there was an apoplectic roar from somewhere behind them: the sort of thing a colossal creature might emit, but a hundred times louder than anything natural.

They sped up, and emerged in a panic onto a deserted country lane. They joined hands and began to run. An instinct for survival had kicked in, and it told them to put every last scrap of their energy into flight. Nothing else mattered, and curiosity was the biggest luxury of all.

"You're going too fast!" Cecily yelled at last. *"You're going to pull me over!"*

He stopped. He threw his arms round her, squeezed her tight and buried his head in her neck. "My God!" he said. "My God! *My God!"*

V.

They walked and ran, and walked and ran, in silence. Within forty-five minutes, they'd arrived back at Headingly Grove. They had a quick conference and decided this was as safe as they were likely to get. They were dimly conscious of being caked in mud. They didn't want to dirty the furniture, so they sat on a couple of hard kitchen chairs for half an hour, with their heads in their hands.

Being back in familiar surroundings gradually calmed them. Cecily went upstairs, changed out of her torn clothes and had a bath. Trevor sat on the patio with a large brandy. He looked out across the countryside to where the wood was, as if he needed to keep an eye on it. He trembled. At one point, he said The Lord's Prayer.

Cecily came downstairs after twenty minutes in a new dress and a woollen cardigan. She stood on the patio's threshold, clutching the door frame on either side. "Your turn," she said dully. "I've put some of father's clothes on the landing, for you to change into."

"I can't do that," he told her. "I don't have his permission."

"At least come into the house then. It's freezing outside."

"We need to keep watching the woods."

"The sun will be going down soon. You - *we* - can't watch forever. What did you feel under the pond?"

"We'll have to tell them everything, Cecily. Your parents, I mean. We can't keep them in the dark." He took another sip of brandy and looked back at the woods. "I'm not even sure whether we should go to the police or not. The trouble is, the police might come to *us*. Then we'll be in even more trouble. Oh, my darling, I'm so sorry I got you into this!"

She sat down next to him and put her hand over his. "We're both in shock, I think. Now, I'm going to ask you again, and I need you to answer this time; not for my sake: we've got to share something like this if we're going to deal with it, and especially if we're going to tell Mummy and Daddy. What - *what did you feel under the water?*" Despite her build-up, the question came out as if she'd rather it hadn't.

"A face," he said. "Like a human face. Nose, mouth, eyes, the entire gamut."

He took a deep breath and looked at her, apparently to see if he was scaring her *unnecessarily*. She did her best to maintain an impassive expression, and she must have succeeded, because he continued:

"That was bad enough, but then I went back to have a look, after we'd walked away. I hadn't lost my watch, incidentally. I'd taken it off and left it there, expressly so I'd have an excuse to return. You see, it wasn't just that I felt a face. I got the distinct impression it was *alive*."

"You said, '*like* a human face.' What do you - "

"Much bigger. And somehow… not quite as solid. I don't know how to put it… *Oily*."

"And what did you see when you went back for your watch?"

"Whatever it was had sat up. I saw a huge head, arms, a torso. Just like a monstrous – I don't know: bigger than anything I've ever seen before, even in a book or at the pictures. I couldn't make out a face anymore. It was exactly as if it was sucking in the light. And then when we heard that horrendous bellow… That was *it*, I'm sure. Oh, God. What *was* it?"

She laughed nervously. Dusk had arrived and the fields and hedgerows had turned grey. An unnatural calm lay over the landscape, as if it had arrived with a view to extinguishing not only all the usual sounds of life, but all the movement too. There was no birdsong, nothing flying, nothing grazing, no wind caressing the treetops. Everything seemed to be waiting for some newer, stranger phase in the history of the world.

"Maybe it was just a big man," she said at last, as if she was talking to herself. She began to shake. "Yes, that's what it must have been. We should call the police. Right now. Because we can't deal with this alone. It must be a murder, although not quite, because the victim's still alive, apparently." Her voice rose a tone. "The police will know what to do. We need to tell them, now. Obviously, there's a natural explanation for all of it. It's just a murder. I say 'just'. We'll call the police. We can't deal with this alone."

Trevor put both arms round her and held her tight. "It's settled then," he said. "I'll probably have to go with them. Obviously, I can't leave you on your own, and you need to rest. I could call one or two of your friends. I'm sure they'll be happy to come over and look after you. How about Sarah or Beatrice?"

Trevor's strong embrace, and the thought of her two stalwart companions, gradually calmed her. She took a deep breath and told herself to stop panicking, she wasn't a child. But then another consideration struck her.

"It can't be *friends*, darling. They'll want to know all about it and I'll end up getting a reputation. Oh, they'll sympathise, but later on, they'll tell every Tom, Dick and Harry in the world. Maybe ... I don't know... you could get hold of Daddy at work? I'm sure he wouldn't mind coming home a little early."

"Easily done."

"And maybe don't talk to the police until after we've talked to him. Three heads are better than one. Four, when Mummy gets home."

VI.

It was dark when Mr Welldringham got in, even though he'd left Tunbridge Wells an hour early. He looked incredulously at Trevor, stated the obvious – you're covered in mud – then ordered him to go and get changed into some of his own clothes, and take a bath. After twenty minutes, when that was done, he sat in his favourite armchair in the living room and poured himself a large scotch. He smoked his pipe while Trevor and Cecily perched together on the sofa and told their tale. He oscillated between nodding, chuckling, and looking pessimistically amazed. When they'd finished speaking, he leaned back and raised one eyebrow, as if to say, 'Well, I couldn't *possibly* tell you what to make of all that!'

"And you think you should inform the police?" he said. "Let me ask you, could you have left anything behind, anything connecting you to the scene? I mean, apart from all the obvious slip marks in the mud and what not? You've checked you didn't drop anything there?"

"I'm pretty sure *I* didn't," Cecily said. "I don't have any pockets, and I removed all my jewellery before we went out. Except for my engagement ring, naturally," she added, looking affectionately at it.

"I definitely didn't drop anything," Trevor said. "The same thought had occurred to me: what if there really *has* been a murder, and we've decided not to tell the police? Could we have left something behind that they might find, and which might lead them to us? Because it'll be ten times worse if they think we're trying to hide something."

"They might try and pin it on you anyway," Mr Welldringham said. "Even if you do tell them now." He chortled. "I'd leave well alone, if I were you."

"It's not funny, Daddy!" Cecily exclaimed.

"Sorry, dear," he said, still half-smiling.

"Someone might have seen us on the way to and from the wood," she went on. "I've already told you I'm sure Uncle Ian was watching us."

Mr Welldringham shook his head. "Yet you said he didn't move in all the time you were there."

"What of it?" she replied irritably.

"Presumably," he went on, "if he'd decided to follow you at a distance, it was because he didn't want you to see him. And yet, you *did* see him. And then you called out to him. He must have heard you, and yet he didn't move." He laughed. "And of course, he'd have to have known precisely when you were setting off. Finally, even if you're right, Stangson, and he's living locally – and I give you my solemn word that's news to me – there's his age. It's not so easy to walk briskly over rough terrain when you're as old as he is." He drained his glass. "Listen to me, both of you. I have a theory, and I think you'll find it explains everything."

"Go on," Trevor said sceptically.

"When you set off from this house," Mr Welldringham replied, "you were in a very excitable frame of mind. And after about an hour, you found what you were looking for. So you were probably already a bit euphoric. Shortly afterwards, you both had nasty falls. At that point, you were undoubtedly shocked. But when you reached the bottom of the depression, you noticed a nasty smell. Now, what if that *gas* – because that's what we're talking about here: a gas: there's no smell without a gas - had the power to cause you to see things? Gases are chemicals, after all, and certain chemicals have the capacity to influence the brain. So, let's go back a bit. You've both taken a heavy tumble. You're probably panting with the unpleasant surprise of it, and, in those deep breaths you're taking, you're dosing yourselves up, completely unawares. To cap it all: Trevor, you go raking about in the muck, probably releasing yet more noxious fumes. In summary, you both got befuddled, and that caused you to hallucinate."

Trevor and Cecily looked at each other.

Cecily's face lit up. "That's it! Of course!"

"I'm not so sure," Trevor said.

"You wouldn't be," Mr Welldringham said. "I don't mean any disrespect, Stangson, but as a rule these things *do* seem real. In my line of work, I come across the occasional drug addict, sadly. Some of their delusions are as real to them as I am to you right now."

Trevor shrugged. "Well, I suppose it *is* the most likely explanation."

"By about a million miles!" Mr Welldringham exclaimed. "Listen, I'll tell you what we're going to do, you and I. We're going to wait till Cecily's mother gets in; we're going to eat a hearty dinner, then we're going to go back to that wretched 'field' of yours - we'll take the 'map', for what it's worth - and I'm going to show you there's nothing to worry about. We can drive over there. I'll bring a rope; we can tie it to a tree and let ourselves down, without fear of getting trapped; and I'll get the old gas masks out from upstairs. I'll prove the truth of my theory to you, and you can come back and tell Cecily, and we'll all live happily ever after. How does that sound?"

"Like a very good idea," Trevor said. "Thank you, Mr Welldringham."

"Mystery solved," Cecily said. "Thank you, Daddy."

They heard the front door open and close. A moment later, Cecily's mother appeared in the living room in her overcoat and hat. Everyone stood up. She was accompanied by a man of about Trevor's age in a suit. He had thinning blond hair, and he was small and slightly overweight.

"This is Mr Adkins," she said. "Clive Adkins, from Harker and Adkins in London; the firm I took your bit of parchment to, Cecily. Mr Adkins is an expert on antique documents. He's having dinner here, then he's staying the night. I asked him to come back with me because the things he told me are literally unbelievable, and I need you to hear them from the horse's mouth. It turns out Cecily's document really *is* from the sixteen-hundreds, but that's just the tip of the iceberg. Mr Adkins, this is my daughter, Cecily, her fiancé, Trevor Stangson, and my husband, Douglas. Douglas, pour Clive a drink and make him feel at home. I'll go and put the dinner on. Clive, save your story for dinner, please. I'm bound to think of more questions while I'm cooking."

VII.

Mrs Welldringham went into the kitchen and when, after twenty minutes' talk about Adkins's experiences at Dunkirk and Normandy, the conversation turned to cricket, Cecily went to set the table. Then she went to her room to change and listen to the radio on low.

At seven o'clock, Mrs Welldringham announced that dinner was ready. They all filed into the dining room, and sat at a table covered with a white cloth. A silver candelabra had been drafted in, but most of the light was provided by two dull standard lamps either side of the doorway. The evening meal - steak and kidney pie, sprouts, boiled potatoes and gravy - had already been served onto plates, which Cecily helped her mother bring in. White wine was served in crystal glasses. Trevor said grace. Everyone put on napkins. They ate.

"Before we get down to hearing what Clive has to say," Mr Welldringham said, "I think you should know, Viola, that Stangson claims to have seen our uncle Ian in the village."

"In Wadhurst?" Mrs Welldringham said. She sipped her wine. "That doesn't surprise me. He's up to no good. I suspected it from the start."

"I'm inclined to think it was a nasty practical joke," Mr Welldringham said. "I'm taking Stangson out there after dinner – to the 'oil well', I mean - to look the place over again."

"'Again'?" she said.

A short pause. Cecily and Trevor, sitting next to each other, exchanged apprehensive looks. They joined hands under the table while Trevor related the day's adventure. As he did so, he thought he detected Adkins becoming increasingly uneasy. Mr Welldringham followed up by reiterating his argument that it had all been a sustained delusion.

His wife listened impassively. "I suppose you *are* entitled to look the plot over," she said at last. "It's what I would probably have done, although why you're contemplating a return journey is beyond me."

"Why, to clear up the *misunderstanding,* of course!" Mr Welldringham exclaimed. "I can't very well do it in the morning: I've got work. And I did come home early this afternoon."

"I'm prepared to accompany you," Adkins said, "if you think it'll help."

"The more, the merrier!" Douglas replied. "Another witness to the strange birth of the oilman!"

"Don't, Daddy," Cecily said.

He turned to Adkins and his voice descended a tone. "Sorry to make light. What did you say to Viola that persuaded her to bring you all the way down here?"

Adkins swallowed a particularly chewy piece of steak and washed it down with a gulp of wine. He wiped his mouth with his napkin.

"When Mrs Welldringham came in to see me at about eleven this morning," he said, "I'd already managed to do a fair bit of research. She'd rung ahead, I'd taken down a few details of the document she'd procured, and I knew I'd come across something just like it before. I was quickly able to locate what I was looking for.

"In case you didn't know, Wadhurst's a veritable treasure trove of maps and unusual manuscripts. And there are all sorts of legends connected with the place. I've even heard it said that The Holy Grail's buried deep beneath the parish church!" He laughed politely. "At any rate, I find myself coming down here two or three times a year sometimes. The item I'm talking about, the one which threw light on your document, came into my hands just after I'd started in the job in '47. The war threw up an awful lot of interesting historical artefacts, all for tragic reasons: when people were killed, sometimes their more singular bequests went up for auction, or their houses were at least partially destroyed and some of the salvage was simply dumped on antique shops, that sort of thing. And the various different items changed hands a lot once the war was over, as the market endeavoured to assess their true value. Mrs

Welldringham's document falls into the 'still undecided' category. It is seventeenth century, but it's a copy, not an original, and it's been defaced."

"Defaced?" Cecily said.

"There's an inscription in Latin at the bottom that says something about a virgin inheriting great wealth," Adkins continued. "The rest of the document's authentic, but that bit's a forgery. Very convincing, but bogus none the less. And it was added recently. Within the last year."

"Didn't I say so at the party?" Trevor said. "Uncle Ian's own contribution."

"I didn't disagree with you," Cecily said. "I just thought it was rather touching, him personalising it like that."

"By alluding to your *sexual* condition?" Mr Welldringham said. "I don't see that as a permissible subject for reference by a virtual stranger! Especially at your engagement party!"

Viola sighed. "We've been through this, Douglas. Let Mr Adkins finish his story."

Silence.

"Apologies," her husband said, holding up his still half-full glass. "Too much plonk maybe. And a bit of scotch, before that. Perhaps you should drive, Stangson."

"The point is," Adkins continued, "My firm owns a much earlier version of your document, and we've assigned it to the ninth century. Ours has many points in common with yours, but I think there must have been many copies – now lost – between the two; the Chinese whispers effect. For example, where yours speaks of 'a *coloured substance* which defileth all things', ours has, 'a colour*less beast* which defileth all things'. And our Latin addendum is much longer than yours. Most importantly, whoever forged yours completely reversed the meaning of one crucial section."

"What do you mean?" Trevor asked.

"Whereas yours speaks of a virgin coming into possession of the field and becoming rich," Adkins said, "ours speaks of a virgin coming into possession of the field, awakening the beast by means of physical contact, and thus bringing about the end of the world."

Another short silence. Mr Welldringham laughed. "Well!"

"But I didn't touch the… beast," Cecily said.

"The *illusory* beast," her father put in.

"Trevor touched it," she finished.

"I appreciate the point you're trying to make," Adkins told her, "but I'm afraid the document doesn't specify the virgin's gender."

Everyone turned slowly to look at Trevor. He blushed. "I don't think it's anything to be ashamed of," he said quietly. "Quite the contrary."

"It's something to be *proud* of!" Douglas burst out. "The only embarrassing thing is that it's an explicit verbal reference to your *sexual* condition! Which, as I said earlier, is always unnecessary."

"Hear, hear," Cecily said.

"What does Uncle Ian get out of this?" Trevor asked, in an obvious attempt to change the subject.

"According to our document," Adkins said, " – and I should point out that I don't endorse *any* of this, far from it! - the 'beast' will awaken of its own accord at some point anyway. The document states that someone who can pre-empt that might be able to control it. And the interesting thing is, he or she would be controlling it to *stop* it bringing about the end of the world. It makes reference to a third century Alexandrian scroll, in which certain 'magical incantations' are contained, supposed to constitute a formula for restraining the 'beast'. Of course, we no longer have that scroll."

Mr Welldringham frowned. "I'd just sold my daughter and her fiancé on the very plausible hypothesis that it was all a delusion. Now, you've come in here, and you've overturned all my good work. Don't take that the wrong way, Adkins. You're only following my wife's instructions. Can I ask you, though, do you agree with me that it's all a case of intoxicated brain cells, or do you have some other theory? Surely you don't believe there's anything whatsoever in it, do you?"

"I've thought about it a lot in the course of my job," Adkins said. "And I'm closer to you than you might think. My 'theory' - since you put me on the spot - is that certain places sometimes provoke specific visual images. The human mind may be full of 'archetypes' - of the kind discussed by the psychologist Carl Jung, for example - which are constantly evoked in the same form and manner, across history, by the application of the same stimuli. If the physical-informational input remains invariable, in other words – specific gases, say, gloomy expectations, a certain environment – so may the mental output. Same shape, same substance."

"So, someone in the ninth century might think he sees a beast down there," Trevor said, "and, for the same chemical and perceptual reasons, a person in the twentieth century might think the same thing?"

"And yet there's nothing actually down there," Cecily said.

Everyone seemed to mentally nod. It seemed a valid suggestion. A bit too cerebral, perhaps, but better than giving credence to some Dark Ages superstition.

Viola finished eating and smiled serenely at everyone in turn. "I think there *is* something down there," she said eventually. She waited for someone to contradict her, but after noting the disquiet, she continued: "I'm equally sure, after what you told us, Trevor, that it's gone now. I doubt it'll return. I'm sorry, everyone, but there are more things in

Heaven and Earth than can possibly be contained by your neat materialist explanations. Don't forget, I've lived in Wadhurst all my life; my family's been here for generations. There's something 'not quite right' about the place by ordinary standards. It's not anything you can ever put your finger on. It's a kind of deep-down *strangeness* most people not only never encounter, but never even imagine. I see it on a daily basis. I see it every time I walk onto the patio and look out over the fields. It's here now."

Cecily and Trevor looked awkwardly at each other. She gave her fiancé's hand an apologetic squeeze. Douglas and Clive exchanged puzzled looks. Clive sipped his wine. His eyes swept the room, looking for something to fix on.

"I – I never knew you felt like that," Douglas said after realising that the others were waiting for him to break the silence. "What about last year, when I said we should move to Langton Green? Or the year before that, when I took you to see that lovely house in Molyneux Park on your birthday? We could have relocated in a jiffy! I had it all lined up, mortgage and everything. All you had to do was say the word. Why on earth didn't you say yes, darling?"

She turned to look at him, and her face filled with affection. She stroked his face with her index finger, as if they were they only ones in the room. "Because I love it here," she said passionately. "I'll never, ever leave. I couldn't, Douglas. Not if my life depended on it."

A chill seemed to fall, as they waited for her to elucidate. But she turned to look opaquely at the candles. For a moment, Cecily thought she saw a distinct resemblance to Uncle Ian.

Mr Welldringham scraped his chair back. "I'll, er, go and bring the car round," he said.

VIII.

The car was a two-door black Ford Prefect. Douglas drove it from the garage to the front of the house, and handed the keys to Trevor. "Be careful with her," he said. "I'm only not driving because I've had a big scotch, but so have you. Your youth trumps my age, that's all. I'm going inside to make a telephone call now. I know a farmer, halfway to our destination. He'll let us park the car in his drive so it doesn't get scratched or stolen. Viola, I need to get the gas masks from upstairs. They're in the tea chest in the spare bedroom. Stangson, you take Adkins and get a long length of rope from the hook at the back of the garage. I'll bring the torch and some proper shoes for you two. You might have to be prepared to get dirty. At least it's not raining. From your point of view, Stangson, at least it's not your own clothes you'll be muddying! Not this time, eh?" He laughed.

"I'll try to be careful," Trevor said.

Ten minutes later, they were all set. The women stood just outside the front door with their arms folded, looking anxious. Douglas sat in front next to the driver. Adkins occupied the back seat. Trevor started the engine, switched the headlights on and pulled onto the main road. In the wing mirror, he saw Cecily waving, apparently in tears.

They drove a few hundred yards and turned into Tidebrook Road. The darkness was almost absolute down here. Were it not for the headlights, they could have been back in the bad old days of blackouts, anticipating bombs. Mr Welldringham navigated. He told Trevor to slow down until the car was barely moving. Further up the road, and around a corner, lights appeared in the distance.

"The farmhouse is somewhere along here," Welldringham said. "There it is."

Trevor turned left onto a gravel driveway.

"What were those lights farther up ahead?" Adkins asked.

"I saw them too," Welldringham remarked. "No idea. We'll find out soon enough, I'm sure. Sheep wandered onto the road maybe, got hit."

Trevor switched the engine and the headlights off. In front of them lay the farmhouse. All its lights were on. The front door opened, and a middle-aged woman in stout shoes came out with a serious expression.

"That's Mrs Porter," Mr Welldringham said. "Nice of her to come out. I'll introduce you, but if she invites you in for a sherry, the answer's no. I know Mrs Porter of old. Lovely woman, but we'll never get away."

Trevor had seen expressions like Mrs Porter's in France. She looked more than worried; she looked scared for her life. She kept looking up at the sky, as if something was going to fall on her. Two policemen came out of the house behind her and trotted up to the car as if they'd been briefed to impound it.

The first one leaned through the window. "Are you Mr Welldringham, sir?"

"This is Mr Welldringham," Trevor said.

"You live on the Wadhurst to Mark Cross road?" the policeman said.

"What's happened?" Mr Welldringham said. "Is something the matter? Has something happened to Mr Porter?"

"I'd like you all to get out of the car," the policeman said. "We'll continue this discussion inside, if you don't mind."

The three occupants disembarked and followed Mrs Porter and the two policemen into the house. In the living room, Mr Porter sat on an armchair in front of a glowing coal fire. He barely looked up when they entered, then he nodded to Welldringham. "Good to see you," he said. "Sorry about the police and everything."

"Come into the kitchen and have a sherry, the three of you," Mrs Porter said.

"That would be lovely," Mr Welldringham said.

They went through. The policemen and Mr Porter followed them. Adkins, Stangson and Welldringham sat side by side on a long settle at a table with a chequered oilcloth covering. Mrs Porter poured them each a sherry.

"Get those inside you and I'll do you all another," she said.

"What's going on?" Welldringham said.

"Would you mind telling us where you were going and why?" the first policeman said.

The three guests turned to each other, and shrugged.

"Mr Porter's already told us you were on your way to the woods," the second policeman said. "We simply need to know why."

"It's a queer story," Trevor said. "I'm afraid it'll make me look mad, and I know my fiancée, Cecily, wouldn't want me bandying it about, but I'm not in the habit of saying no to the police."

He proceeded to summarise the relevant events with as much accuracy as he could, from Uncle Ian's appearance at the party, to dinner at the Welldringhams' an hour beforehand. As he piled detail on detail, he noticed his inquisitors' faces change from morbid curiosity to something approaching tightly subdued terror.

"So *now* are you going to tell us what's going on here?" Mr Welldringham said at last.

"That roaring noise you mentioned," Mr Porter said. "I don't know whether I credit your story, but it's been going on all evening. I've had to bring my livestock in. I've got two missing horses, cows stampeding, or trying to. I won't pretend it hasn't affected me either, nor the Missus. And all the tree trunks in the woods are covered in… crude oil. At least, that's what it looks like."

"That's right," the first policeman said. "We've had it tested. It's oil all right."

"And there's been a murder," Mr Porter said, "or at least, a death."

"A man whose description very much fits that of your great-uncle Ian," the second policeman said. "Anyway, you can forget all about your little excursion tonight. Right now, the entire woods are a restricted entry zone, which means no one's paying visits for any reason. We need all three of you to come down to the station with us and answer a few more questions."

"Would you like another sherry before you go?" Mrs Porter asked.

IX.

I have read, and listened to, many ghost stories in my time, and I've noticed that, at a certain point in the narrative, close to the end, they generally involve the use of a specific technique, a certain *sleight of hand,* you might call it. The first part of the story usually concerns events to which the narrator feels reasonably confident of giving a naturalistic explanation; on those, he usually dwells in some detail. The last part concerns the unknowable. Here, he speeds up. I regard this as good practice. If the narrator doesn't know how to explain something, it seems pointless burdening the reader with long-winded speculation.

The remaining events in this story are as follows.

Firstly, Welldringham, Stangson and Adkins were transferred from the Porters' farmhouse to the police station, where they were questioned separately for an hour. None of the three requested a lawyer, partly because they considered their own innocence obvious, but also because they trusted to the integrity of the police force. After two hours, Welldringham and Adkins were released; Stangson alone was detained. Cecily Welldringham was then brought in, accompanied by the solicitor her mother insisted upon. Her story was identical to her fiancé's. Both she and Trevor were then discharged on a provisional basis.

As regards the victim himself – 'Uncle Ian' - the preliminary report described his cause of death as 'drowning in oil'. He died in the crater into which the couple had fallen only a few hours earlier, and which, inexplicably, was now full almost (but not quite) to the brim with oil.

However, at the very minute the autopsy was due to take place, the corpse exhibited infinitesimal signs of life. Ten astonishing minutes later, the initial medical verdict was completely overturned. (The man who'd pronounced it was subsequently reprimanded, but not severely: a coma is frequently impossible to diagnose without specialist equipment to hand.) In any case, the invalid made a speedy recovery. Seven hours later, he abruptly discharged himself from hospital, leaving no forwarding address.

The roaring in the woods vanished. For three whole months, the mysterious oil coating given to the tree trunks was the subject of an investigation by the Ministry of Defence, during which time the area was sealed off. Nothing significant was ever discovered, but then I think the inquiry was flawed from the outset. This was the beginning of the West's UFO craze - Project Sign and Project Grudge had just given way to USAF Regulation 200-2 – and I think the MOD was hoping to find evidence of extraterrestrials in Sussex.

Eventually, however, the 'No Entry' signs were removed, and, as usual in England with things that defy explanation, everyone forgot that anything at all had ever happened.

X.

I came to know Cecily Welldringham on a professional basis two years after the events I've just described. She was Mrs Stangson then, with a one-year-old son named Thomas. She'd begun to have bad dreams; bad enough to stop her sleeping at night. After she described them to me, and I'd suggested that they might be connected to the now long-dismantled exclusion zone in the woods near Tidebrook, I was given pretty much the whole story in one long burst.

However, it wasn't until a year before her death in 2017 that she confessed to having seen 'Uncle Ian' in and about Wadhurst on five separate occasions in the last six decades. She didn't think he'd seen her, and obviously, the older she got, the less likely he was to recognise her. But his visits always seemed to coincide with an appearance of 'The Oilman', as she'd come to call it.

Of course, such sightings aren't usually spectacular enough to merit a mention on the various social media outlets (no one wants to look too obviously like a crank), far less in the newspapers. She got to hear about them by having lots of acquaintances, showing a healthy degree of curiosity about others, and keeping her ear close to the ground. They took the form of asides in pubs, or conversations at bus stops, and always concerned a-friend-of-a-friend. They began with a depreciating, 'I know this sounds crazy, but…' then went on to relate the subject's strange experience at dusk, 'when the light's so low, of course you're *bound* to see things', before finally coming to the point: a rather too-detailed-to-be-entirely-inconsequential account of a monstrous humanoid thing that was obviously several miles away – thank God – but which, 'so she said: *seemed to be looking right into me!'*

As for Uncle Ian, he hasn't aged. According to Cecily, he still looks no older than he did in 1953. He must have changed his name several times. It's difficult to tell whether The Oilman is pursuing him, or the other way around, or whether they're somehow inextricably joined.

My suspicion – though I never mentioned this to Cecily - is that they're actually one and the same being.

The Wealden Excelsior

I.

You probably won't remember Tony and Sandy Metcalfe. They used to own a little bed and breakfast on Faircrouch Lane. And yes, I know how implausible this sounds, but they'd tapped into a market no one else knew existed: non-drivers who couldn't decide whether they wanted an urban or a rural break. Their guests arrived by rail, and spent their holiday going by train to towns and cities (Hastings, Tunbridge Wells, Sevenoaks, London), or exploring the countryside on foot (Wadhurst). Tony drove them to and from the nearby station, as required. He also did most of the cooking. What he served up was supposed to be very good, although there probably aren't many ways you can go wrong with bacon, egg, a potato waffle and a few mushrooms. Sandy was the business brains and what I'd call 'front of house', nothing ever too much trouble to keep a guest happy.

They'd both come from the sort of backgrounds you wouldn't think would segue naturally into hospitality. He'd been a singer in the 1980s, one quarter of a 'New Romantics' band called In Your Wake. Actually, he looked a little like he still belonged in the '80s: T-shirt tucked into his jeans, tall, gawky, bit of a mullet, an eager-to-please-the-fans general demeanour. Sandy had been a model and, although she'd put on a bit of weight over the years, she also hadn't altered much: well-conditioned blonde frizzy hair, a mouth that looked as if it did a lot of smiling, clear green eyes. She liked to wear big earrings and bracelets with gemstones, and, despite all her commitments, she never missed weekly Mass at the Sacred Heart.

The story I'm about to tell you took place four years ago, in November 2018. At that time their inn keeping career was probably at its zenith. Things went downhill soon afterwards, and they eventually got out of the business completely. Good thing, really. They'd never have weathered COVID. A lot of far better businesses than theirs went under during the pandemic.

What finished them off as B&B landlords, and later hoteliers, is the subject of my story. It began when a seventy-six-year-old millionaire called Sidney Crees put his five-bedroom house up for sale. Faircrouch Manor was built in the Georgian style with hood moulded sash windows, steps to a large front door, and a portico supported by Ionic columns. It was half a mile along the same road as the Metcalfes' cottage, and they got to hear about it just before it went on the market. Their surprise - it was a mere two years old, and the owner had only recently moved in – was tempered by Crees's reputation: he was widely supposed to be one of those people who loves a challenge, but quickly tires of completed projects. The asking price - one and a quarter million - wasn't out of their reach, though it did stretch them. Meanwhile, Crees was the perfect vendor: he unconditionally declined all the better offers he subsequently received; he introduced his buyers to an influential estate agent in London who got them ten thousand more than they expected for their existing business; and, as he handed them the keys, he gave them his phone number and told them emphatically that, if Faircrouch Manor ever gave them any problems *at all*, they shouldn't hesitate to contact him.

Once installed as the new owners, they negotiated a Change of Use agreement with the council, fitted fire doors, alarms and external steps as instructed by the safety standards people, built an in-character extension to add another two rooms, created a small car park at the side, hired a few staff, gave it a rather pretentious new name - 'The Wealden Excelsior' - and opened for trade that October. They'd created space for fourteen guests. All the rooms were doubles, and obviously an overnight stay cost an arm and a leg.

Their next focus was a seven-day 'Christmas package', beginning on 21 December, which they took for granted would be a runaway success. Next year, 2018, they could raise their prices, depending on how many people they had to turn away now. Best case scenario: Christmas might turn out to be the goose that perpetually laid golden eggs. In that eventuality, obviously, they'd have to forfeit their own celebrations indefinitely, but that didn't bother them: they didn't have or want children, and they weren't that keen on all the seasonal kitsch anyway. They tended to have 'Christmas' in Barbados in June: a couple of *pina coladas* on a secluded beach at sunset.

Sad to say, though, despite all their efforts, the Christmas 2017 package was a flop. Their only guests that year were a phlegmatic young couple who were actually fleeing the festivities: a man and woman very much like themselves, only without their bonhomie. Tony later told me that it was like having 'the ghosts of Christmas death' to stay.

Running a hotel was much harder than they expected, with the result that they didn't get around to conducting the seasonal package *post mortem* until the following October. They decided the root problem was that they, themselves, weren't Christmas aficionados. They were trying to perfect something they didn't even believe in. First, they needed to humbly kneel before whatever made the whole thing special to people. They had to bottle that magical little Ingredient X, then pour it liberally into their business plan.

And that was just for starters. As always in business, you had to stay one step ahead of the competition. You had to offer something new.

So, one evening in early October, they had a brainstorming session. Up for consideration: a series of short-distance excursions to local seasonal markets, a fancy-dress ball, an on-the-premises performance of *A Christmas Carol* by a local theatre group, and four or five other things. They even briefly contemplated mining the seam their two 'ghosts of Christmas death' had exposed: their hotel as a safe haven for Christmas-haters. *The Wealden Excelsior: Where December 25 is Just Another Miserable Day*. But that was always going to be a step too far for Sandy. She might not be a fan of Christmas, but she liked it in the background. Money, she insisted, wasn't everything.

After an hour's discussion over two bottles of Chianti, they still hadn't found what they were looking for. The problem with local seasonal markets was that there just weren't that many, not within a few days of Christmas. As for a fancy-dress ball, not everyone would want to participate, so it would probably be necessary to bring in outsiders, and, for some guests, that might ruin The Excelsior's 'peace and quiet', one of its putative selling points. And *A Christmas Carol*: well, you'd probably be better off watching it on TV, and Tony's suggestion of a big screen in the lounge struck Sandy as way too downmarket.

For a while, they were stumped. Then Tony had a brainwave. They could host a *murder mystery party*. He'd never taken part in one himself, but he knew what they involved. They were puzzle games, played by a group of people – which could be smallish – rather like *Cluedo*, but with role-play instead of a board and pieces.

"It sounds like a lot of fun," Sandy said. "but in what way is it Christmas-y? Don't get me wrong, Tone, but Christmas is supposed to be about presents and decorations and overeating; it's not about people killing each other."

He shrugged. "What about *Hercule Poirot's Christmas?*"

"I think it's more the 1920s vibe people go for with Agatha Christie. Poirot's antique, and anything vaguely antique's a *bit* Christmas-y. Besides, if a murder mystery involves dressing up, which I think it does, we're back to fancy-dress."

"'Anything antique'," Tony echoed pensively. He was ruminating.

"Besides, if it's a good idea," she went on, "you can bet other hotels will be doing it. And they'll be making a better job of it than we could, if only because they've had a head start."

"I was just thinking about that word of yours: *antique*. Ghosts are always Christmas-y. Well, not always, but often. More so than murders, definitely. We've already implicitly acknowledged the fact, really. Weren't we thinking of putting on *A Christmas Carol?* You can't get more Christmas-y than that."

"So, what's your suggestion, Babes? We get some sort of raconteur in?"

"Possibly, but I think we can go one better than that. All the ideas we've had so far have one thing in common: none play to our strengths. What we've been trying to do is compete with the big players - hotels in Tunbridge Wells, Brighton, London - all of which can do everything we've discussed, but probably better. What we need to make use of is our unique asset."

"I thought our unique asset was that we're relatively small and intimate."

"That's one of them. What's the other?"

"You mean, the lovely countryside?"

"Miles and miles of it in all directions! Us being in the middle of nowhere, really. There's no way Tunbridge Wells, Brighton or London can compete with that!"

"So, what's your plan?" she said. "Spell it out for me."

"We need to get a specialist in. Someone who can cook up a quality Christmas ghost story, make it interactive, and utilise our wonderful, bleak midwinter landscape to bring it to life. It's a tall order, but it should be do-able."

Sandy stroked her chin. She nodded. "It's vague, but, yes, I can see what you're driving at. All right then, we need to hire an expert; someone who does that sort of thing for a living. As far as I know, you're proposing something that's very original – and I admit, that's it's beauty: it's what we wanted – so such a person's probably going to be difficult to find. But we can certainly try."

It seemed a reasonable plan, and at least worth investigating. As soon as they'd finished talking, however, they each had a strange, incommunicable sense of having – how can I put it? - *let the spectres in*.

II.

It took them four weeks to find anyone suitable. Twenty-nine-year-old Ben Stoppard from Northampton had an advert in the classified section of *The Stage,* which wasn't a publication Tony and Sandy ever normally looked at, only it was thrust in Sandy's direction by one of her showbiz friends during a late-night Skype on her laptop. "He's supposed to be *very* good," this friend said. "He did Wanda's murder mystery party, about eighteen months ago – Wanda raved, but that's Wanda - and then he put on a lovely show for Giles when he married Rodney; had the guests *enthralled* over dinner. Of course, there were only a few people there. Tragic, really. Giles's parents still haven't come round, you know. Ignorance still rules the world."

'A few people' was fine by Sandy: it described the capacity of the Excelsior. She took a screenshot of the advert and called Stoppard the next day. The truth is, she was running out of options, and since Stoppard had already come with one recommendation, and could (so the ad said) supply others, she was prepared to break the bank.

To her surprise, his fees were well within her budget, and yes, he was available. She had long experience of dealing with hired hands and she got the impression he was slightly reluctant but trying to conceal it. She may have been mistaken – her intuitions weren't infallible – but she didn't mind. He was obviously daunted by the challenge, yet at least that meant he understood it. He sounded like a nice young man, and times were hard: if she could give him a leg up, then even if, in the end, he turned out to be a let-down, Christ would be pleased with her. That was all she needed.

I sometimes wonder if she'd have been so sanguine had she known all the facts about him. Other hoteliers might not have been. A lot more information emerged about him after he died.

He made several preparatory trips to Wadhurst before presenting himself at The Excelsior. He did a tour of the local area, and the environs of The Excelsior in particular, without telling anyone.

III.

Sandy Metcalfe's first face-to-face meeting with Stoppard occurred in the reception area of The Excelsior in early November 2018. He made an ambiguous first impression on her: besuited, tall, well-built, but with an anaemic complexion, badly scuffed shoes and a noticeable tremor. Her sentimental half felt instinctively sorry for him; her business half wanted to keep him at arm's length. He carried a small suitcase and a haversack. They'd agreed he needed a week to explore the local area before finalising anything, and that that would require him to stay on site. They shook hands perfunctorily over the counter. She invited him into the office at the back.

"So, what have you got for me?" she said dubiously, as she sat down behind her desk.

He undid his haversack and took out a map, which he unfolded in the space between them. "I've already done a bit of scouting about, Mrs Metcalfe. I don't know how good your map-reading skills are." He pointed. "This is The Excelsior, here. You can see I've marked a number of X's around it in a rough circle, at a radius of about half a mile. I'll come to those later. Now, have you ever read, *Oh, Whistle and I'll Come to You, My Lad?* It's by MR James, and, apart from *A Christmas Carol,* probably the best ghost story in the English language."

"I think I might have seen it on TV," Sandy said, unexpectedly warming to him. At least he'd given it some thought. "Was John Hurt in it?"

"I, er, don't watch much television. Maybe."

"Anyway, go on."

"It's about a confirmed sceptic called Professor Parkin who discovers an ancient – I say 'ancient': dating from the time of the Templars, so no earlier than 1231; I mean, unless the historical records are wrong, but that's unlikely because ..." He swallowed. " – Er, sorry, this, er, Professor Parkin discovers a whistle. He blows it, and he's pursued by a ghost, which, at one point, turns into a bed sheet. At the end, he throws the whistle into the sea, and he's never bothered again."

"Okay..."

"What you need to do, Mrs Metcalfe, is produce the impression that The Excelsior's *haunted.* I can help you with that: it's the sort of 'fake news' that it's still possible to manufacture on social media."

She laughed humourlessly. "Sorry to sound negative, but apart from anything else, I rather think that might be bad for business."

"It would certainly be off putting for some people. However, it'll attract others like bees to a honeypot. Everyone loves a bit of haunting at Christmastime, providing it doesn't get too intense."

"What about the rest of the year, though? What if you're wrong? What if it backfires? I could be permanently lumbered with a white elephant."

"Maybe that would have happened in previous eras, I admit. But Britain's now officially one of the least religious countries in the world. Even amongst those people who still believe in life after death, hardly any of them believe in ghosts. Ghosts are for funfairs, Christmas and the movies."

She scoffed. "Well, then, if no one believes in them, surely we're never going to persuade anyone The Excelsior's haunted!"

"It's the *suggestion* that counts, not the conviction. Just as people love ghost *stories* and *films* about ghosts and they love to go on the ghost *train* at the amusement park, so they'll also flock to the ghost *hotel*."

She frowned. "This isn't quite what I hired you for. It strikes me as taking a big risk. I was thinking more in the way of a ghost story with interactive bits."

"I understand that," he said, "but a ghost story isn't like a murder mystery. In the latter, you've got to have a perpetrator, and he or she has to be identifiable. But a ghost story isn't like that. Ghost stories are much more nebulous: they're about sudden, eerie *impressions*. What you need to do, if you're to make this proposal a success, is to lure people here, and subject them - without making them aware of the source - to those sorts of impressions."

"Scare them, you mean?"

"Impress the uncanny upon them, that's all. If we identify our market correctly, it's what they'll have come for. They won't *mind*. Quite the contrary, they'll leave here highly satisfied. They'll tell like-minded others, and we need never do it again. It'll run itself, in other words. Next year, you'll get a bunch of new arrivals who've heard about the haunting, and can't wait to try their luck."

She took a deep breath. "You're effectively talking about a huge con trick."

"It's not a con trick. Sometimes people *want* to be scared. So, for example, they know the ghost train's not real, but they pay through the nose for a ride on it, in the desperate hope that they can adopt an appropriately credulous mindset for just ten minutes; sufficient to be really scared. They willingly suspend their disbelief. Why? Because the rewards of the unfettered imagination are greater than the deadly boring solace of knowing the universe is entirely regular, that you've got eighty long years of life in which to experience it, and that you'll never, ever encounter anything that's genuinely inexplicable. We're doing them a favour."

She folded her hands. She nodded. "I must admit, you talk a good talk."

"I can walk a good walk, if you'll let me."

"Okay, let's just say that, in principle, you've persuaded me that we're not doing anything morally reprehensible. What, specifically, is your plan?"

"I subtly use social media to suggest The Excelsior's haunted, as discussed. I put all the hints on the right sites in the hope that they'll be picked up. You lower your prices slightly, if need be. Just for this year. You can raise them next year, once the buzz gets out."

"Okay. I'm assuming there's more."

"What you advertise for your Christmas break is 'a walk through the local countryside with qualified archaeologist, Ben Stoppard.'"

She hooted. "*Are* you a qualified archaeologist?"

He reached into his haversack, took out a large hard plastic folder, opened it, and passed her his degree certificate.

"Very impressive," she said doubtfully.

"I can also provide references from Sussex university."

"Thank you." She sighed. "Okay, so, I'm going to be advertising you as an archaeologist, conducting some sort of guided tour of the local area. What then?"

"We get them to do a little digging. At the sites marked by X's on my map. In the next few days, I'm having a very small booklet, produced by a local printer, called *Local Tales and Legends of Wadhurst*. Ten pages, mostly copied and pasted sections of Wikipedia. Twenty-five legends, one of which is a complete fabrication. I know, because I made it up. It concerns the lost dagger of a Saxon noble. When the dagger is found, said noble will re-appear on Earth to fulfil some who-knows-what dark purpose."

"'Who-knows-what'?"

"Best to keep it obscure. Obscurity's ninety percent of the game."

She hmm-ed. "And so – I think I'm beginning to get it now – you manipulate one of our guests into 'discovering' the dagger in question?"

"That's the idea, yes. It doesn't have to be a dagger, of course. It could be anything. A whistle, I thought, originally, but that's been done. We manipulate all the guests into reading the booklet. Which won't be difficult: like I said, if we tap the market effectively, they'll all be keenly interested in that sort of thing already. Picking it up and reading it will probably be the first thing they do after they've unpacked."

"And the guest who 'finds' the dagger?"

"I appear from a long distance away, in a head-to-foot grey garment, and I'm just ... *watching* him or her from afar. Then I disappear. Then I reappear. I know the route they're likely to take from where I've buried the dagger back to the hotel."

She nodded. "Okay. And is that it?"

"If necessary – we'll have to play it by ear, to some extent - we can arrange for said person to be 'haunted' for the duration of their stay. We can discuss the details later."

"Let's hope Scooby Doo and his friends don't turn up," she said drily. "Okay, it sounds like a plan. There are risks, and I'm relying on you to manage them - "

"Just to set your mind at rest, Mrs Metcalfe, if the worst comes to the worst, and someone does twig that the whole thing's a setup, they're probably not going to be angry. On the contrary, they'll most likely congratulate themselves on their own sharp-wittedness. As I pointed out earlier, no one really believes in ghosts, not even their biggest cheerleaders. People just want to be scared. No one's going to sue you because the thing that shadowed them wasn't *a real ghost*. I doubt they even could."

She smiled. "Actually, that does set my mind at rest. Now, I understand you want to stay on site for seven days? That's fine. We haven't any free rooms, but we do have a reasonably spacious summer house, right at the bottom of the garden. This time of year, it would normally be shut up, but it's weatherproof, it's got a very effective heater, and I've put a bed in there. You need to be up early every day. I don't want you scaring my guests just yet! You can use the bathroom facilities next to the kitchen, and Carlo, our chef, will do you a bit of breakfast. If you've got any special dietary requirements, let him know. You probably need to be out and about during the day."

"I definitely will be. There's a lot of work to be done. Have you a spade and a trowel I could borrow? If not, I can buy one in the village."

"There are three or four in the gardener's shed behind the ash tree at the side. It's usually locked, but I can open it up and you can have a rummage around. I'll introduce you to Tony – that's my other half – when I get the chance. He's off doing a few odd jobs now. The whole 'ghost experience' was his idea, which is why I'm the one who's talking to you: he's got a bit too much invested in it, emotionally speaking. I like to see myself as the level-headed one."

"I'll try not to disappoint either of you."

IV.

The summer house had large low-level windows and an ornamental lantern light. Inside, was a sofa bed, a sleeping bag, an electric heater ('I'd keep that on throughout the night, if I were you,' Sandy said, as she showed him around), and a matching table and chairs. As soon as he was alone, Stoppard sat at the table and spent an hour re-examining his map over an egg and cress sandwich. He drank a bottle of Coca-Cola and set off to explore the area.

Tony was repairing a curtain rail in one of the first-floor bedrooms, and saw him leave briskly by the front entrance at 1.30pm. He saw him return in the same way six hours later. Even through the darkness, he noticed he looked gaunt and unhappy. When he relayed this to his wife over dinner, she told him that, sadly, it might well be 'his normal look'.

"I really didn't know what to make of him," she admitted. "Some good ideas. I mean, *radical,* but not completely off the wall. I'm not regretting having hired him yet, which I half thought I would be by now. I mean, how *do* you make something like this work?"

"You mean, make *my* idea work?" Tony said.

"Looks-wise, he could make a bit more of himself," she went on, ignoring him. "He's definitely let himself go at some point. He actually had a bit of a tremor."

"Maybe he's an alcoholic. We might need to keep an eye on him." He laughed. "Although, given that he's living at the bottom of the garden, how can we not?"

"He's very intelligent. He's a qualified archaeologist."

"I can believe it. It's not like there are lots of jobs in that area. No wonder he's branched out into the entertainment business."

"I should take you down there, really, introduce you to him."

"Let's leave it till the morning, eh?" He didn't need to state his reasons. Guests to see to, chores that still needed completing, the usual tiredness.

"I suppose it's best to let him settle in. I hope he's got enough to eat."

"He looked old enough to take care of himself."

"I suppose so."

They helped clear the tables. Tony pitched in with the washing up while Sandy updated the hotel database and emailed an advertising company. At ten-thirty, she checked the staff itinerary for the morning. They'd lately hired two cleaners from an agency, and, a month earlier, a part-time receptionist named Madeleine, and a factotum called Paul. Then they went to bed. They watched a bit of TV, propped up against the headboard. Sandy drank her cocoa. At eleven, they switched out their bedside lamps and got down.

Both usually slept well, but lightly, in case there was an emergency: a guest might have lost something, or there might be some persistent noise outside, or someone might have forgotten to pack aspirin. Sandy usually dealt with whatever it was; Tony tended to become grumpy between the hours of 11pm and 7am.

At 2am, she awoke to the sound of a persistent rap on their bedroom door. She looked at her watch, and mechanically followed the drill: dressing gown, slippers, smile. She opened the door to find Dr Patel, a middle-aged GP, in his pyjamas. He looked sheepish.

"I'm terribly sorry to bother you, Mrs Metcalfe, but I thought I'd better let you know there was someone *digging* in your rear garden. I thought you might want to call the police."

"Digging?"

"Rather a big hole. I knocked on the window at him – which I probably shouldn't have done – and he ran away like a hare being chased by a greyhound. I didn't knock particularly hard. Not aggressively. Just a kind of, 'What are you doing?' Like a genuine question. Anyway, I can describe him. There's a full moon, so I got a fairly good look at him. I thought I'd better tell you now, because I may have forgotten some of the details after I've gone back to sleep. A young man. Quite tall, but with a hunchback."

"A *hunchback?*" She realised she probably sounded like an echo.

"Sorry, wrong word. *Kyphosis*. A pronounced convex curvature of the spine around the areas of the sacrum and thorax."

"I'm terribly sorry you had your sleep disturbed, Dr Patel. Just leave it to Tony and I. We'll call the police, just to be on the safe side. You go back to bed, and thank you for being so considerate."

He seemed pleased, as people usually did when she praised them. "Don't mention it, Mrs Metcalfe," he said. "I hope it's nothing serious. Don't hesitate to call me if you and Tony need any assistance."

She thanked him again, got Tony out of bed, and rang the police. Then she went into the garden. She already had an idea who the mysterious excavator was … except for that one detail: *hunchback*. But then, that was probably an optical illusion: harsh moonlight had a way of casting odd shadows.

The garden surrounded the house at a radius of about forty metres on each side, but only a small portion was visible from the Patels' window. Shrubs of different varieties, and a few young trees, bordered a wide, well-cared-for lawn. Sidney Crees had warned them before they moved in that it was inexplicably difficult to get anything much to thrive in this particular soil; even so, there were lots of hiding places for armed thugs.

She found Tony in his wellingtons and dressing gown by a large mound of soil, peering into what was obviously the hole behind it. Judging by his body-language, all danger had passed. The cold was biting, and a frost was already beginning to form on the grass.

"Whoever was here, he's long gone," he said. "I'll have to cordon this off, obviously, stop anyone falling into it. Our friend Mr Stoppard's nowhere to be seen. He's certainly not in the summer house."

"So, you think…?"

"It's obvious, isn't it? What do *you* think?"

"Okay, yes, so maybe it was him. Only he doesn't have a hunchback."

"A shadow from one of the trees. No disrespect to Dr Patel." He directed the torch beam to a spade lying on the grass. "That's ours. And we gave him access to it. Anyway, he's done a runner. We need to give the police another ring, tell them it was a false alarm."

"What do you think he was looking for?"

"I don't know. We'll talk about it in the morning. We really need to get a guard dog or two, see this as a wake-up call."

V.

Tony kept an eye on the hole from the lounge window till 7am, when Sandy came downstairs. The sun was rising now, and the garden was gradually filling with light.

"You go and get a bit of sleep," she told him. "I assume nothing's happened?"

"There's still no one in the summer house either. I last checked five minutes ago. But I've kept looking. Whatever he was doing, he obviously knows he's in trouble."

Sandy sat down next to him. "What about his things? He had a small suitcase, and a haversack."

"Still there."

"So, what do you think he was up to?" she asked. "Sorry, I'll have to go and help Anita with the breakfast things in a minute. And it's only polite to update Dr Patel. I'll need to do that myself, in person."

"He was obviously looking for something. He's a qualified archaeologist. He knows something's buried there, and, whatever it is, it's worth his while to dig it up. Ye Olde English dagger of King Whatever of the Saxons, maybe. Buried treasure. He went to an awful lot of effort to dig a very big hole. He didn't do that for nothing."

She clicked her tongue. "I take it you're not going back to bed, then?"

"I've been up since two in the morning. I think I'm both duty-bound and entitled to find out what's going on."

"Agreed. I'll get Paul to come and help you. There's at least one other spade in the shed. But I very much doubt you'll find anything."

He frowned. "What makes you say that?"

"Think about it for a moment. We chose him. He didn't choose us. And after we've chosen him, he *suddenly discovers* there's buried treasure here? Goodness gracious, talk about a lucky coincidence!"

Tony shrugged. "On the other hand, lucky coincidences do sometimes happen. People win the lottery."

"Okay then, let's go with that for a moment. He realises there's buried treasure here. He invented plausible enough reasons yesterday for digging up the local countryside; why couldn't he invent a plausible excuse for digging up our back garden? I'd probably have let him, providing he put everything back again and made the turf level. Why does he then get up in the middle of the night and start digging, when there's a full moon and a cloudless sky? He must have known that would increase his chances of being seen. He's here for a week. Why not wait for clouds? It's not like they're rare at this time of year. And why make my acquaintance at all? Now Dr Patel's seen him, we know who the culprit is. He could easily have cried off ages ago, long before I got the chance to meet him in person, then snuck over the wall and dug. Had he been noticed then, no one would have been able to identify him."

Tony nodded. "We did suggest he might be an alcoholic, as I recall. If that's true - "

"Have you searched his things?"

"Yes." He cleared his throat. "And no, there wasn't any sign of alcohol. But that doesn't mean he hasn't got mental health issues. I mean, going by your description of him. *Definitely let himself go at some point? Bit of a tremor?* That was what you said, wasn't it?"

"Mental illness: my thought too. We should really call the police yet again. Get them to file a missing person's report."

"It's still early days. It's only been five hours."

"It was minus four out there last night, Tone. If he's wandering across the fields, probably not properly dressed – I didn't ask Dr Patel what he was wearing – he's likely to come to grief."

"Okay, granted. I hadn't thought about that, although I should have done. Send Paul out here, though. I'll have to do a bit of digging. Just because he's got mental health issues, it doesn't mean there isn't treasure. And before you accuse me of being greedy - "

"I wasn't going to."

"It's not about us coming into sudden wealth. If there really is something buried down there, and he's heard about it, it won't be long before others get to hear about it. We'll never be shot of chancers digging our lawn up, and some of them might well be a lot more reckless than he was. We could be putting ourselves and our guests in serious danger. If I don't find anything, we should probably get a team of professionals in with an excavator."

She let out a miserable sigh. "This is turning into a bit of a nightmare."

"I've got a good idea. I'll do an hour's digging. That should tell me whether there's anything worth discovering. You call the police, then brief Dr Patel. If, after an hour, I haven't found anything, I'll ring Mr Crees."

"Mr Crees? Sidney?"

"When he left this place, he said we could call him about anything, remember? If there are crackpot rumours of buried treasure in the garden, he'd probably know. Because that's all we might be dealing with here: a single crackpot."

"That's a very good idea, Tone. Okay. I'll let you know if I find anything. You do likewise."

"Is there something wrong?" he asked.

They'd been married for over thirty years, and sometimes they knew each other better than they knew themselves. Was something wrong? She hadn't noticed until he put the question, but yes; yes, there was something wrong.

Hard to put a name to it for a second. Then she could. A strong sense of approaching menace.

"I feel weirdly as if something bad's going to happen," she told him. Then, because her own words unsettled her, she couldn't resist clarifying. "Something *really* bad."

Tony looked at her without smiling. "Check," he said. "You be careful in that hole."

VI.

She'd learned long ago that nearly everything in the hospitality business takes longer than you'd ever expect. The police kept her waiting on the phone for thirty minutes, and when she went to brief Dr Patel, she got talking to his wife about intruders in general, then about the inadequacy of the police, then about the dire state of the country, then the uselessness of Westminster. An hour and a quarter passed in which she made no dent whatsoever on the necessary daily chores. To make matters worse, she didn't feel any happier than she had earlier. Setting the world to rights with a guest – especially one as intelligent as Mrs Patel – usually gave her a bit of a boost. Not this time.

When she finally got back downstairs, she found a large boxed parcel behind the counter at reception, addressed to 'Mr Ben Stoppard c/o The Wealden Excelsior, Faircrouch Lane.' She inspected the label. *Royale and Stimpson, Printers, Yapton.* Then she took it into her office and cut it open, using the heavy-duty scissors in the stationery-organiser. She already knew what it was. He'd want her to see it, and it *was* addressed to her hotel.

As she expected: *Local Tales and Legends of Wadhurst.* Two hundred copies was probably far more than they'd ever need, although possibly Stoppard thought people would purloin them when they left, along with (sometimes) the towels. He was probably right. Good that he was thinking ahead.

She hoped he was okay, despite the big hole. In some ways, because of it.

She might as well browse what he'd written. People would probably ask her about it at some point. She wondered if she'd be able to spot the dummy story. Shouldn't be too difficult: presumably, it involved a buried something.

She skimmed each potted tale in turn. Odd stories of snakes living under hillocks and 'oily' creatures buried long ago in deep pits with binding imprecations. There was the usual headless horseman, a huge obelisk, and two ghostly friars. When she got to page ten, however, she read something that almost made her fall out of her chair.

The Wealden Excelsior

Despite its apparent grandeur and ornate Georgian appearance, The Wealden Excelsior is no more than five years old. It was not originally intended as a dwelling-place, not even for such temporary visitors as now comprise the majority of its occupants. Rather, its chief function was always to conceal an altogether different, more ominous structure which lies at an indeterminate distance beneath the ground at the exact spot on which it was built.

The individual responsible for its construction must remain anonymous for the purposes of this booklet, although, if the reader is at all curious, a little research will doubtless reveal his identity. For the time being, we shall call him Mr X. In 2011, his son and five others were archaeology undergraduates at the university of Sussex. One of them – not the son of Mr X

- during the course of some direct, unpremeditated fieldwork in the Wadhurst area, chanced upon clues strongly suggesting a single underground structure, on the northwest village outskirts, of pre-Roman, possibly even pre-Celtic, provenance. He assembled an impromptu research team from the ranks of his contemporaries. They pooled their resources, waited till the winter vacation, and, with significant financial help from Mr X - who simply wanted to help his son shine in his future career - embarked on a major dig. The whole enterprise was conducted with the utmost secrecy. These were men and women at the beginning of their careers, and they believed that, should word of their discovery be leaked, the press would react with its usual hysteria, and more experienced, tenured heads would discover nefarious ways of edging them out.

For the first few days, the dig was an unqualified triumph. But each successive layer seemed to take them further back in time, and finally, into prehistory. Meanwhile, the artefacts they uncovered stopped being mappable onto any hitherto known historical culture. Each was completely unique, and, in the final stages of the dig, they all featured insects rather than humans. The project came to an end before the central hoped-for structure could be uncovered. By now, all the participants had the inexplicable conviction that it was a temple of some kind. It was almost certainly there. One of the team later said – only half tongue-in-cheek – that she felt as if it was sinking, and the further they dug, the more it seemed to withdraw downwards. *Impossible, of course, but, at the time, somehow disturbingly plausible.*

Just before the whole undertaking was due to come to an end – the long winter vacation was within a day of drawing to a close – something horrendous happened.

Precisely what, must necessarily be a matter of speculation. For now, let us err on the side of sanity and say that the entire team fell prey to a mass hallucination whose content was that they were being attacked by monstrous, intelligent insects.

The dig was abandoned. The earth – all of it – was painstakingly replaced. Mr X's son had a breakdown from which he never recovered. Four members of the team died within a year of each other, in circumstances too disquieting to relate. One of them – if you ask him, which no one ever will, since no one else even suspects it – will tell you that he has a ten-legged invisible creature wrapped around his back. This man will be the next to die. Such, dear reader, is The Wealden Excelsior.

Her stomach fell into her legs, or that's what it felt like. Questions raced through her mind at a million miles an hour and, at first, they were all purely instinctive. How *dare* he? What could have *motivated* him to play such a *nasty trick?* He obviously expected to be found out in advance, so why the *hell* was he making such *vicious fun* of her and Tony? What had he got against the Excelsior? Who was *behind* him? What *sort* of a human being –

Then, horribly, she realised. It was all true. *This man will be the next to die*. He was talking about himself. Somewhere out there, in the fields, he might already be prone and lifeless.

The door opened. Madeleine, the receptionist, came in. She hadn't knocked and she looked pale. "We've got a bit of an emergency, Mrs Metcalfe," she said. "Some of the guests are leaving and one of the cleaners... well, I don't know any Filipino, but I've been on the phone to the agency, and they're sending the district supervisor over. He can apparently interpret. From what I've been able to gather so far, though, it appears we may have a bit of an *insect* problem."

VII.

Sandy emerged into the reception area to find four guests checking out. She asked them humbly and regretfully why. Mr Peters mentioned the 'discordant noises', and she got the strong impression he didn't want to make this his principal reason, in case she told him she could do something about it. Mr and Mrs Taylor had an unexpected emergency and Mme Saussure cited an overlooked diary conflict. The truth was disturbingly obvious: they were leaving for reasons they couldn't explain, and which might embarrass them if they tried. They were experiencing the same sense of rapidly approaching danger that she was. She expressed her heartfelt disappointment, lingered to underline her sincerity, then followed the receptionist upstairs to interview the cleaner in the room she was supposed to be making up.

But the room was empty.

"I left her sitting on the bed," Madeleine said. "I don't know where she can have gone. She seemed terrified, though. I probably shouldn't have left her alone, only I didn't want her frightening the guests."

"She probably went to find her friend. Which one was it? Belen or Carmelita?"

"I don't know them that well. Belen, I think. The smaller one."

"You go back down to reception, Madeleine, and process the leavers. I'll sort this."

Once she was alone, Sandy put on her best 'compassionate employer' expression, adjusted her skirt and ascended the next flight of stairs. She noticed, just before she reached the landing, that the door to 3A, at the end, was slightly open. Maybe Belen was in there.

For some reason, however, she'd stopped walking. It took her a split second to realise: she couldn't go and look. Not because she was physically incapable, but because she was suddenly overwhelmed by the feeling that something unspeakable was waiting for her down there.

"Belen?" It came out in a croak. "Belen? Are you up here?"

What had come *over* her? It was simply a *vacant room* in an empty, well-lit corridor! She couldn't -

But then, something appeared. A jointed limb, like a tarantula's, but much bigger, and in many more sections. It curled around the door with a hideous clicking sound.

She'd stopped herself from going into 3A, but she was far from being completely paralysed. She turned and ran downstairs so quickly she almost tripped.

Two seconds later, she stood gasping in the middle of the empty reception area. Madeleine was nowhere to be seen. Where was - anyone? Her heart thumped. She hadn't felt paralysed upstairs; she did now.

She had to act. But do what? Hit the fire alarm and get everyone out on to the lawn?

Tony came in from outside. He looked at her, hurriedly put down the cardboard box he was carrying, and rushed over. "What's the matter? Are you okay?"

"I – I – The guests are all leaving, Tony. I - "

"Come into the office and sit down. Take a few more deep breaths and tell me what's wrong. I'll get you a glass of water."

Madeleine entered from the restaurant direction. "Is everything okay? Did Belen - "

"We're fine," Tony said. He closed the door, then opened it again. "Maddy, could you get Sandy a glass of water, please?" He closed it again. "Start at the beginning."

"There's something upstairs. I don't know, maybe I was seeing things. A big spider? That sounds crazy. But not a spider. *Really* big. Oh, my God. In 3A."

"Sounds like someone's tabbed you for a practical joke, and not a very nice one. I'll go and check."

She grabbed his wrist. "I - "

"Don't be silly." He laughed. "You *must* have been mistaken. Anyhow, *someone's* got to give it the once over! We can't very well never go upstairs again! You stay here."

She nodded reluctantly. "Be careful then."

Madeleine knocked on the door. Tony left as she entered with the water. She put it down hurriedly as the reception bell dinged five times in quick succession.

Tony returned seven minutes later. He shut the office door behind him. "Nothing," he said evasively.

"You saw *something,* though. I can tell from your expression."

"A bigger than usual cockroach, that's all. Nothing like what you saw. I admit, we've got problems, but - "

"'Bigger than usual'? How big?"

He shrugged. "Eight inches?"

She laughed feverishly. "Oh, my God!" She put her hands on her temples. "*Eight inches long?* Tony, there's no such *thing* as a cockroach that's *eight inches long!"*

"I *saw* one, so there must be! And keep your voice down! I've just spoken to Mr Crees," he went on, as if he'd suddenly worked out how to change the subject. "Just this minute. He's coming - "

"We need to get everyone *out* of here!"

"It's raining, so, well, we can't. We can't evacuate the entire building just because you thought you saw a giant spider, and I saw a bigger than normal cockroach. What difference would it make, if everyone's outside? If it was a fire, we'd call the fire brigade and they'd come, and eventually they'd give us the all-clear, and everyone would grumble and go back inside. But they'd understand. We can't put them out in the rain because of a giant cockroach! The emergency services aren't going to come out for that, and the guests certainly aren't going to stand there grumbling. One or two of them will wet themselves. They'll definitely never come back. And for what? It's not going to *eat* them!"

"My God, my God."

"Stop panicking. Sidney Crees is coming down here. By helicopter. He's got his own personal - "

"He's coming *here?*"

"I told him about Stoppard. I expected him to make some polite excuse and hang up, but in fact, he seemed really concerned. Almost like he'd expected something to happen all along. I told him everything, Sandy: I mean, Stoppard, the hole, the guests leaving, your delusion, the cockroach. I… "

They hadn't noticed until now, but during the time they'd been talking, a commotion had been going on outside. They registered it only because it had suddenly stopped. Silence. A door slammed somewhere.

"What's going on?" Sandy said. "Go and get Madeleine, Tone. She'll know what to do."

He opened the office door and looked out. He turned back quizzically to his wife, then looked out again.

"Where is everybody?" he said, in a voice so uncertain it wasn't obvious who he was addressing.

Sandy joined him. They held hands and went through the reception area into the dining room.

No one.

The kitchen was similarly deserted.

The lounge was empty.

"I suppose we'd better check upstairs," Tony said reluctantly, when they were back in the reception area.

Sandy suddenly heard the same clicking noise she'd heard when she was looking along the second-floor landing at room 3A. Somewhere close by.

"We need to get out of here," she told Tony.

He nodded, trying hard to feign insouciance. "Agreed."

VIII.

As far as they could tell – they hadn't checked upstairs, but the ground floor was deserted and the car park was empty - all the occupants had left. Their own car was in the garage at the end of the road, being serviced. Sandy called a taxi and she and Tony walked along Faircrouch Lane, in the freezing rain, to meet it *en route*. They had no idea what they were doing, except that they were fleeing. Neither was dressed for the weather. They briefly discussed whether to call the police, but Sandy said no, that might be putting someone in danger. They knew they needed to call someone with *some* kind of emergency powers – they couldn't leave things as they were - but who? Their taxi arrived before they could decide. When the driver asked them where to, Tony said any hotel in Tunbridge Wells. It was the first thing that came to mind: they needed somewhere warm, safe and far away.

Ten minutes later, they checked into The Travelodge on Mount Ephraim and went to their room. They, removed their wet clothes and put them on the drying rack, then they got into bed, put their arms round each other and shivered. They still had no idea what had just happened, but both knew instinctively that they would never set foot in their own hotel again, even if they wanted to. Something had been decided. They still didn't know who to call. Maybe if they left things…? She told him about *Local Tales and Legends of Wadhurst.* He listened with increasing astonishment, but also as if it somehow explained things.

They ordered a bottle of brandy from room service. Alcohol would warm them up, relax them and perhaps even get them in the right mood to think.

An hour later, Tony's phone rang. *Sidney Crees*. They'd forgotten all about Sidney Crees. He seemed irrelevant now. Tony picked up and put it on speaker for Sandy's benefit.

"Tony, where are you?" Crees said, in a voice that suggested whatever the answer he wouldn't be surprised.

"In the Travelodge in Tunbridge Wells. I won't go into details. We had to leave at short notice. Where are you?"

"Outside The Excelsior. Is Sandy with you?"

"We're both here, Mr Crees. Don't go inside the building. I mean, you won't be able to, because it's locked, but don't try. I'm sorry to have bothered you, and I apologise for making you fly all this way. It would have been nice to see you, but - "

"I'm with the police, Tony. They're *also* outside your hotel, and they want to speak to you. I've been able to give them a little information, so in return they had to put me at least partially in the picture. The man you told me about on the phone, Ben Stoppard: he's dead. He was found about two miles from your place, in a ditch, with his neck broken. He had a letter bearing your address in his pocket."

"Oh, my God," Sandy said. She lowered her voice to a whisper, so her next words couldn't be overheard. "I – I knew it!"

"You're not under suspicion of anything," Crees went on. "Especially after what I told the police. As I've mentioned already, they want to speak to you and Sandy. Of course, they also want to speak to your Dr Patel. I'd like to come and see you. At your convenience, of course, but the sooner the better."

IX.

Tony arranged a rendezvous with Crees in the reception area of the Travelodge in an hour's time. In the interval, two policemen arrived. Tony and Sandy sat on the bed in their still damp clothes and answered their questions as truthfully as they could, without mentioning anything about *Local Tales and Legends of Wadhurst* or the insects. The younger of the two policemen recorded the answers jadedly in a notebook. Both left after thirty minutes.

Crees arrived punctually at 1pm, accompanied by a bearded man in his late twenties who wore a tweed jacket, brogues and corduroy trousers. "Raymond: my son," he said laconically. He didn't introduce Tony and Sandy in return. The reason became clear when Raymond gave no indication of knowing where he was, and looked through them as if they weren't there. "I've booked us a room where we can talk privately," Crees added, "just in case you didn't want us in your own room. The haste with which you left the hotel probably means you're still settling in, and I didn't want to presume."

"It didn't seem to bother the police," Sandy said.

"That sort of sensitivity isn't necessarily high on their list of priorities," Crees replied. "Shall we?"

He led the way along the corridor, guiding Raymond solicitously by the arm, to a ground floor room with a portable electric heater and four armchairs turned towards a central low table. He ushered everyone inside, closed the door behind him, manoeuvred Raymond into one of the chairs and gestured for Tony and Sandy to sit down beside each other. He lowered himself into the chair next to Raymond, then picked up his hand and held it. He gently asked Sandy and Tony to explain why they'd left The Excelsior. They obliged.

"Do you know who Ben Stoppard was?" he asked.

Sandy nodded. She told him about the item in *Local Tales and Legends of Wadhurst*. Crees listened attentively, and seemed to relax.

"Well, he's saved me an awful lot of explanation," he said incredulously, when she'd finished. "I wonder why he put that in. Presumably, because he wanted the truth out there. Idiot. To be honest, until today, I'd no idea he was even still alive. Quite the contrary: if you'd asked me, I'd probably have told you I didn't think he *could* be." He sighed. "In any case, two days ago, he and Raymond were the only survivors of that excavation; unless you count me, of course, but I was never *in situ*: I simply threw money at the thing and kept my distance. Archaeology was Raymond's passion and although it wasn't my first choice of career for him – barrister, architect or surgeon was my firm preference - he was certainly bright enough. And I'd learned enough about him, growing up, to know that, when he makes a solemn decision about the direction of his life, he usually sticks to it. I simply wanted to give him a leg up.

"What I can't understand is what inspired you to get in touch with young Stoppard in the first place. Oh, I know the pretext – a 'ghost walk', of kinds; Tony, you've explained it to me, and I don't doubt you for a second: from your point of view, that was all that happened: you had an original idea, and you chanced across his name. Even so, it does seem a monstrous coincidence, don't you think? Someone with a more credulous mindset might even say you were being directed by a kind of thought-control from beneath."

"Beneath the ground?" Tony said.

"Somewhere far below The Excelsior," Crees replied. "But we needn't pursue that line of thought. It makes no - *humanly* - rational sense, and nothing good can come of it. The point is, as of today, Raymond's the sole survivor of that ill-fated expedition."

Sandy folded her hands. "Ben's account of The Excelsior in *Local Tales and Legends of Wadhurst* mentioned him having an invisible 'ten-legged creature on his back'." She laughed nervously. "I mean, that's insane, isn't it?"

"And yet, from what Tony told me," Crees said, "Dr Patel described Stoppard as having a 'hunchback'. *He* saw it. *You* couldn't. Or didn't want to."

"It's probably true that I didn't want to," Sandy said, "but it sounds like a symptom of mental illness to me."

"Was the thing you saw emerging from room 3A a symptom of mental illness?" Crees asked. "Because, according to your own account, you definitely saw *something*. And you intuited more. You *knew* it was real."

Tony ran his hands over his hair. "I suppose it's academic now."

"Not quite," Crees said. "There's an identical thing on Raymond's back. I guarantee that, if you look hard enough, you'll be able to see it. *I've* seen it. I can see it now if I really try. I have a theory about the matter, if you're interested."

"Well, we might as well hear it," Tony said politely. Sandy nodded.

"Biologically, our five senses filter out objects that are really, really disturbing to us, but which, normally, are harmless. At the time of the dig, those 'creatures' believed they were being attacked, I think, and so they counter-attacked. As a rule, I genuinely believe they're happy to keep out of our way. That may change, I don't know. Maybe in the usual course of things, they can't see us, either. But I doubt it. I think they know everything we're doing. And I'm pretty sure they roam the Earth."

"I still don't understand why Stoppard chose that night to dig our garden up," Sandy said. "I mean, it was a full moon. He had a week with us. Why that night?"

"And why not tell my wife he was going to dig in the garden?" Tony asked. "Prepare us, so that when we saw it happening, we'd condone it?"

"We'll probably never know," Crees said. "My guess is that he took the summons from you – to mastermind your 'ghost experience' – as a sign. As I said earlier, on the face of it, it does look like a gargantuan coincidence. He may have believed he was being beckoned back, possibly even that he'd been invited to put things right."

"He thought he'd been forgiven," Tony said.

"Precisely," Crees replied. "And he had things to return: artefacts he'd taken with him from the dig. My conjecture, Tony, is that when you were looking in the hole he'd created, you chanced across broken pieces of pottery, that sort of thing."

"As a matter of fact, I did," Tony said. "They didn't look like much. I certainly didn't think they could be the purpose of the hole."

"You're saying those things were what he was 'putting back'?" Sandy asked.

"The full moon illuminated him," Crees said, "so in that respect, yes, it was a risk; but it would also illuminate *them*, and in that sense, it was a safety precaution. As for not asking you for permission to dig your lawn up, do you *really* believe you'd have granted it?"

Sandy took a deep breath. "Probably not, when I actually think about it. And I suppose I don't know what pretext he could have invented. Digging up an ornamental garden's not like digging up field."

Crees paused portentously. "What are your plans for The Excelsior now?"

Sandy and Tony exchanged pained expressions.

Sandy sighed. "We can't go back. Even if we wanted to, the guests will already be slating us on TripAdvisor and

Trivago. We're finished, really, if we're going to be honest. We can't sell it on, that wouldn't be right. I wouldn't want anyone else to undergo - "

"The only reason I sold it to you, Mrs Metcalfe," Crees said, "was that I happen to know you're a devout Roman Catholic, and I was superstitious enough to imagine that might keep whatever's down there at bay. It turns out I was badly mistaken. In any case, I want to make you an offer. I'd like to buy The Excelsior back for half a million more than you paid for it."

Tony sat up. "Er, what?"

"You can't be serious," Sandy said. "That – that would be - two million pounds?"

"I assure you I'm in *deadly* earnest," Crees said. "I've actually put my solicitor on standby. It's just a matter of signing the relevant forms. She can arrange for the money to be paid into your business account before midnight. There are only two conditions. One: you need to accept right now, if you're going to accept at all. This very instant. Two: you'll be required to sign an affidavit committing you to never, ever mentioning anything whatsoever about what happened in The Excelsior to another living soul. You're not to speak about it, or write about it, or leave anything behind after you die that so much as mentions the events of the past twenty-four hours. I think you'll agree that those two conditions are more than reasonable. If you're amenable, we can get the process started right away."

Tony and Sandy looked at each other. They wore stupefied expressions. They joined hands.

X.

The rest of my story can be told in a few short paragraphs.

Sidney Crees became the new owner of The Wealden Excelsior within two hours of his offer to buy it back. That same night, a neighbour, a quarter of a mile away, switched off his upstairs lights before going to bed, and noticed an unusual glow in the far distance. From his attic window, a row of fir trees screened the precise cause. When he went outside onto the road to investigate further, he found himself amongst several others, all looking at the same thing. The Excelsior was on fire. From this distance, and discounting the effect of the trees, it looked like a raging inferno.

By now, the fire brigade was on the scene, although it had come too late to save anything at all of the building. It concentrated exclusively on preventing the spread.

The police appeared an hour later. The elderly man who had first spotted the fire, and who had called 999, described having seen a couple of men – one old, one much younger with a pronounced hunchback – holding hands and walking into the blaze.

The next day, the investigators confirmed what everyone already knew: arson. Two bodies – or the very little that was left of them - were discovered amongst the ashes.

Suspicion at once fell on Sandy and Tony, as it was bound to. However, at this point, the Creeses' solicitor stepped in. She produced a document written and signed by Sidney Crees, and witnessed by her and one of her colleagues, to the effect that he had decided to 'destroy' his own property 'as soon as possible'. The vagueness meant she couldn't be accused of knowing precisely what would happen. Because, on Sidney Crees's instructions, she had sat with the Metcalfes all night, they couldn't be suspected of having aided and abetted anything. The police obviously sensed that the Metcalfes knew why Crees and his son had killed themselves, but since they couldn't assemble a remotely plausible charge – it wasn't even clear a crime had been committed - they closed the investigation.

Anyway, Sandy and Tony are living in Cornwall now. Last time I heard of them, he'd re-formed his old band, and he was preparing to tour the country with a new collection of songs ('The World Tour', he called it). She was writing a children's book. They're still very much together.

As for Sidney Crees's admonition not to mention what went on at The Wealden Excelsior, well, that's where I come in. Crees was a typical specimen of his age and social class, you see. He took into account the wealthy bigwigs – Tony and Sandy, to you and me – but he completely overlooked what he would doubtless have called 'the lower orders': Madeleine, Paul, Belen, Carmelita and Carlo. They all had their stories to tell. As did the various guests.

So, I've managed to unearth the truth. If he was still with us, Crees would doubtless beg me to leave it at that. He'd say it was bad enough me uncovering it; that I should publish it as well, is reckless in the extreme.

I disagree. Truth is an ultimate value. Nothing else trumps it, and everyone deserves to know it.

So here it is.

I *am* right, aren't I?

The Wadhurst Obelisk

I.

I probably wouldn't be telling you this if I didn't want the kudos of being first to 'go to press' with it. Others will almost certainly retell their own versions in the months and years to come, and that's fine, but I'd like you to remember that you heard it here first. I suppose I've a competitive nature, and everyone wants to be the first to break a great story. And actually, it is *my* story. It's the story of *moi*, of how I used to be lonely but now I'm not anymore.

Let me begin by telling you who I am and what I do. My name is Lucinda Bridgen, I'm a journalist by profession. Forty-six years old, dark hair, unmarried, wears spectacles. I don't usually smoke but I do have twenty cigarettes on my birthday. Yes, I drink a bit. I live in Wood's Green and I work from home most days, but I'm required to report to HQ in London twice-monthly, and I regularly do a fair amount of driving from A to boring B, interviewing people and investigating incidents. I'm attached to my paper's Southeast desk: Kent, Sussex and a bit of Surrey. Some days, that's a *lot* of driving.

Luckily, I have a hobby to stop me going insane. Antiques: buying and selling rather than collecting. On 'bad' days – when it's pouring with rain, say, and I've got to be in Maidstone by 5pm, and it's 4.25 and I'm stuck in traffic in Ashford, and the car engine's making a funny noise – I kid myself that I could make a business of it.

My favourite place to sell is my home village, Wadhurst, in East Sussex. Every few months, on a Saturday morning, there's an antiques fair in the 'Commemoration Hall' just off the High Street: lots of trellis tables covering a large floor space; bit like an upmarket boot fair, with a token entrance fee. Obviously, not everyone likes antiques, or lives in the sort of house where they can be advantageously displayed, but that doesn't matter: some people just like to browse, or they buy a curio because they find it interesting to take out and look at once in a while (I own a few medieval coins that fit that description: I simply like the thought of having them to hand. I don't see them as an investment).

Traders come from far and wide, relatively speaking, but each one brings something unique to the event. Which is why people come, of course. Most town centres are identical nowadays – *Next, Boots, M&S* - and a good antiques fair offers the possibility of something genuinely different. I always make a reasonable profit, and over the years I've learned that I'm likely to do especially well with Wadhurst-related items, the older the better. Lots of locals are amateur village historians. Which is true of many villages, of course.

I source my items through contacts I've made in auction houses in the course of many years' travelling round, reporting; friends, most of them, rather than professional acquaintances. Gorringe's in Lewes has always been particularly helpful. Frank Cave, one of the auctioneers – stout, fifty-ish, with a grey beard, and prone to wearing a blazer - keeps me informed of anything with a Wadhurst connection. If I'm interested, I'll put in a bid. If I'm *really* interested, I'll attend the actual auction. I say 'actual': usually remotely, via webcam.

About a year ago now, Frank sent me an email with a JPG attachment and a short description: *'Wadhurst Obelisk': 18th century oil painting in the style of Claude Lorrain. Artist unknown.*

I'd never heard of a 'Wadhurst Obelisk', so I was straightaway intrigued. The picture's dimensions were 5 by 10 inches, and its orientation landscape, so I didn't open it on my phone, because I knew I'd be disappointed. Even the best paintings tend to look poor when they're overly reduced. I went directly to my laptop.

Now, I'm not an expert on art, so I didn't know who 'Claude Lorrain' was. But it turns out there are as many local artists in Wadhurst as there are local historians, and I've shown it about a bit, so that now I can describe it more meaningfully than I could when I first clapped eyes on it. I might as well give you the benefit of others' authority.

Claude Lorrain was a seventeenth century French painter. Some of his work involved idealised pastoral landscapes. One or two of my interviewees claimed to detect the additional influence of a 'Nicolas Poussin', working at about the same time as Claude, who also painted bucolic idylls. The Gorringe's item was about a century later than both of them, so not remotely original at its time of production. What it depicted: gentle rolling hills, with a field in the foreground, and a castle in the distance to one side. The subject proper was a huge standing stone – it definitely wasn't an obelisk: obelisks are manufactured and regular, this was irregular and unworked by human hands – with a shepherd standing about ten feet to its left, leaning on his crook, and gazing up at the stone's pinnacle in admiration. This human figure seemed to have been placed there mainly to give a sense of scale: the stone – I'd call it a menhir: I repeat, it categorically wasn't an obelisk, despite the original designation – was at least fifteen times taller than the man, and perhaps twice as broad. Its bottom part was lodged in the ground. It listed significantly to the right, clearly the effect of time and gravity. The only 'obelisk' thing about it was that it was covered in what looked like hieroglyphs, though I couldn't match any one in particular to anything I'd ever seen in a book about Ancient Egypt. The colours were significantly faded: pale beiges where there had probably once been bright pastels.

I think my initial reaction was mingled annoyance and puzzlement.

Annoyance because there was nothing like this … *menhir* anywhere in Wadhurst, or even nearby. The castle in the background could conceivably have been Wadhurst Castle, except that Wadhurst Castle didn't exist before the nineteenth century. Considered thus – as a faithful depiction of an actual reality - the whole thing was clearly a fake.

Puzzlement, however, because I couldn't see what the purpose of such a fake could have been. The appellation, 'The Wadhurst Obelisk' was of a piece with the painting, and had definitely, so Frank assured me, been added by the artist. In a deeper sense, it wasn't a fake at all: it was a true report of an egregious case of mistaken identity. Including 'Wadhurst' in the title, in the eighteenth century, couldn't conceivably have added a *sou* to the value of the thing.

But at least as interesting as the painting itself, was the man to whose estate it had belonged. John Stafford had died recently, aged one hundred and three, in Brighton, where he'd lived since the nineteen-sixties. 'The Wadhurst Obelisk' had reached Gorringe's through a house clearance, and it had come as part of a collection of occult objects in which it was very much the 'odd item out'.

Apparently, Stafford had been part of the original 'Bricket Wood Coven', which probably doesn't mean anything to you, as it didn't to me, but, well, thank God for Wikipedia. It was founded in the 1940s by the inventor of a modern religion (which you've almost certainly heard of) called 'Wicca'. Along with my picture, Stafford's rather morbid collection included a handwritten copy of Gerald Gardner's 'Book of Shadows', a first edition of a novel called *High Magic's Aid*, a short letter to John Stafford from Aleister Crowley, another from a woman called 'Dafo', a postcard from Robert Graves, one or two objects which Doreen Valiente shared with the 'Museum of

Witchcraft and Magic' in the 1950s, along with ten or twelve related artefacts. The collection had been broken up for sale, but all told, it was expected to fetch an awful lot of money. When Frank Cave sent me that JPG, it was already attracting a lot of international interest.

Now, call me superstitious, but the whole thing gave me the creeps. I'm not a Christian by any means, but I have an aversion, probably atavistic, to anything with black magical overtones. Or maybe I'm just prejudiced. So be it. In any case, 'The Wadhurst Obelisk' was – as I said earlier, and as Frank Cave agreed – the glaring anomaly in this collection. It had no obvious occult significance; it featured a figment of some unidentifiable painter's imagination, one in which he or she had been unable to interest a single other being on Earth as far as anyone knew (excepting possibly Stafford, and even he might have come into possession of it by accident). It was simply an oddity.

The guide price said £75-150. I put in a bid at the bottom end of the range, just to please Frank. Not only did I not expect to end up owning it, I actually hoped I wouldn't. Because I certainly didn't think I'd be able to shift it at a Wadhurst antiques fair. With the auctioneer's fee to consider, and other expenses like delivery, I'd have to sell it for around £90 just to break even. Since there *is* no Wadhurst Obelisk, and never *was*, and since the thing in the picture doesn't even *resemble* an obelisk, I think most buyers would understandably peg me for a scammer, and not a very intelligent one at that. I'd be better off just putting it in the bin.

Of course, seventy-five pounds is seventy-five pounds, and it's far too much to pay just to keep Frank Cave happy. In reality, I didn't think there was the slightest chance I'd win. Despite all I've just said above, I thought the guide price was too low even at the hundred and fifty mark. Its value lay not in its intrinsic merits (it didn't have any), but in the reflected glory of the other items in The Stafford Collection, and in its once having been owned by an individual who'd been present at the birth of Wicca. Yes, on reflection, I suppose it did have a certain mystical whatnot about it, a hint of the other-worldly maybe. But perhaps only if you already knew it depicted something unreal. In strictly aesthetic terms, its value was negligible.

Even so, I spent a few sleepless nights wondering if I'd been reckless. Seventy-five pounds – ninety, really - is a lot to lose, and what if I'd miscalculated?

II.

The auction came and went. I had a lot of work to do that particular Monday, so I didn't log on to follow the proceedings online. Besides, what would have been the point? I'd either win or I wouldn't; whatever happened, me watching via webcam wouldn't change the outcome. If the worst came to the worst, I'd have lost nearly a hundred pounds. Senseless to add insult to injury by wasting time fretting in front of a screen.

All through the late afternoon, I half-expected to get a text saying, congratulations, you've won, you can come and collect it any weekday between nine and five. It was eight o'clock in the evening before I began to relax. I finally went to the Gorringe's website and saw that it had been sold.

But irritatingly, it didn't say for how much, or to whom.

My heart sank again. It might be me.

I texted Frank. I couldn't take another bloody restless night. I wished I'd never even seen the stupid picture.

Five minutes later, I got a reply: *You didn't win this time, Lucinda. Better luck in future!* accompanied by a smiling-apologetically emoji. I texted back, *Thanks! Oh dear, well, there's always the next auction!* with a sad face emoji. I poured myself a nice big glass of Shiraz.

There's nothing like knowing the executioner's axe has missed your neck. I played a bit of Sheryl Crow, watched *EastEnders* on iPlayer, then went to bed and slept like a log.

III.

I didn't think any more about it for precisely two days. Then, on Wednesday evening, I was sitting in The Greyhound, in front of the log fire, with a glass of Prosecco and a schoolfriend called Tabby Veldrett, when in walked a young woman – mid-twenties, long hair, gabardine, smart jeans, leather shoulder bag, rather a pinched face – and began looking around. Her search stopped when her eyes met mine. I knew right away she was a journalist: takes one to know one, I suppose. She was alone, obviously looking for someone specific, and she wasn't, as far as I knew, anyone I'd ever seen in the village before.

She didn't come racing up to me, like an amateur, with an 'Are you Lucinda Bridgen?' But she visibly relaxed when our eyes met, as if she'd finally tracked me down. She sat at the bar and calmly ordered an orange juice. She'd already registered that I was with a friend, and past experience must have taught her that barging in isn't likely to get a result. Far better to bide your time. She might even be waiting for me to go to her. *Oh dear, why was a journalist here to see me? I had to find out!* That might be her thinking.

If so, she'd miscalculated. I didn't have that sort of curiosity any more. Journalists usually want more from you than they can conceivably offer in return, and if you're in any sort of trouble, it's usually the police you have to deal with. If you're sensible, you do that in the presence of a solicitor. You definitely don't go blabbing to the first journo on the scene.

I ignored her and carried on talking to Tabby. We'd already raked over my adventures with the auctioneer. She was telling me about how Jake, her youngest, was doing at school, and how this one teacher, you know, said his potential was 'massive'. Mumsnet stuff. After five minutes, something happened that I should probably have foreseen. Chloe, the serving girl, came over with two drinks on a tray. "Compliments of the young lady at the bar?" she said, as if asking our permission to put them on the table.

"Wow," Tabby said. Not a good 'wow'; more of a suspicious one. She leaned towards me. "Do you know her? I saw you make eye-contact with her when she came in. She's – I assume she's some sort of acquaintance of yours?"

"Sort of," I said. "I'll probably need to go and speak to her in a minute."

Tabby shrugged. "I need to be getting home anyway."

"I didn't mean it like that."

"Neither did I." She picked up her drink and toasted the buyer. "Thanks," she said. It was a Wednesday evening. There were only six people in the bar, including us three, so she didn't have to raise her voice.

"You're welcome," the woman said, raising her orange juice. She didn't smile. Cool customer.

"Who are you?" I asked her.

"I'm a journalist," she said simply. "Like you."

"I didn't say 'what'," I replied. "I said, 'who'."

"I'd like to talk to you in confidence," she said. "Make you a mutually beneficial offer. I can see you're here with your friend, and I'm not here to interrupt that - "

"You already have," I said.

"Lucinda, it's *okay,*" Tabby put in. "I've got to go anyway. It's a school day tomorrow, and I've got packed lunches to make." She stood up, downed what remained of her wine – nearly a full glass - and grabbed her coat. "Ciao. I'll call you."

I watched her walk out - there wasn't much else I could do - with mounting anger.

The woman from the bar came and sat on the seat she'd just vacated. "I can give you a lift home to Wood's Green if you like," she said. "It's a long way from here."

"Who do you think you *are?*" I said loudly, making everyone else in the bar jump. "Do you do this sort of thing as a matter of policy, or are you just tactless by nature? Either way, do you really think it's the sort of behaviour that's likely to endear you to other people? I can walk home, thank you." I got up, pointedly not touching the drink she'd bought me, grabbed my coat, and headed in the same direction as Tabby.

"Wait!" the woman said. She followed me outside onto the forecourt. It was dark. "Sorry, I'm sorry. I'm really sorry. Please, I'm sorry. My name's Beata Gryniewicz. Here's my ID card. I work for *The Guardian* - "

"Wow, good for you."

"That picture you bid on at Gorringe's," she went on breathlessly: "do you know how much it went for?"

I turned to face her. For some reason, I hadn't expected anything about the picture. I'd been stupid enough not to speculate about her motives. Anger had blinded me. Big mistake.

"What picture?" I said in a feeble attempt to gain the time I needed to reappraise the situation.

"Two hundred and fifty thousand pounds," she said.

Every smart aleck reply I could possibly have made dropped onto the floor and expired in silence. I don't know how long we stood staring at each other. I must have looked thunderstruck, because I certainly felt it. In any case, something had changed between us. We'd connected.

"Where's your car?" I said.

IV.

Beata owned a battered old Volvo whose interior smelt of diesel. We drove in silence, partly because I assumed she already knew the way, which she did. She parked in the little lane that runs down to Osmers Hill and we walked side by side to where I lived. When we got indoors I poured us both a Jack Daniels – I didn't ask her if she wanted one, and she didn't object, even though she was driving – and we sat down at opposite ends of the sofa. My house is never very tidy, but she gave no indication of noticing.

"Before we get to talking about all this," I said, "I might as well ask the obvious question. Are you sure you're not mistaken?"

She shrugged. "You've got a friend at Gorringe's. Why not ask him?"

"How do you know that? About my friend, I mean?"

"I'm a journalist."

I laughed. "A better one than me, apparently!"

"You were the first bidder. You could only have got in that quickly if you had an inside contact. But look." She reached into her bag and passed me a single-page document. "That's a copy of the bill of sale. I shouldn't have it, only I've got a contact at Gorringe's too. Name of Frank Cave."

She was beginning to irritate me again. She seemed pretty puffed up with her own brilliance. So far, the only decent thing she'd done was not comment on the nuclear explosion which is my living room. That goes a long way with me, but it's not a panacea.

I skim-read her photocopy and gave it back. "What's your angle?"

"How do you mean?"

"Why have you come to see me? Surely, *Obscure Picture Fetches Two Hundred and Fifty Thousand at Auction* is story enough. I don't see why you need my input, unless you think there's something deeply suspicious about the whole thing. Which, since you're here, drinking my Jack Daniels, you must do. So, I'll ask you again, Beata Gryniewicz: what's your angle?"

"Well, *of course* I think there's something suspicious about it! Two hundred and fifty thousand! Don't *you?"*

I sighed. "You have an annoying habit of not answering a direct question. Have you ever considered a career in politics?"

"Sorry, I'm just excited, that's all. I'd like you to help me. I can probably tell you more than you can tell me, and I'd like us to work together. There's a story to break, and we can both enter the journalistic hall of fame."

I laughed again. "'The journalistic hall of fame.' Why me? There must be lots of other fat, middle-aged hacks around, a fair number of them much closer to *Guardian* Central Command in London."

"Because you're a Wadhurst person. This is a Wadhurst story, and in order to get to it, I need the help of a Wadhurstian."

I frowned. I was finding it hard to gauge how intelligent she really was. She seemed to alternate between perspicacity and crassness. "You're barking up completely the wrong tree."

"In what way?"

"I've had a good look at that picture, and believe me, the only thing 'Wadhurst' about it is the single word in the title-inscription. Besides, you can't *seriously* think that whoever bought it had any interest at all in the subject? The most obvious explanation is that the buyer knew something no one else did about the true identity of the anonymous painter. Presumably, it was a genuine Claude Lorrain, or a genuine insert-name-of-Old-Master-here."

"Let me tell you what I know," she said, "because I was actually *at* that auction. And I spoke to Frank afterwards. So I know what went on."

I scoffed. "'What went on'? You make it sound like a gunpowder plot." I realised I sounded truculent. "Sorry, you said you were going to tell me about it, and I'm sitting here, picking faults that aren't even faults. Go on."

"I attended solely because of The Stafford Collection. Apart from that, 'The Wadhurst Obelisk' wasn't even on my radar."

"So, what 'went on'?"

She drew her feet up onto the sofa. "Most auctions have a lot of regulars, as I'm sure you know. But obviously, there are always at least a few first-timers, especially when something unusual is up for sale. So, on Monday, as you might expect, there were a lot of newcomers. Amongst them, there was a fairly distinctive sub-group of middle-aged and elderly men and women in smart dress. They didn't speak to anyone, they held themselves aloof, and they came across as rather disreputable, despite their expensive clothes. They arrived early, but they didn't sit in the first three rows where the big notice says the web cameras are. They obviously didn't want to be seen by the world at large.

"Most of the items in The Stafford Collection went for a fair price – the shadows book went for five thousand, and the Crowley letter for nine hundred and fifty – but none came close to two hundred and fifty thousand.

"Anyway, this little clique of strangers made no attempt to bid for anything in that collection other than the obelisk landscape. When it came up, the bidding was dogged and relentless. You should have seen the auctioneer's face when it passed the two thousand mark, and especially when it showed no sign of slowing down. When it broke ten thousand, he seemed to relax a bit, as if he'd suddenly twigged. *Aha! I know what's going on here: we've got a conspiracy of practical jokers!* It must happen from time to time, I suppose, but I'd be surprised if it's not as rare as hen's teeth. Still, what's more likely? Ten thousand pounds for a piece of obvious tat like 'The Wadhurst Obelisk', or a cabal of pranksters? Even *I'd* say the latter. So, the auctioneer put on an air of forbearance, as if to communicate to them that he knew what was going on, he'd seen it all before, he might as well see this infantile charade to its bitter conclusion, but boy were they going to be in trouble afterwards.

"Anyway, up in price it went, up, up, up. After a hundred thousand, the atmosphere changed again, and it suddenly became obvious – even to the auctioneer, I think – that this was a genuine contest. For a start, there were none of the little conspiratorial nudges and smirks you'd expect from a sendup. Something angry and unpleasant had entered the mix: sneers, scowls, winces, sudden trembles, grinding teeth, perspiration. It looked as if the bidders both hated and were afraid of each other, which is exactly the sign of a really intense auction for something genuinely coveted, I suppose.

"The successful bidder looked both relieved and scared out of his wits. Small, bald, about sixty, slightly obese: name of Mark Tennyson. He asked specifically that Gorringe's keep the whole thing quiet. He paid, there and then, *in cash,* and took it away.

"Of course, Gorringe's *couldn't* keep the whole thing quiet. Everyone there was amazed, and I'm sure everyone online felt the same. Obviously, the participants talked about it. They shouted it from the rooftops. Why wouldn't they?"

"What are you waiting for then?" I asked. "You've got your story right there. Write it up and submit it."

"I already have."

I nodded. "Of course you have, yes. Only you think there's an even bigger story."

"*Obscure Picture Fetches Two Hundred and Fifty Thousand at Auction* is a scoop, but a minor one. And I happen to believe it's only the tip of the iceberg."

"Well, my professional guess is that you've arrived at the scene too late. Like I said earlier, the picture was probably painted by some famous artist, just unsigned. Word got out about it and a bunch of collectors turned up, probably bidding on behalf of zillionaires. Its true value was realised, end of story. I'm sure it's only a matter of time before a committee of experts authenticates it, and, well, *that's* your story. You should really be concentrating on likely panels of art historians. Or even unlikely panels: there are bound to be rumours, and rumours of rumours, and disaffected players of various types looking for a sympathetic ear to moan into. If you keep your nose to the ground in the right places… Well, it's a long shot, but you might conceivably hit gold."

"And yet, I'm sure that's not it."

"Your reason being?"

"Before I go into that, I need your word that if I convince you, it does have a Wadhurst aspect, you'll agree to work with me. Yes?"

I shrugged. "You've got your work cut out. But, fine, knock yourself out."

"I happen to know – I discovered it yesterday - that Charles Stafford considered 'The Wadhurst Obelisk' the most important item in his entire collection. And yet, he wasn't an art collector. More than that, he had no interest whatsoever in art. The pictures on his walls were considered too commonplace to appear at auction, even as a job lot. And Tennyson has no interest in art, either. I've asked *The Guardian*'s cultural editor about him, and the associate editor. He's a complete unknown."

"'Tennyson' could have been a false name. And unless there's footage of him bidding, I don't see how they can pronounce definitively. They'd need to have seen his face, at least."

"He may not have appeared on the auction's webcam. That doesn't mean he wasn't caught on the security cameras."

"Fair point."

"But it's not just Tennyson. *None* of those people were art collectors. What they do have in common – the few I've been able to identify – is a passion for the occult."

"As you'd probably expect," I said, "since this was the sale of The Stafford Collection. And, well, *there's* the solution to your mystery. They knew that Stafford himself set a high value on the painting, so that persuaded them to follow suit. The straightforward transmission of a delusion from a master to his acolytes. Not very interesting. Hardly an 'iceberg beneath the surface'."

"But don't you see?" she burst out. "They weren't interested in the painter. They weren't interested in the painting, not as a piece of art. They weren't even interested in the rest of The Stafford Collection, which they should have been, since they were occultists. Just *this*. Just this *one thing*. And by a process of elimination, that means they must have been interested in the subject."

"The 'obelisk'."

"Exactly. Now, don't get me wrong. Whatever they believe about it is almost certainly going to be total bullshit. But even so, there are types of bullshit. There's harmless bullshit – the healing power of crystals, fairies at the bottom of your garden, that sort of thing - and there's powerful, potentially dangerous bullshit: The Elm Guest House Hoax, QAnon, the Sabmyk Network. And there's lots of in between points. What I want to know is, what do they actually believe? And what do they intend to *do* about it?"

"I see, yes. I wouldn't call that earth-shattering, but it might make an interesting story."

"Depending on how potentially lethal the bullshit is. What's interesting about it is that almost all of them were willing to pay upwards of a hundred and fifty thousand to gain entry to whatever they think it is."

I yawned. "Sorry. Tired. Okay, we can work together. I'm still not sure what use I can be, though."

"Isn't it obvious? If they're interested in the subject, then sooner rather than later, some of them are going to turn up in Wadhurst, and they're going to be asking questions. What you've got to do is 'keep your nose to the ground', as you put it earlier. You know the locals. They'll tell you if there are 'strangers in town' asking weird questions, and if you put it about that you're interested in the whole thing, and you're doing a little research of your own – keep it vague, obviously – then you'll probably find said 'strangers' coming your way. All you've got to do is pump them."

"What's your part in all this?"

"I'm going to find Tennyson. At the very least, I'm going to find out about him. I've got his address. He lives in Rochester."

"Okay, let's exchange phone numbers, then we'll discuss how this is going to work."

"What do you mean?"

"I've been here before," I said. "A fellow hack turns up, out of the blue, with an offer of 'working together'. So, you put in a lot of legwork, then suddenly, there it is, *your* article, in print – suitably reworked, of course: the 'author' wouldn't want to be accused of plagiarism - and there's no sign of your name in the byline, just his."

"Suits me. Can I spend the night? I mean, on the sofa or something?"

"Only if we get the wording right."

V.

After we'd talked, I gave her a copy of my front door key. With two hundred and fifty thousand pounds in the mix, either one of us could make enemies, and she might need a place of relative safety at short notice. She thanked me but said she didn't think it would come to that. I insisted. Last thing I wanted on my conscience, avoidable death of my sole collaborator. And to be honest, I liked her. Once you'd got past the hardened journalist, she was nice.

She got up at six o'clock while I was still asleep. She showered, went downstairs, made herself a cup of tea, had some Frosties, plus a slice of jam on toast, and left the house at seven.

As soon as I heard her close the front door, I got up. I went on Facebook. I've been a member of 'Wadhurst Village, East Sussex' since it was created. I still had the photo of the painting that Frank had sent me, so I posted it to the group with a short announcement that I was busy writing an article about it. I didn't say for who, or what I thought I'd discovered. The vaguer, the better. I poured myself a big bowl of Honey Monster Puffs, drank two cups of coffee, and headed into the village to check out The Word on the Street.

I did a bit of shopping and went into The White Hart for another coffee. Old Raymond sidled up to me. He knew all about 'The Wadhurst Obelisk', he said. Which, after buying him two beers and listening to him for twenty minutes, I concluded was a complete lie (for 'all' read 'zilch'). I bumped into Sheila Rioddas in One Stop, who also thought she knew something about it. Hadn't it been an exhibit in one of the recent village fetes? I was polite. I listened for twenty minutes. Finally, we decided she must be thinking of something else. Then, she had a sudden flash of insight. Yes, yes, it *was* something else! That's right!

And so it went on. As always happens in these sorts of cases (and believe me, I've been involved in a lot), the people most eager to provide information are the people who know least. Total ignorance is never a disqualification; quite the opposite.

I checked Facebook. Twenty responses to my post. No one there had ever heard of 'The Wadhurst Obelisk'. Ten or twelve people tactfully pointed out what I should have mentioned in my announcement: that it wasn't an obelisk at all: it was a standing stone, which was a completely different thing. All were adamant: the scene in the picture wasn't located in or about Wadhurst. How *could* it be, unless that castle had been painted in later (a consideration which, I admit, hadn't occurred to me till now). And the title-inscription: was it original?

I ended up having to answer a lot of questions, and getting nothing much back in return; but then how could I get anything back? As I'd known from the beginning, there *was* no 'Wadhurst Obelisk', nor had there ever been such a thing.

The important thing, maybe, was that I was establishing my credentials in the local community, as the person to come to for information. When Beata's 'strangers' turned up – if they ever did - I stood a good chance of hearing about them, and possibly being their first significant port of call. I hadn't told her that it wasn't necessarily possible to identify 'strangers' in a village with a population of nearly five thousand. Maybe that didn't matter.

I went home about two o'clock: chores to do for 'the office'. I called my editor and told her what I was working on, and that I'd teamed up with a journalist from *The Guardian*. I expected an indulgent so-long-as-it-doesn't-interfere-with-your-real-work, but, to my surprise, she was supportive. Incredibly, news of the quarter of a million pounds painting had reached Reuters (I don't know if she was winding me up:

who cares?), and everyone in 'the office' was just a little bit curious. 'Good to know we've got an iron in the fire' was her parting salutation.

Beata called at seven o'clock that night. We exchanged accounts of our day. She'd tried to see Tennyson, but not only was he absent: his large terraced house had a 'Sold' sign outside. None of the neighbours knew where he was living now, or whether he'd be back before the new owners moved in. In the meantime, she'd found out a little more about him. His wife had died about six months ago, and he had a twenty-five-year-old daughter called Jilly, who was worried about him. He wasn't coping with being a widower very well at all; he'd shown signs of being on the verge of a breakdown. All hearsay, perhaps highly unreliable, but based on several incidents of symptomatic behaviour within a short time-frame. Midnight walks, public drunkenness, bouts of amnesia, a marked decline in personal hygiene: all the usual suspects.

Her next step was to try and find Jilly, which might be difficult: she might be married, in which case, she could well have ditched her maiden name. None of the neighbours seemed to know where she might live. Beata believed it was irrelevant. Both she and her father would turn up in Wadhurst within the next twenty-four hours.

I told her I'd be on the lookout and hung up.

I couldn't help it but, despite all our wrangling over rights to the story and mutual contractual obligations, I had the strange feeling she was the one in charge, and she knew it. She had her own agenda. I was just her servant.

VI.

I got up at seven the next day, looked at my Facebook post. The comments had dried up, as I suppose I expected. I ate more Honey Monster Puffs, drank more coffee, set out for the village once more. When I was passing the primary school, my phone pinged: a Facebook alert.

The signs were promising: a direct message from someone I'd never heard of before, name of 'Derek Martin'. *Hi, Lucinda. I understand you're the local go-to woman re the so-called Wadhurst Obelisk? Could we meet for a drink and a chinwag? Give me a bell. Sooner the better.*

Bingo. I looked at his Facebook page, though I'd already deduced a lot. No one says 'give me a bell' or 'chinwag' any more. He was middle-aged or older, probably unmarried, probably middle-class, probably not one for going out on an evening.

I called Beata. "The Eagle has landed," I said.

"What?" She sounded annoyed. "What do you mean? *What* 'Eagle'?"

Whoa. I'd expected a bit more encouragement. "Someone's made contact via Facebook. A 'Derek Martin'. He wants to talk about the painting… or the object; the fictional object. I'm not sure which. Is something wrong? You sound a bit grumpy."

"Something terrible's happened," she said. "We've got a story all right, but it wasn't the one I was hoping for. I know a story's a story, but - "

"Calm down," I said firmly. Familiar journalistic territory. "I need you to tell me what's happened."

I got the distinct sense I'd need to sit down for whatever she was going to say next. I left the pavement and plonked myself down at one of the picnic benches outside the fire station.

"Okay," she said, "here goes. You know Jilly? Tennyson's daughter? Well, I found her. Found out where she was living, I should say. I was on my way to meet her. Which I didn't get to, because the police beat me to it."

"The police?"

"And I backed up as fast as I could in the opposite direction. She's not under suspicion of anything. They were just there to inform her, apparently. Someone dug her mother's grave up and removed the corpse."

I took an involuntary breath. "Oh my God… Who would do a - ? Do you think her *father*…?"

"That's the assumption the police are working on, yes. And they've got evidence. I'm surprised you don't know about – about - something even worse than the excavated grave! But they probably haven't made an official announcement yet. It's still a crime scene, I suppose. I wouldn't go there if I was you. Not now you're known for being the local obelisk woman. Do you have an alibi for last night?"

"Beata, *calm down*. You're supposed to be a journalist! I need you to keep a clear head. What's this 'something worse' you're talking about? And why the hell should I need an alibi?"

"Tennyson's dead. He died in the woods somewhere in Wadhurst. The corpse – his wife's corpse, they think: they *know*, obviously, more or less - was found about a hundred yards behind him."

I let out a flute of air, then recovered my perspective. "How macabre. Terrible story. Poor old Tennyson."

"Do you have an alibi for last night?" she asked a second time.

I chuckled darkly. "Come on, Beata. I appreciate your concern, but they'll have difficulty pinning *that* one on me. What, just because I've shown an interest in a seventeenth century painting, and asked around the village a bit? No way. Relax."

"You're right, you're right. I don't think that's really what's bothering me. Things have taken a turn for the strange, and I really wish I hadn't asked all those questions."

"What questions?"

"The cemetery officials called two men to come and investigate the grave robbery. I got talking to them. They said that, if they didn't know better, they'd swear the grave had been excavated *from the inside out*. I asked them why they thought that. Because, they said, the hole was larger the deeper it got. Given a few hours, the whole thing would likely cave in, and no one would ever be able to tell the difference. But it was as if the earth had been hollowed out at the lowest part, and a small exit created near the surface."

"Whoa. So, someone came and took the body, and deliberately tried to create the impression that it had returned to life? Bloody creepy, but you've got to admire their dedication. And Mark Tennyson's the prime suspect?"

"Oh, yes," she replied.

I waited for her to elaborate.

"I take it you've something else to tell me," I said eventually.

"I've got a contact in the police. *Obviously*, I have, yes. Anyway, the initial verdict is that Tennyson died of a heart attack, brought on partly through exhaustion. At the time of death, he was *running away*, or that's what they said it looked like."

"And the corpse…You say that was about a hundred yards behind him?"

"Mm-hm."

"Wow. Looks like we've got a full-blown case of the supernatural on our hands. I'm not saying it *is* supernatural, obviously: Sherlock Holmes would probably know what to make of it; I don't. We need to write it up, pronto. The general public loves this sort of thing. If *we* don't break it, someone else will. And we definitely don't have to commit ourselves to a fixed interpretation: just a here-are-the-facts kind of account, leaving the how-creepy-is-that entirely implicit. People will talk about it for years. My God, it's the kind of thing people will write *books* and make *TV shows* about! It could be our ticket to fame and fortune!"

"Yes, I guess so," she said sadly.

"We need to get it in to tomorrow's papers: yours and mine. We've still got oodles of time before the press deadline. Get yourself over here, to Wadhurst. You need to find Jilly. Since her father died here, this is probably where she'll be now. She almost certainly won't want to talk, but she might. *I* can't go looking for her. I've got to rendezvous with whatshisname - Derek Martin – and find out what he knows. Not that we need him: we've got enough for a stupendous article already. But if he can tell me anything *at all* – and he will: I'm not known as The Grand Inquisitor for nothing – it'll be the icing on the cake. Call me when you get here. We'll meet up and compare notes. Then we'll file the copy."

As I ended the call, I realised: our positions had reversed. Right now, I was the one in charge. She was my servant.

But God, how horrible to think like that. What had I become, over the years?

VII.

Before speaking to Beata, I'd half-begun to wonder how I should deal with the mysterious Mr Martin: should I perhaps play hard to get? Yes, probably, because, by and large, potential sources are less likely to disclose secrets if they think you're desperate.

As I got up from the picnic bench and put my phone away, however, I was in no doubt. I had my story now, and it didn't need his input. I'd meet him, drink his drinks, and see what he had to say. I wouldn't feel obliged to proffer anything in return. I certainly wouldn't divulge what had happened to Tennyson. He could discover that for himself, later.

I got my phone out and called him.

"Who is this?" a brusque male voice said.

"Lucinda Bridgen, the go-to woman for The Wadhurst Obelisk, at your service."

"Ah! Lucinda! I presume you got my message! We need to talk. I very much doubt you can tell me anything, but I can tell you a lot, and I'm happy to buy you as many drinks as you like. Believe me, you're going to need more than one. You're a journalist, I take it. I hope you work for the *Fortean Times*. The White Hart okay with you?"

"I'll be there in two minutes," I said.

"I'll be waiting."

When I hung up, I was just passing the village sign, when I had an odd sensation. Something I'd never felt before. On my left, a big house behind a brick wall. On the opposite side, a fairly uninterrupted view, across rolling fields, into the far distance. I don't know what made me turn my head in that direction at that moment, except maybe … the weird feeling that I had to.

What I saw: the thing in the picture, about three or four miles away.

The Wadhurst Obelisk.

I stopped dead. I laughed. No, no, *no,* absolutely *not!* I blinked slowly, twice. How the hell…?

No, it wasn't really there. It *couldn't* be.

And yet… it was. I stepped onto the grass verge. I went to the very edge of the road, trying – pathetically, since it was a matter of inches – to get a closer look.

It definitely *was* there. Yet I'd never seen it before.

Of course I hadn't! No one had: I knew that from Facebook alone. It *couldn't* be where it appeared to be! Or anywhere! *For God's sake, it didn't exist!*

Only, it did.

I wanted to grab a passer-by – ask him or her the obvious, stupid, 'can you see that?' - but there weren't any.

Not that it would have made the slightest difference anymore. Somehow, I'd just passed the point of no return. *I* could see it. Whether anyone else could didn't matter, not even a thousand other people. *I was right;* they were... well, it didn't matter what they were.

Then suddenly, I felt *exhilarated!* like ten thousand volts had just shot through my body. I looked up.

What I saw quite literally took my breath away. Something like a rainbow, except that it filled the entire sky. Seven concentric semicircles, each a thousand miles higher than the other. My fingers tingled. When I examined them, they were covered in little worm-like threads of lightning.

Another thing: the sun was no longer the brightest object in the sky.

I had no idea what was happening to me. And the strangest thing of all was I didn't feel frightened or disturbed, or even particularly curious. It all felt perfectly natural. *More* than natural: as if I'd never *been* natural before, and I was returning to what I was always meant to be.

I knelt down. There were hundreds of Wadhurst Obelisks down here! each no bigger than a blade of grass, stretching away as far as the eye could see! They vibrated together, making a strange kind of music. I couldn't help myself: I burst into tears of joy.

Then I laughed. I saw what Tennyson had done. I actually saw him *doing* it. I put my hands together in front of my face. Contradictory emotions. How *good* of him! He'd been a truly generous man! Was, still.

Another pulse of power, and I was above myself, looking down ... upon myself. Then I was everywhere at once. In the air, on the grass, in The White Hart with Derek Martin, in London with Beata, in the woods with the dead body of Mark Tennyson and the investigative team, and everywhere beyond and in between.

It struck me I had an appointment with Derek Martin to be getting to. Not that it mattered what he had to tell me. I knew everything now.

And I don't mean that in any trivial sense. I mean, I was literally omniscient.

VIII.

All this sounds as if I was on something like LSD. I've actually taken LSD in my chequered past; I wouldn't now. But this was nothing like that: it was hyper-lucid. I remembered everything I'd ever done, and I realise this sounds crazy, but I remembered all my past lives, like the Buddha or Mahavira or something. On a more trivial level, I knew before I got to The White Hart exactly what Derek Martin would look like – younger than I'd expected at about forty, ponytail, single earring, closely cropped brown beard – and I knew that he'd bought me a large Prosecco, and I knew Janine would be sitting at the bar, though she never did that as a rule, and that Hillary and Walter would be in the corner with a pint of *Larkins* each, sharing a plate of triple-cooked chips on which they'd put vinegar but not salt. For God's sake, I knew everything that had ever happened - and ever *would* - to every single one of them!

To prove how cogent I was, I'm going to write down what Derek Martin said to me, verbatim. At no point during our encounter did he turn to me and say, 'Are you okay? You seem preoccupied.' Believe me when I say it didn't even occur to him.

He stood up. We shook hands. We sat down. He seemed pathetically, brazenly proud of the fact that he'd known my 'choice of tipple' in advance. I was in no mood to deflate him (some men hope you'll be all, 'Ooh, if you knew *that* about me, what *else* do you know?', as if finding out your drinks preference is on a par with getting a higher degree in Advanced Maths, ergo impossible.)

"You and I have something in common," he said, when we finally got down to brass tacks. "We both put in a bid on 'The Wadhurst Obelisk'. I was willing to go up to two hundred and twenty-five thousand, and when the final stages of the auction were reached, Mark Tennyson and I were bidding against each other. Our closest competitor had dropped out at a hundred and ninety-five. I pushed to my limit, but what I didn't realise was that Tennyson had wisely sold his house and everything else he owned. He actually had the means to go up to seven hundred, had it come to the crunch. I'm pretty sure that, when the bidding was over, he congratulated himself that he'd got a bargain. If so, he'd have been exactly right. Have you ever read Jesus' parable of The Pearl of Great Price? *The kingdom of heaven is like unto a merchant man, seeking goodly pearls: who, when he had found one pearl of great price, went and sold all that he had, and bought it*. I'm fairly certain Tennyson wasn't the only person in Gorringe's who considered 'The Wadhurst Obelisk' in that league. I'd imagine the others left cursing themselves for not having had the foresight to do what he had.

"But how could they have foreseen it would go for that much? I do know that when they got to Lewes, they were each horrified to find themselves amongst their rivals. They all thought they were the only ones who knew. You see, the picture went up for sale in amongst a bunch of other stuff that it simply didn't belong with: the assorted contents of the all-singing, all-dancing 'Stafford Collection'. A heap of worthless junk, really: letters from X, postcards from Y, bulls' horns, pentacles made from twigs, a copy of Gerald Gardner's unreadable novel, etcetera, etcetera. Bric-a-brac not intrinsically fit even for a charity shop or a car boot sale. Stafford *himself* didn't consider it valuable. I happened to know him. He kept the 'Stafford Collection' in a cardboard box under his stairs, along with four worn-out pairs of shoes, a set of garden implements, a washing up bowl, a raincoat with a tear in it, and a ton of other rubbish. He'd been roped into the whole 'Wicca' thing in the forties by accident, largely because he was well-known as a proponent of a very specific set of non-Christian mystical beliefs, and well, the Wiccans never were much good at making distinctions. All pagans were, and are, the same to them: part of a broadly homogenous, wholly affable pre-Christian mish-mash. But Stafford was never a Wiccan. He couldn't abide it. No, he was a Hermeticist from beginning to end. A Hermeticist, in case you don't know, is a follower of the philosophy of a certain 'Hermes Trismegistus', an immortal teacher of supposed great antiquity, who, so Stafford reliably informed me, actually visited Wadhurst in the fifteenth century, and wanted to stay here. Anyway, the basic idea of Hermeticism is that humans are one with the divine, that their true condition is a love of nature, and that by inducing a kind of mystic inwardness, they can reunite with God. Or something along those lines. Don't hold me to that reading: it's a complex package, and like a lot – not all - of those things, I find it self-contradictory and downright zany in places. Stafford didn't go along with the whole of it. He called himself a 'modern' Hermeticist. He believed the broad outlines, but not necessarily the cosmological or magical appurtenances. He was a one-off, and knew it.

"In any case, 'The Wadhurst Obelisk' was the only thing in his house on which he placed any value whatsoever. The reason he lived to such an advanced age was that he was waiting for it to 'activate', as they say. Tragically, he died just a little too early. 'Tragically', because he'd have known how to use its power properly. In short, the painting *is* the obelisk, which *is* the standing stone; they're the same thing in different forms: oh, in different places at the same time, of course, but then, space and time aren't actually real, are they? Just let me know if I'm losing you, by the way. They – it – the obelisk - was created by magic, supposedly by Hermes himself, to allow it to exhibit magical powers at specific points in its lifetime. One of those temporal points is now, and one of the things it can do is bring the dead back from the grave. You're probably beginning to get some idea of why Mark Tennyson was so eager to get his hands on it. It should be in the Ritman Museum, really. They may even had been bidding for it, but I doubt it. My personal opinion? Tennyson will turn up here within the next two days, at the latest, and it won't be pretty."

His phone rang. He took it from his pocket, looked at the screen and turned pale. I already knew what it was, but I thought I'd surprise him. He apologised, left the bar for three minutes to take the call 'privately'. When he came back, he looked even more shaken than before he'd left.

"Everything okay?" I asked innocently.

He took a deep breath, expelled it slowly and looked me in the eye, one of those, 'I'm afraid I've got some very, *very* bad news' gazes meant to prepare you to sink to the floor. "It's very much *not* okay," he said melodramatically. "I've just been informed by a hugely reliable source of mine – so trustworthy I can't doubt it – that Mark Tennyson's body has been discovered not fifteen minutes away from here. And that, not too far behind, the police found *another* dead body … in an advanced state of decomposition. Apparently the late Mrs Tennyson's grave has – in London - well, someone broke into it, or… " He was suddenly overwhelmed by his own revelations, as if he was hearing their import for the first time. "From what I've been told," he went on, "Tennyson's body was in an attitude of *running away*. My friend didn't want to say so, it's unbelievable, but it's as if – and no one in the investigative team's on board with this interpretation, incidentally, but they're having a hard time coming up with a scientific narrative – as if the corpse was *chasing* him. Or maybe Tennyson and the corpse were both running away from the same thing." He'd reached the glassy-eyed stage of talking to himself, articulating hypotheses that might keep his world view – determinedly secular, despite his pretensions - intact in the face of a relentlessly hostile barrage of adverse evidence from without.

I downed what was left of my Prosecco. I wasn't really feeling like alcohol, but I didn't want to offend the bar staff. I grinned, reached across the table and patted his hand. I felt genuinely sorry for him.

He looked at me in mild revulsion. "What are you – smiling for?"

"Tennyson wasn't running *away* from anything," I said. "Neither was Valerie, his wife. They were running *towards* something. He only ran ahead because he knew she couldn't fail, any more than he could. And because the thing they were going to meet was so fabulous. It was literally irresistible. They both made it, in case you and your friend are worried. They left the least important part of themselves behind, that's all."

His disgust had redoubled. But something else had joined it. Fear. "How do you know that?" he said feebly. "And how did you know the name of his wife?" The fear ousted the disgust until it was the only thing left. His next three words were exclusively motivated by it, and came out in a croak. "Oh, my God."

He backed away as I stood up. I laughed. 'Tipple', what a stupid word.

But what a fantastic one!

IX.

The next fifteen hours were easily the best of my life, and I'm confident that, if you were to rank them alongside the best hours of the lives of everyone who's ever lived, they'd come out *número uno*. My God, I can't even put them into words.

It began with me running. A long way. Out of the village and deep into the wooded countryside. Finally, I was 'alone' in the conventional sense, by which I mean there were no other human beings within sight. But of course, that's not real solitude. I had the birds, and insects, and everything beneath the ground, and everything I couldn't see because, well, animals are mostly used to keeping themselves hidden. I loved them. I lay prone. It rained. I picked myself up. I took all my clothes off. I sat under a tree. The obelisk was everywhere I turned. I felt strangely warm. The heavens opened.

I knew it couldn't go on forever because I knew the past and the future. I knew that yesterday, sometime after arriving outside The White Hart with 'The Wadhurst Obelisk' tucked under his arm, Mark Tennyson - not knowing precisely how things were going to play out, but confident he'd done enough to bring his wife back - had wandered around the village for three hours, trying to work out where the 'obelisk' was situated at the time of the painting. During that period, he asked for help from precisely four passers-by, including Sheila Rioddas. Sheila steered him in my general direction, as did Ted and Fiona.

At that point, things gathered pace. Suddenly, he wasn't just confident about his wife anymore; he *knew*. He knew an almighty summons was imminent and that he wouldn't be able to take anything along. So, as a last act of spontaneous generosity, he went into the Post Office, bought an envelope and posted the painting to me. He knew my address because, of course... well, let's not go back through all that: he just knew. My transformation began the moment it dropped through my letterbox in Wood's Green.

It would end sometime later that evening, and the course of events leading up to that termination would be exactly as follows. Beatta arrives in Wadhurst but she can't find me. She bumps into Derek Martin, who somehow recognises her as a journalist, and guesses she's working with me. He tells her about our conversation, but not everything: he says he thinks I may be on the verge of a nervous breakdown. She wisely decides to keep looking for me on her own. On the way round to my house, she realises Martin is following her. Not just him either, but two others, all with an air of menace. She suddenly remembers what I told her when we first met: *either one of us might need a place of relative safety at short notice.* She lets herself into my house. She locks and bolts the door as her pursuers – five of them now, and she has the strong sense that they're *not quite human* - hammer on the other side. Then she spies the envelope. She knows instinctively what it is. She knows that destroying it is her best chance of survival. She goes into the bedroom, opens the front window and sets fire to 'The Wadhurst Obelisk' in front of their eyes, using my birthday cigarette lighter. Then she flutters the ashes over them and calls the police. She still can't see their faces, and she has the horrific feeling that's because they haven't any – not even Derek Martin. In any case, five minutes later, they've scarpered. She pours herself a Jack Daniels and, for reasons I'll explain in a moment, savours the last remnants of an unutterable peace of mind. The police never arrive.

In the interim, I've dropped to Earth with a bump. Not too brutal, because I knew it was coming, but horrible none the less. In the final hour beforehand, I'd gone back as far as I could, through all my past lives, through everyone's, to our earliest human ancestor. What I saw: myself looking into nature like it was a glassy pond and falling in love with it, and that love being reciprocated. And that's the best way I can think of to put it, though it doesn't remotely do it justice. It's not even very interesting, put like that. Shame.

I retrieved my clothes, pulled them back on and walked home. Thank God it was dark. I must have looked like a bomb had hit me.

An hour later, I got in to find an empty bottle of Jack Daniels on the coffee table and a fully clothed, rat-arsed journalist asleep in my bed.

My birthday wasn't for another six months, but what the hell. I lit a cigarette.

X.

Sometimes you have an experience, and no matter how intense it is, you can't discover any way of integrating it into your life, with easily retrievable memories, clear implications for action, manageable affective repercussions. Most dreams are like this: we find it difficult to recall even the most overpowering ones. Why? Because we just can't clip them onto anything we've ever done before. So, with the best will in the world, we forget them.

Obviously, I was never going to forget what happened the day I met Derek Martin, but forgetting isn't the only option: sometimes, you simply tell yourself it must have been caused by some natural process (a near breakdown, say, or stress, or a sudden release of the wrong sort of chemicals from the nether regions of your brain). You *ought* to forget about it, but you can't. So, you 'explain' it in such a way as to make it easier to file under the category 'ought to be dismissed'. Henceforth, the problem's yours alone. A personal one, but it could be dealt with.

In my case, neither of those options is necessary, because I'm not alone. When Beata tore open Tennyson's envelope, she says the hieroglyphs on the 'obelisk' 'sparkled' like they were alive. She asked herself *why* for a split second, then it ceased to matter. She'd caught what I had. In a flash, she relived, with me, the cosmic dawn of humanity. When she set fire to the picture, it was because that was its destiny. She didn't feel bereft. On the contrary, she felt ecstatic.

My experience lasted several hours, hers lasted a few minutes, but we were both outside time and space. And where there's no space you can't have two individuals, nor can you really contrast 'several hours' with 'a few minutes'. If you ever manage to re-enter the world, then you'll know its physical boundaries aren't real. And that knowledge won't go away.

I'll cut to the chase, shall I? We live together now, in a little house on the Lower High Street. We couldn't be apart. And we became Christians six months ago. I don't mean tub-thumping, The-Bible's-an-instruction-manual-for-life, evangelical Christians. No, we signed up to Greek Orthodoxy. *Theosis*, becoming one with God. It's the only thing in the modern world that remotely encapsulates what we both know to be possible. Our once and future selves.

By way of a postscript, as far as I can discover, Derek Martin doesn't exist. I've asked Jilly, Tennyson's daughter (whom we found in the end). I've even been through her father's papers with her. Martin's claim to have known him simply doesn't hold up.

Anyway, virtually no one remembers the mysterious death in the woods now, or the corpse, or the empty grave, or even the auction. It's almost as if those things never happened. All anyone recalls is crazy Lucinda Bridgen bandying a whacky picture about on Facebook.

And I still don't know why the painter called it an *obelisk*. Maybe just the hieroglyphs ... if that's really what they were...

So, Beata and I are alone with what happened. But then, *of course* we would be. It's not possible to reconcile something like that with 'common sense'.

And we're completely fine with that. It doesn't bother us a fig.

The Never House

7 May, 1976. Norfolk

Dear Professor Bastford,

Please find enclosed everything relating to the 'missing episode' in my father's career. I do not consider myself much of a writer and I admit that, to compensate for my deficiency, I have 'cheated' slightly - albeit in a way which I hope will be of value to future researchers: I have inserted unredacted primary sources wherever I could. These consist of an exchange of letters between my father himself, Dr David Rosembaum, and his good friend and close colleague (also now deceased), Professor Charles Atkinson. They make up the bulk of what I have sent.

All ten letters were written in the space of a six-month period beginning in December 1934 and ending in May 1935. At that time, my father was a splendidly rotund figure with a distinguished gait and considerable charm. Four years later, when war arrived, he retired, and for a while he seemed to go into decline. Around 1942, he rallied. However, his mode of writing was always rather antiquated. He and Professor Atkinson were really products of the 1880s, and remained so until the day they died.

Unfortunately, as you already know, the letters do not cover the entirety of the aforementioned 'episode'. I have therefore concluded with my own account of the event which allegedly brought it to an end. I have taken care not to embellish what I myself was told in 1954.

In your last communication, you asked why all this is missing from Tom Ruttinger's otherwise excellent, *Dr David Rosembaum: A Life* (1968). The answer is: I do not know. Mr Ruttinger had full access to all the letters and the diaries, and over the course of several face-to-face interviews with him, I did recount the terminating event. One possibility is that he thought that, not being a psychoanalyst myself, I would not understand my father's work (in other words, that I was not a reliable witness). However, I prefer to think that since the *Life* is, above all, the scholarly biography of a *scientist*, our author simply did not know how to include what I told him. And with that, I sympathise.

My father kept all the letters transcribed here under lock and key during his lifetime. He bequeathed them to me when he died. Besides myself and Mr Ruttinger, you will be the first to read them since they were penned over four decades ago. If you can discern a useful meaning, or even a moral, I would be interested to hear back from you. Otherwise, please consign them to the archive, and take care about granting future access. While they could, as you say, be useful for some yet-to-be-invented science, they could, in the wrong hands, seriously compromise my father's reputation.

Yours sincerely,
Sir Matthew Rosembaum

****

Friday, December 14th, 1934. London

Dear David,

I hope this letter finds you well. It gave me great pleasure to see you again at the recent meeting of the British Psychoanalytical Society, and at Lady Rollehampton's society dinner a month later. As I am sure you gathered, Her Ladyship is seeking to have Freud elected as an honorary member of the Royal Society of Medicine. If she is successful (and of course she is not working alone), it should enormously advance the prestige of our discipline in this country. I thoroughly agree with you that we are presently at a crossroads. Far too many in the establishment concur with the idiotic National Socialist evaluation. The Marxists are scarcely less hostile, and influential in a different way. We have made great strides, but we cannot afford to relax.

I am writing to you partly as a result of all this. Her Ladyship feels it would help our cause to publish a volume of case histories (with all names, etc. suitably anonymised) for popular consumption. At her insistence, I agreed to coordinate the enterprise. I am therefore writing primarily to ask if you have anything worth contributing. Of course, you would need to give *me* the real names, dates and, where relevant, locations referenced, in case we were ever to be accused of 'making it all up'. In that eventuality, the facts could be verified *in camera*; we could prevent their transmission, at the same time as mollifying the mischief-makers.

In sum, it would be a great help to me if you could look back through the entries in your casebook, and, if any in particular seem appropriate, send me the details. I know that this will inevitably lead to an increase in your workload, for which I apologise in advance. I will take care of the anonymisation. It will be thorough.

I hope your left knee is better. At your age, a walking tour of the Lake District is a courageous choice of holiday (as it would be at mine)! Please give my regards to Ada. Tell her I saw the Chinese piece she recommended in the British Museum, and that it was every bit as astonishing as she suggested. I hope Matthew continues to excel at Cambridge.

With deepest regards,
Charles

*

Sunday, March 10th, 1935. Tunbridge Wells

Dear Charles,

regret at having nothing suitable for your highly commendable anthology. But now, I really think that may have changed. If you have already gone to press, please disregard what follows, although I think you will still find it interesting. If you feel inclined to offer any advice, however succinct, I would of course be very grateful, though I am sure you have many more pressing concerns.

It concerns a thirty-six-year-old new patient of mine called Michael Braithwaite: a tall, bearded bachelor with a sombre demeanour and a slight lisp. He appeared in my consulting room last week, complaining of disturbed sleep. Now, most of my cases are, like yours, clinically straightforward - acute stress, phobia, repression, neurosis, anxiety, obsession - and on first inspection, this one looked to be equally routine. I directed him to the couch then got him talking while I took the occasional note and smoked my pipe.

To my immense gratification – although it quickly evaporated - the solution seemed evident in the very formulation of the problem. You see, he had recently finished reading a volume of collected ghost stories, amongst which was one in particular. I don't know whether you're familiar with Oliver Onions's, 'The Cigarette Case'. It tells of a chance encounter between a pair of young gentlemen and two ladies – all English - in the Provençal countryside, rather late at night, in the latter years of the nineteenth century. The men gallantly return a dropped handkerchief. By way of showing their gratitude, the women invite the men home. They all spend a very enjoyable hour or so conversing in the women's 'rather old-fashioned salon'. The next day, one of the men realises he has left his cigarette case behind. When he finally locates the house, he hardly recognises it: it has been derelict for at least a century. Inside, it is exactly as he recalls it in terms of furnishings and fittings, yet everything is time-worn, decayed, and overlaid with several inches of dust. He finds his cigarette case, shiny and apparently as good as new, on the 'rickety old round table' where he left it. At the same time, the men's host – a long-time denizen of that part of France – assures them that there are 'no English ladies' to be found anywhere in that area.

To me, ghost stories work best when they highlight something of the eerie strangeness of life *as we normally lead it*. When the two protagonists stand up to say goodbye, they somehow know their acquaintance with the women cannot continue. And yet the reader gets the impression the single hour spent in their company has been abnormally happy and intense. If the narrative was to end there, with, say, a final meditation on memory and the loss of youth, it would still be excellent. It might remind the knowledgeable reader a little of Alain-Fournier's *Le Grand Meaulnes*.

But I digress. The point is that something in 'The Cigarette Case' prompted Braithwaite to have a recurrent nightmare with several interesting features. Let me describe it, and you will see what I mean.

Firstly, its temporal setting is very specific - about fifteen years ago, just after the war, when he and his friend (whose name he cannot remember) were twenty-one. In terms of its narrative-pictorial content, the dream runs as follows. The two men are staying in an inn called The Queen's Head. One afternoon they are hiking in the local countryside when they find themselves behind a trio of young women, walking arm in arm. One of the women drops a book. Braithwaite's friend runs forward, picks it up, and politely returns it. The women are delighted – possibly a little *too* delighted, says Braithwaite (though this may be a *post hoc* appraisal, external to the dream) - and they invite both men back to their house. When the five reach the front door, the women – all three of whom are inconceivably beautiful, by the way, but of indeterminate racial stock (I find this detail very interesting) - go inside. The friend follows, but before Braithwaite can cross the threshold, the door slams rudely in his face. At first, he thinks it must be a mistake. He knocks gently. Silence. He waits and tries again. Silence. At this point in the dream, Braithwaite either awakes, or time speeds up. In the latter version, he is aware of still standing outside the house at sundown. Then he goes back to The Queen's Head. There is no sign of the friend there either. Finally, three days go by, and the friend has still not returned. He informs the police. The friend never reappears.

I have my own theories about this, of course – the women obviously present a siren aspect - but I would be interested to hear your assessment.

Please give my warmest regards to Lucy, and pass on my condolences regarding the recent death of her aunt in Wales. I hope Tom, Ella and Pip are still enjoying life to the full! Give them each a kiss from me.

Yours as ever,
David

*

Saturday, March 16th, 1935. London

Dear David,

Thank you enormously for your letter of 10th March. I managed to obtain a copy of 'The Cigarette Case' from a second-hand bookseller in Pimlico. Superficially, it already presents highly salient psychological features!

Before I get more narrowly 'to business', it may interest you to know that Mr Braithwaite's case possesses several features in common with another that was recently brought to my attention. Of course, I have been inundated with interesting studies since I first sent out my letter in December. I will not share the details of the one I have in mind, lest it subliminally affect your judgement about Braithwaite. I mention it solely because, if they do end up following a similar trajectory, it might be good idea to bring them together, under a single heading, in the anthology. Obviously, in that case, I would also seek permission from the psychoanalyst concerned to share his findings with you.

You asked for my advice. Well, from a professional point of view, there are several important differences between Mr Braithwaite's dream and the short story, and, as is universally acknowledged to be good practice, those should be our starting point.

To begin with, we have the named inn: The Queen's Head obviously suggests an Oedipal element; '*The* Queen' from which both men – and human beings in general - emerge. The idealised mother.

The second point of divergence has to do with the women, and has three parts. In the literary antecedent, one of the women is much older than the other. And both are English. And Onions makes no mention of their beauty or otherwise. In Braithwaite's dream, however, there is an extra woman, all are the same age, of uncertain race, and astonishingly beautiful. Presumably, in the dream, they represent the conventional focus of the libido. I am not sure why there are three of them, but that will doubtless become clearer in time (NB. interesting parallel in that Braithwaite also waits *three* days for the friend to reappear).

In the story, it is a handkerchief that is dropped; in the dream, a book. But notice that the friend picks it up, and, in the dream, it is he who ends up in the company of the three women. This may symbolise a sense of educational inferiority on the part of the patient. The Queen's *Head* may indicate that the patient's mother was a woman of unusual learning, and that this is his yardstick for judging potential mates. If his own accomplishments in this area are unimpressive, that may be the entire secret of the dream. *To wit*, he wants a woman who possesses his mother's learning, but feels he himself will be unable to satisfy such a woman intellectually. In my experience, that sort of thing often issues in misogyny. It might be an avenue worth investigating.

Notice finally, the ambiguous ending. We do not know what ultimately becomes of the friend. He may actually be better off inside the house… but not necessarily. You mentioned at the beginning of your letter that Braithwaite is unmarried. The friend's disappearance may represent a deep equivocality about the fairer sex, which would confirm my analysis in the paragraph above. It may even be that the whole dream presents a homosexual aspect, but I consider that unlikely. From what you have told me, I get no sense that his attachment to the friend is erotic. More likely, Mr Braithwaite is suffering from a form of misogyny, possibly even gynophobia. That would be only its most superficial aspect, and once brought to light, hardly likely to solve the problem.

In any case, perhaps the most significant part of the story is that he returns to The Queen's Head and calls the police. The return to the mother as a symbol of security and protection.

These are only my first analytic impressions. I am sure you have already considered all the above, and it may be that you have rejected it. In that case, forgive me. But please keep me informed.

With very best wishes,
Charles

Sunday, March 24th, 1935. Tunbridge Wells

Dear Charles,

Thank you for your encouraging words. I find it gratifying that our thinking on Michael Braithwaite is so similar. A part of me had hoped that, in articulating his dream, he might 'talk' himself into a cure, but alas, no: he had the same nightmare this Wednesday, unchanged in its detail and equally distressing. So, we are no closer to a resolution.

I have not yet shared our professional analysis with him. Up till yesterday, I had hoped to do so – suitably translated into lay terms, of course - in our next session (he has another appointment with me at 4pm this coming Saturday, the 30th). But in our last meeting, I asked him a few indirect questions about his relationship with his mother, with women in general, and his friends. He did not seem overly surprised at the apparent re-direction of emphasis – the focus of psychoanalytic inquiry in general is a matter of common knowledge nowadays - and he was not reluctant to talk. But the results were not as auspicious as I had hoped. I anticipated a deep attachment to a brilliant mother, an unwillingness to let her go, and an irrationally negative assessment of other women in general. What I got was nothing like that.

Let me outline the relevant biographical details. Braithwaite was born in a village not far from Tunbridge Wells, called Lamberhurst. He lived there until the age of twenty, when he moved to Hastings to take up a position as a clerk in a solicitor's office, a position which he still holds. His mother, Alice, was a housekeeper, one of several employed by the owners of a local manor called Scotney Castle. She does not seem to have received much in the way of a formal education, although obviously that is not to say she was unintelligent. She died, in 1925, at the age of fifty-three, of an organic heart disease. Her husband, Gerald, some ten years older than her, a retired gardener on the same country estate, is still alive, and has remarried. He is on formally good terms with his son, although they are not especially close. Michael Braithwaite was their second child. The first, Ian, was killed at Passchendaele. I had hoped that Ian might be the source of the 'friend' in Michael's dream, but in fact the two men had little in common – ten years separated them - and they may even have actively disliked each other. Michael signed up for the war effort in 1917. He saw action in France and was demobbed shortly after the armistice. He does not seem to have been unusually affected by his experiences, which were, he assures me, 'relatively uninteresting'.

As regards his relationships with women, he is engaged to be married to a Miss Lorna Smith, a barmaid at a Hastings public house called The Jenny Lind. She is four years younger than him. They hope to have the wedding in September. From what I could ascertain, they are as devoted to each other as any normal engaged couple. He exhibits none of the symptoms of misogyny.

Friendships? He has the usual work relations with colleagues, and one or two other men, all former schoolmates. He is not unusually outgoing or popular, but nor is he particularly shy or disliked.

In short, I have been left with very few leads, and the case is turning out to be anything but simple.

As I said earlier, I had hoped to present our 'Oedipus' analysis to him in our next session, but after delving into his background, I do not yet feel I possess sufficient warrant for such a gambit. Possibly, there are details in the dream that he is concealing. For that reason, I intend to devote our next session to hypnosis.

Yours as ever,
David

Saturday, March 30th, 1935. London

My Dearest David,

Thank you for your update on the mysterious Mr Braithwaite. I am sorry to hear you are disappointed, although I rather think you were too optimistic in the early stages. Please do not take that as a criticism. From time to time, we have all been tempted to find an easy solution to our patients' problems in their superficial aspects; as if we are receiving a golden key on a silver platter. In my long experience, however, those sorts of cases often turn out to be the most obdurate.

I heartily endorse your decision to go with hypnosis. My dear fellow, this is the unconscious we are dealing with: it cannot be relied upon to yield its secrets so easily! No, we have to dig deep. I completely share your view that there is more to this dream than your Mr Braithwaite is yet able to tell us. Obviously, I do not mean that he is deceiving you. But of course, people cannot be expected to know their own minds; otherwise, what would be the use of us psychoanalysts?

Have faith! By the time you receive this letter, I am sure you will have made solid progress, and will no longer be feeling so despondent.

With very best wishes,
Charles

*

Sunday, April 7th, 1935. Tunbridge Wells

Dear Charles,

Well, what a week this has been! Hypnosis produced new insights, as we both suspected it would. Again however – how frustrating! – not the ones I'd hoped for, or even expected. The 'mysterious Mr Braithwaite', instead of yielding up his secrets, simply added detail to his existing ones.

The Tuesday session began with me putting him into a deep sleep. I asked him to re-experience his recurring dream and describe it to me as it unfolded, then I plied him with questions: *does this hike with your friend remind you of anything? What is the first thought that comes into your mind when you catch sight of the women? How do you feel about them emotionally? Is there anywhere specific in 'the countryside' that ties it to a specific location? What does 'The Queen's Head' mean to you?* and so on.

As his account progressed, I got a peculiar sense that he wasn't so much describing a dream, as something that had *actually happened*. The Queen's Head isn't, as we thought, a symbol of his mother (or at least, not primarily), but an actual place in a village called Wadhurst, about seven miles southeast of my consulting rooms. The generic 'countryside' he initially described is actually (so he claimed) Cousley Wood, a small hamlet within the Wadhurst parish boundaries. He even gave me the name of his friend: Simon Francis Geffers.

And it was that last disclosure which unsettled me. A middle name seems just a detail too much.

After I'd brought the patient back, he seemed as surprised as I was, and at a complete loss to know what to make of it all. We parted in the usual convivial manner, half an hour later than usual, at 5.30pm.

You mentioned me feeling despondent in your letter. I felt a lot more so after Braithwaite had left. I was tempted to spend the next day in Wadhurst parish, trying to find that wretched house of his. Maybe I would find it in the same condition as the one in the Onions story: broken down, vacant, infinitely disturbing.

But I am not a detective. My rational self said nothing could be gained from making such an expedition alone. Now if Braithwaite were to accompany me… Suddenly, I had a firm idea for our next session.

In the event, I did not need to suggest it. Braithwaite got in touch with me by telephone on Saturday morning, and made the same proposal.

We met up just before 3pm by The Queen's Head in the High Street. He had been inside the inn ten minutes earlier and bought himself a beer. Public houses close at three, and I think he was hoping someone there might remember him. The interesting thing about that is – and it took me a few minutes to notice it – he'd reached exactly the same conclusion I had: at the most basic level, we weren't dealing with a malady of the unconscious; rather we were dealing with a series of *actual occurrences in historical time*. Of course, that is not to say they were not overlaid with mental constructions, and that I therefore had no further role to play. Whoever 'Simon Francis Geffers' was, in the dream he had clearly become a cipher; the women equally. Their real counterparts had long since dropped out of the equation. In short, Michael Braithwaite still needed help of the kind only a trained psychoanalyst could provide.

I think the beer had given him a degree of Dutch courage, because he was no longer as meek as I was used to finding him in my consulting room. He had a proposal for me, he said. I should hypnotise him right here, in Wadhurst, and instead of getting him to talk through the events of that fateful day, I should get him to *re-enact* them.

I was not sure whether such a thing would be possible. I had never tried it before, and to be truthful (though I was reluctant to admit it), I am not a particularly skilful hypnotist. I find the procedure helpful in my clinical practice, but only occasionally. It is just one weapon among others in my armoury. My least preferred!

I kept all this to myself. The doctor-patient relationship requires that the former maintain a certain mystique, and at the very least, an aura of authority. This was not the time to confess to chinks in my armour. I agreed to his suggestion.

We needed privacy: the sight of one man publicly hypnotising another is sufficient to raise eyebrows anywhere in the world, and I had a sense that, at some point in the days and weeks ahead, we might need to come back here. I did not want us to acquire 'a reputation'. We went into the churchyard of Saint Peter and Saint Paul and I performed the operation whilst we both stood between the north transept and where the gravestones began. To my relief, it went entirely smoothly. I suppose it always depends on how cooperative the subject is.

Once Braithwaite had regressed, I asked him the question I suppose I should have asked in our last session. Given that he had grown up in Lamberhurst, why had he decided to come on holiday to the neighbouring village? Why not go somewhere farther afield? And why not stay with his mother (who, assuming he had got his dates right, was still living at that time)?

I am ashamed to say, it did not occur to me until I had actually posed these questions how interesting they were!

But his answers were deflating. When he and 'Simon Francis Geffers' originally decided to holiday together they had very different ideas about the specifics. Braithwaite wanted to go to Great Yarmouth or Bridlington, but Geffers was emotionally attached to his home village: he wanted to holiday there and nowhere else. (He'd recently moved to Brighton to work in a stationery store, and he was deeply homesick.) Eventually, the two men reached a compromise. They would holiday near to Lamberhurst (as Geffers wanted), but not too near (to satisfy Braithwaite), and they would not stay with Mrs Braithwaite (as Geffers suggested), but somewhere more like a hotel (as Braithwaite wanted). The

Queen's Head was Braithwaite's suggestion, and Geffers – wisely, probably realising most of his demands had been met - fell in with it. In other words, the entire thing was the result of a compromise. However strong Geffers's feelings might have been, it was no evidence of an *unnatural* affection on the part of either man for the place where they had grown up, or any revelatory attitude towards Braithwaite's mother. Once again, I had the dispiriting sense of a return to the start.

After that, we set off to retrace the steps the pair had taken that day. I asked him the date. *April 12th, 1920* came the reply. I asked him what day of the week that was, although psychologically speaking, nothing much hung on it. I have since been able to confirm that his answer – Monday – was correct.

Apart from that, we proceeded in silence until we came to Cousley Wood. Then I invited him to alert me at the precise moment he spotted the women. When he did so, I bade him describe his feelings. But of course, I'd miscalculated. In the dream, you will remember, Geffers put on a spurt, and Braithwaite ignored me, and ran ahead, in an attempt to draw level with his imaginary friend.

My left knee, as you already know, has not been quite right since that walking tour last year. I found it incredibly difficult to catch up, but I did learn something. Those women – if Braithwaite's pace was in any way an accurate reflection of the historic reality - were obviously in a hurry. In the Onions story, one gets the impression of a leisurely stroll. This was nothing like that. The word 'sirens' came disturbingly to mind again.

And then, suddenly, we were standing outside the 'house'. I saw Braithwaite flinch. Then he went through the motions of knocking on a door.

But there was nothing there. Certainly no house. Just empty land on the fairly flat crest of a minor hillock. I could see he was about to become distressed so I awoke him. It took me a moment to calm him. I showed him the vacant patch on which we were standing, I related events since the churchyard from my point of view.

Yet he remained convinced that there must once have been a house here. He was even able to describe it. It had a thatched roof, Tudor beams, lattice windows, a climbing plant. I pointed out the complete dearth of evidence. Even if such a dwelling had existed, and had been demolished, or collapsed as a result of some unforeseen calamity, there would still be traces here, and they would probably be hard to overlook.

Which meant, he said, that we must be in the wrong spot. So, we spent the next hour and a half going over what felt like (and probably was) every square inch of Cousley Wood. Needless to say, there was nothing that even vaguely matched his description. In any case, he claimed he would *feel* it when we reached the right place. But he never did.

It was getting late. We made our way back to The Queen's Head rather than go straight to the railway station. Braithwaite clearly wanted another shot at seeing whether anyone there remembered him, and I'd offered to buy him another beer. I was very tired.

We left Cousley Wood just as the sun was setting. Still, the sky was clear, and there was still sufficient warmth in the day to make the journey relatively unobjectionable. We crossed a field of sheep, with a shepherd at work in the far corner. Against my advice, Braithwaite politely enquired whether there had ever been a house on the crest of yonder hillock.

And this is where it becomes even odder. The man looked at us askance. He scratched his head and said, "Some folks say so." The gist of the elaboration which Braithwaite educed, was that sometimes a house *did* appear to be there, but only under certain conditions of light and usually in the early evening. "Yet everyone round here knows not to pay it any mind. It's just one of them mirage-y-type things people see in deserts and those sorts of places." He couldn't say whether it had a thatched roof, or what the windows were like. It was known locally as 'The Never House'.

We walked back to Wadhurst in silence. Not the hostile kind. I could see he was thinking deeply and did not want to be disturbed. I bought him the promised beer at The Queen's Head. He told me Miss Lorna Smith, his fiancée, had broken off their engagement and left Hastings to marry a veterinary surgeon she had met in St Leonards. Apparently, the illicit relationship had been going on behind his back for some time. She and her vet were due to marry in Eastbourne next week. Since she did not want any bad feelings, he'd been invited. He didn't think he would go. As he was telling me all this, he managed to knock his beer over. It poured across the table and soaked both of our trousers. He apologised repeatedly, and I could not help feeling there was ample raw material for a lifetime of Freudian misery for both of us in the day's events. I told him it didn't matter. I even tried to laugh (and I would have, had it not seemed insensitive, coming in such close proximity to his revelations about his engagement. After all, what do *I* care about a *pair of trousers* at my age?) Above all that, I felt infinitely *sorry* for him. I know that one should not get too involved with one's patients (although that does not seem to have stopped Professor Freud meddling in the affairs of Horace Frink. - Sorry, Charles, as I write this, I am a little melancholy). Braithwaite reminds me forcefully of my older son, Theodore, who, as you know, we lost at the Somme. I feel very strongly that he is a good man. Why do such awful things always happen to the best of us? *What is my strength, that I should wait? And what is my end, that I should be patient?*

We parted half an hour later on the village railway platform. By that time, he had tactfully told me that he wished to terminate our connection. He was very grateful to me, but felt we had reached the end of the problem (though probably not its solution). He did not believe it was essentially psychoanalytic. Something had actually happened that day. Something possibly supernatural, although he knew I could not entertain such a thing. We shook hands. I wished him the best. He thanked me again. As his carriage pulled away for Hastings – mine, going in the opposite direction, was ten minutes later – I waved him off. I may be mistaken, but I think he cried a little. Just as Theodore did all those years ago. I may have imagined it.

I wonder what you must think as you read this? The psychoanalyst needs psychoanalysing, perhaps. Nothing new there, of course. Professor Freud himself in his forties. But I wonder whether anyone who lived through the war, even as a non-combatant, can really be 'normal'. To be such, after all that - *filth,* would be at least *historically* abnormal! And we may be about to become even worse. I cannot shake the conviction that another war is coming. Hitler and Stalin and Mussolini? The crises in France and Spain? The Blackshirts? God preserve my Matthew and your Tom. (Though, tragically, I doubt He will.)

It turns out my Mr Braithwaite was not suitable material for your anthology, after all, and for that, I sincerely apologise. Perhaps my failure with him reveals my failure more generally. Tomorrow, neglecting both my patients and my professional responsibilities, I will spend the day in Lamberhurst. Mr Braithwaite may think he has cast me off, but I will not be dissuaded so easily. I will go door to door if necessary, in an attempt to find out who his 'Simon Francis Geffers' was.

Please give my regards to Lucy, &c.

Best wishes,
David

*

Wednesday, April 10th, 1935. London

Dear David,

Thank you for your long letter of April 7th. I feel nothing but sympathy for your opinions and emotions, and I am genuinely touched – and grateful – that you felt able to express them to me so frankly. Ours really is a degenerate age, and, horribly, as you say, war may yet be inevitable. We can only hope saner heads will prevail. With Oswald Mosley and Lady Houston holding the reins and The Prince of Wales probably about to ascend the throne, that seems unlikely.

You will notice that I am writing to you rather earlier in the week than usual. You were correct about Braithwaite in several ways. Firstly, you have probably not finished with him; secondly, whatever the outcome of your investigation, it cannot go in the anthology. Indeed, I rather hope you will refrain from publishing it at all – for your own good, as well as that of psychoanalysis generally. I trust you will see why in the lines that follow, for I have what might be called 'good news'. I use the term advisedly.

You may recall that when you first wrote to me about Mr Braithwaite, I said his case possessed several features in common with another. I am now in a position to share its details. It concerns a woman, unmarried, of exactly Braithwaite's age, who happened to read a story about a young lady whose fiancé unexpectedly abandoned her, and who then began to have dreams in which she was the forsaken person. The usual curatives failed to have any effect, and the dreams continued unabated. The psychoanalyst – you probably know Albert Collins: he has a consulting room in

Norfolk now – put her under hypnosis. All this was five years ago, in 1930, when Collins was based in Tenterden.

I shall pause a moment here to remind you that intended hypnosis is the exact stage you had reached with Mr Braithwaite, in your last letter but one (March 24th). I mention this by way of showing that I have not withheld any information that could have been useful to you.

Collins's patient – a Miss Margaret Keys – was from Lamberhurst (as was the dreamed fiancé). The specific backdrop of the dream was the same place. She claimed that, as children, she and her fiancé had attended the village school together. The fiancé's name? *Simon Francis Geffers*. They had become engaged secretly.

I can tell you the remainder of this wholly singular story in very few words. Collins came to the same conclusion as you did: the delusion was so firmly entrenched that, in order to extinguish it, it was necessary to take the patient to its supposed location. So, he and Miss Keys travelled together to Lamberhurst. They went door to door, exactly as you said you intended to do. No one remembered a Simon Francis Geffers, although one or two thought the name sounded very vaguely familiar, including the local school's headmaster. A school photograph dating from 1908 showed roughly two hundred and fifty pupils, including a gap, the size of a single individual, on the back row. Miss Keys looked hard and closely at it, and actually claimed to see her Mr Geffers there, very faintly! In his case notes, Collins remarked laconically on the stubborn power of 'hysteria'. Of course, he said nothing to her at the time.

Their day ended in the same way yours and Braithwaite's did. She thanked Collins and terminated the treatment. She even said she thought the real problem might be a supernatural one! He did not see her again until quite recently, and only by chance.

I contacted him by telephone after receiving your letter. He had met her in Tenterden, having returned there for three days to stay with friends. She was shopping with her mother. She still lives there; she is still unmarried. Curiously, she knew that she had once been one of Collins's patients, but she could not recall why. Geffers's name meant nothing at all to her: she could not even remember having heard it before.

At first, Collins thought she must be joking, or perhaps she was embarrassed about the whole affair in front of her mother. But the longer the conversation went on – and I gather it lasted nearly twenty minutes – the more he felt she was telling the truth. It was this that persuaded him to refer the entire case to me, as suitable for my anthology. Such a profound forgetting is surely rare, and may reveal something valuable about memory in general. He wanted to know whether he should invite her back, and offer to treat her *gratis* for scientific reasons. He felt such a case might turn out to be as ground breaking as Little Hans and Anna O, and could therefore make his name! Naturally, I gave him every encouragement.

Of course, this was before I received your last letter. Now, I do not know what to think. The obvious course of action would be to bring Mr Braithwaite and Miss Keys together, and put them both under hypnosis. Please let me know your views on the advisability of this.

I finish this letter with an overwhelming sense of *gloom*. Something even deeper than the morbid sense that the world is poised on the brink of a new conflagration. It seems to be something to do with this case. I cannot suppress the disturbing feeling that we have stepped entirely outside science into something deeper and less salubrious than anything within our professional experience.

Please send me your reply as soon as you can.

My very best wishes,
Charles

*

Saturday, April 13th, 1935. Tunbridge Wells

Dear Charles,

I am writing this letter to you quickly, and it shall be brief. Following my outing to Lamberhurst on Monday, and again the following day, I have become convinced that there was once *a real individual* in Lamberhurst called Simon Francis Geffers. He was born there, he grew up there, he became engaged there (secretly, and I think the real reason he insisted on holidaying there was so that he could rendezvous with his sweetheart), he intended to get married there, and then he disappeared. For some reason, his disappearance was accompanied by a general … erasure. His entry into 'The Never House' – if that is what happened, and I am actually beginning to think it may have – somehow changed the past. It gradually expunged him from the history of the world. I feel as if I am going mad.

Given this, and what you told me in your last letter, *obviously* we must bring Mr Braithwaite and Miss Keys together… Or so one might think. But to what end? To resolve the psychological problem? Only, Miss Keys's problem disappeared of its own accord, and there is every reason to think Braithwaite's will follow suit. To bring Geffers back? But how? To honour Geffers's memory? What memory?

Nevertheless, I think we have an abstract duty to the truth. I agree, we *are* out of our depth, but even so, we have an obligation to do the moral and correct thing. That surely means telling Mr Braithwaite and Miss Keys about each other (whilst keeping everything vague for now, and certainly making no initial mention of Geffers). It further requires arranging for them to meet so they can be put into a concurrent hypnotic trance.

In terms of a venue, my consulting room seems the obvious choice, since I am geographically closest to both parties, but I am open to suggestions. I am also happy to perform the procedure, although, given its potential significance, I think you and Collins ought to be at least present. If anything of scientific interest emerges, I am perfectly content to let either or both of you write it up and take the credit.

I hope all this strikes you as just and reasonable. I look forward to hearing from you very soon.

Yours as always,
David

****

Editorial note by Sir Matthew Rosembaum:

My father was not a great diarist, but he did keep a very occasional record of significant events, amongst which, as a student of the mind, he included his own mental states. On April 14th and 15th, 1935, he mentions 'very peculiar dreams.' On 16th, he mentions 'receiving an anonymous message' at his consulting rooms, delivered apparently 'by hand'. It read: *On no account must you bring Michael Braithwaite and Margaret Keys together*. It subsequently 'got lost'. He writes of his suspicion that he may have inadvertently stumbled onto some kind of government business connected to foreign affairs. From the 15th onwards, he feels he is being watched whenever he steps outdoors. He experiences a continual sense of looming menace. As a result, he begins to have second thoughts about 'the moral and correct thing'. But even so, his resolution remains. On 17th April he writes: 'Even if Heaven and Earth fall, we must choose the sole moral option.'

Two days later, he received a reply from Professor Atkinson.

****

Wednesday, April 17th, 1935. London

Dear David,

Thank you for your letter of April 13th. It arrived on the 15th. I immediately got in touch with Albert Collins by telephone, and he was convinced that we should bring the two young people together 'as soon as is humanly possible'. He agreed with everything you wrote, and, from what I could gauge, was highly enthusiastic about charting fresh territory in the discipline. 'Opening new vistas', he called it.

To my infinite perplexity and annoyance, however, he has now completely changed his mind. I received a letter from him this morning in which he states baldly that, 'at the risk of demolishing his credentials as a scientist… there seems to be a decidedly supernatural element to all this.' He mentions being 'warned off' the case; he does not say by whom. He hopes I will appreciate his honesty, he knows I can be relied on to respect his confidence, etcetera, and he ends by announcing that he is taking a sabbatical. Another psychoanalyst who needs psychoanalysing!

Afterwards, I telephoned him with a view to getting a more thorough overview of the situation. But he is absolutely adamant. He backtracked a little on his 'supernatural' claim, but not much. I really believe he thinks he is being pursued by some kind of ghoul.

Please re-read my last sentence, David. Consider: it would be natural for me, under normal circumstances, to end a sentence like that with an exclamation mark.

But the truth is, I have some inkling what Albert is going through. I am undergoing something similar myself. I feel I am being continually followed. I happened to catch sight of my pursuer in Hyde Park last night, on my way home. He looked small, and hairy, and somehow… *unspeakably simian*. I do not know how else to put it.

However, the labyrinths of the mind are many and various. How can we hope to map them if we are afraid of exploring our own? Yes, I feel terribly maudlin, but my better self tells me we are on the brink of something momentous. Which we two must now explore alone!

Yours in perpetual friendship,
Charles

*

Wednesday, April 18th, 1935. London

Dear David,

This is extremely difficult for me to write. I hope you will forgive me after all I wrote yesterday but, at the risk of sounding mad, I have become convinced that Albert may not be half as deluded as I initially believed. We are getting old; there are many, many things we still do not understand. In short, I must beg you to exclude me from your experiment. More than that – for my own sake, and Albert's: because we are *all* apparently implicated in this, and share the responsibility – to *abandon* it; to proceed as if there had never been a Mr Braithwaite.

In the name of all we have ever felt for each other, I hope you will comply.

Charles

****

Editorial note by Sir Matthew Rosembaum:

My father did not immediately reply to Professor Atkinson's letter. Despite his own depressed mental state, and the unrelenting feeling that he was being scrutinised by unfriendly eyes, he decided to press ahead with his project. In his diary (apparently his sole confidant at that time), he reiterates his resolve to put the truth first, come what may. I have the feeling that he also considered his two colleagues cowards, and did not wish to despise himself. I am certain he compared himself with my older brother, Theodore, who died courageously on the Western Front. That loss had affected him powerfully, and he was frequently prone to feelings of inadequate valour.

It was while he was in this fragile mental condition that the event occurred which should be considered pivotal to the whole affair, and which ultimately enabled him to transcend it. He arrived in his consulting room one evening (I do not know where he had been beforehand), to find a young woman sitting in the armchair next to his desk. The housekeeper had let her in after she had announced herself as 'one of Dr Rosembaum's patients'. She had a refined accent and a spotless outfit – pale yellow summer dress, hat and matching shoes - so she was eminently plausible. The window and the setting sun were behind her, so when my father entered, he could only see her face dimly. He noticed that she was 'extraordinarily beautiful and dark skinned', and that she did not stand up to greet him. He had an immediate intuition of who she was.

Allow me to digress about the detail I have just mentioned: he said she was 'extraordinarily beautiful'. That was very unlike him. He always disapproved of descriptions that rely on 'beautiful', as if the word states anything useful: it is, he held, at best vague, and usually both lazy and misleading. For my father himself to have used it, he must have been powerfully affected, and in context, it must mean something more than the usual subjective banality. In my strong opinion, he took it as signifying *who she was*.

She did not introduce herself. She asked him politely to sit down, and, although it was his office, he felt constrained to do so. He did not feel afraid. He got the powerful sense from the start that she bore him no ill will; that, if anything, she felt genuinely sorry for him.

She asked him why he was being so stubborn.

"I don't know what you mean," he said, his nerve beginning to return. "Who are you?"

She laughed politely. "I don't think I could tell you in words that you would believe. Luckily, I don't have to. You already know who I am. Mr Braithwaite was quite mistaken, by the way. There's only one of me."

His heart beat hard enough to restrict his throat. "What - what happened to Simon Francis Geffers?"

"Nothing at all. He lives with me now."

They sat in silence for a few moments. She looked at him seriously and intently from her position of deep shade. He was about to ask what she wanted when she spoke again.

"If it helps you to come to terms with all this," she said, "you can bring Mr Braithwaite and Miss Keys together. And you can hypnotise them to your heart's content." She smiled. "It won't get you anywhere. I'm here because I care for you.

Do you remember what you wrote to Professor Atkinson, just over a month ago? You outlined your theory of 'a good ghost story'. I too have opinions on that subject, especially when they're *true*. To me, such things are essentially cautionary phenomena. In any decent one, really bad things cannot happen to truly principled people. Oh, they can get a scare, yes, but no more: the universe simply won't allow it. Now, Dr Rosembaum – or may I call you David? - you've arguably exhibited the sin of hubris, but only *arguably*, and in any case, that's entirely counterbalanced by your desire to be worthy of your son's memory, and even more by your commendable attachment to the truth."

"Why are you here?" he croaked.

"To tell you I've called off the evil angels. There will be no more harassment: no menacing, no furtive watching, no following. The ground has entirely closed over Simon Francis Geffers. Go after him in the name of 'science', if that's what you want. We won't hinder you. To put it in the kind of trivial language you will understand – and please do not take that the wrong way - I want you to *look after your heart*."

She stood up gracefully. And then somehow (I can only repeat what my father told me: the word is his) she 'disappeared'.

The diary suggests a degree of confusion as to whether he dreamt the whole encounter (you will recall he was sitting in his armchair throughout their interview). But he spoke to the housekeeper, who owned that she had admitted a young woman to his rooms, and - uttered with a kind of ecstatic fervour - 'Oh, but she was *beautiful!*'

The rest of the story is as you might expect. After several weeks of intense searching, my father managed to track Margaret Keys down. A small, blonde woman with large brown eyes and a Sussex country accent, who rather diffidently agreed to cooperate with him. He'd used the period of his search for her to hone his hypnotic skills.

In a trance, however, she remembered nothing at all, not even why she had ever gone to see Dr Collins (Collins himself had mentioned her surface amnesia; my father had expected it to cave in underneath). She had recently become engaged to a London man of her own age, an 'Edward Teller', whom she married three months later. I think this was an added disappointment to my father. I believe he harboured secret, highly irrational hopes of bringing Miss Keys and Mr Braithwaite together. If they were to fall in love and marry, you see, that might go some small way to making Geffers's disappearance meaningful: he had gone because they were meant to be together. As I say, utterly irrational, and I mention it only as an aside.

More astonishingly, Michael Braithwaite proved equally unproductive. Only a week or so had passed since the parting at Wadhurst railway station, yet he had no memory of anything connected to Simon Francis Geffers, even under the deepest hypnosis. He could not remember what had prompted him to go and see a psychoanalyst at all, although he did recall wandering about the countryside in company with my father. To what purpose, he had no idea. Understandably, he considered it disconcerting, although I think he was too polite to say so.

To move several years on in time, it is a matter of public record that, when war broke out in 1939, the National Service (Armed Forces) Act of 3rd September conscripted all men between the ages of eighteen and forty-one, with a preference for unmarried men. Michael Braithwaite was just within the limit, he was still a bachelor, and he eagerly volunteered. He was killed at Dunkirk a year later. Margaret Teller (née Keys) and her husband died in the Blitz shortly afterwards.

My father survived the war, of course. After he retired in '39, he lost a lot of weight, and, notwithstanding his active involvement in the Home Guard from 1940 onwards, he seemed to fade away for a while. But in 1942, when the tide began to turn in the Allies' favour, he rallied, realising, I think, that he still had important work to do, although now it would be charitable work, not scientific. After VE Day, he became an active member of the Jewish Committee for Relief Abroad and, of course, as you know, Save the Children.

Intellectually, he, Atkinson and Collins gradually migrated from Freudianism to what they jointly considered 'the more nuanced' approach of Carl Jung. No practical consequences followed from that (since all were retired), but the conversion of three such eminences did create a minor stir in academic circles, being considered a swipe at what one commentator called 'the Freudian cause'. In his biography of my father, Tom Ruttinger put their defection down to the general 'shake-up' occasioned by the war. Lots of people changed their views on all sorts of things at that time. Knowing what I know now, however, I am sure my father would have disagreed. Rather, it was that single encounter in his consulting room in 1935, which he persisted in seeing as a theophany.

I shall conclude on a purely personal note. Throughout the enterprise of collating my father's letters and recounting his experiences, I often found myself wondering about 'Simon Francis Geffers'. If we accept - as I know my father did (and as Atkinson and Collins apparently did in the end) - that such a person really did exist, then why was he 'chosen' (if that is remotely the right word)? What sort of a character did he possess? Was he unusually pious? Unusually gifted in other respects? Did he have merits no one of us could possibly, at the time, have discerned? Or did he just happen to be in the 'right' place at the 'right' time? Where is he now? More generally, how often does such a complete erasure of an entire human life on this planet actually happen? It all reminds me of that old philosophical puzzle: if the world and everything in it, including our ‘memories’, had only been created five minutes ago, how could we ever know?

Perhaps the Master Craftsman – or woman - is more intrusive than we can conceivably imagine.

Dr Jenkinson's Machine

I.

It was probably typical of Dr Elias Jenkinson that, when asked what had brought him to Wadhurst, he cited 'clues in William Blake', more particularly, in the long poem, *Visions of the Daughters of Albion*. In any case, his sudden appearance as a guest at The Queen's Head in the spring of 1889 created a quiet sensation in the village, and, almost simultaneously, in the surrounding area. He had already gained a reputation for 'new ideas' – actually, outspoken religious radicalism - in London, and his visit here felt like a compliment, especially since he had been obliged to pass through Tunbridge Wells on the way. (We only learned about the 'clues in William Blake' later.)

I was among the first to meet him. I was standing in the post office talking to old Jabez Smith when Mrs Benge entered in a rush. She'd been in the grocer's, apparently, and heard news of the arrival there. She did not know who 'Dr Jenkinson' was, so she had kept her counsel.

Our postmaster was also at a loss, but I had followed something of Jenkinson's career as reported in the newspapers. Unfortunately, I admitted it before considering the consequences. Of course, in reality, I knew hardly anything about him at all; relatively speaking, however, I was an international expert, and so I immediately became the focus of their excitement.

Both Mrs Benge and Mr Smith wanted to despatch me to The Queen's Head to 'welcome' him: that is, they wanted me to find out more about him, but also to gain the credit of being first to make his acquaintance, albeit at one remove. Then they began debating whether to give me 'some small token of salutation' to take, and if so, what sort. I am thirty-one, and a man of means, so I try to avoid being sent on errands. I was attempting to state all this as politely as I could (and getting nowhere), when in walked Dr Jenkinson himself.

Wadhurst is a parish of roughly three thousand people, but between the old tollgates at either end of the main road, only about five hundred, about a fifth of whom were born here. New faces inevitably stand out.

Yet Dr Jenkinson – we knew at once it was him – would probably have stood out anywhere. In his mid-fifties, well above six feet tall, dressed in an old-fashioned suit and a bowler hat, sporting a large black handlebar moustache, a well-trimmed beard, and with a reddish complexion and keen brown eyes, he held in his left hand what looked like an advertising bill. He entered just in time to hear Mrs Benge utter his name. By stopping mid-sentence and blushing, she managed to turn what might have looked like friendly curiosity into the serious likelihood of offence.

"I see my reputation has preceded me," Dr Jenkinson said, in an uncertain tone. He removed his bowler. "My name is Elias Jenkinson. At your service."

This should have been the cue for us to give our names, but we were all still abashed enough to be considering some sort of apology. Mrs Benge clasped her hands at waist-level. "We know who you are, sir," she said, "We were just saying that it's an honour to have such a good and famous person in the village. You might ask, 'How, pray, did you know who I was?' Well, I confess, *I* didn't – though I admit I should have done – but you see, William Jones here does. I heard about you in Corke's, the greengrocer's, only ten minutes ago. Just your name, sir, whispered in awestruck tones. *Dr Jenkinson's here,"* she whispered, as if he might not know what a whisper was otherwise. *"He's a good and famous person.* Everyone there buying apples and nuts, and *very* excited about your arrival. Anyway, William here was just telling us all about you. I honestly believe he's one of your biggest admirers in the entire world. He follows everything you do, William does. In the newspapers."

"William was just asking Mrs Benge and myself," old Jabez went on before I could get a word in, "whether we thought it would be acceptable for him to take a gift over to you, seeing as he's always wanted to meet you." He winked at me. "I said, yes, but don't you go making it too expensive. *You need to be saving your money, young fellow,* I went on. *You're getting married in a few weeks' time.* But he wouldn't have it. Oh, no. He insisted, he did. 'Money's of no importance in a matter like this,' he said, loudly, like he meant his words to be heard by the entire county. And Mrs Benge here, she was halfway through saying, 'I'm sure Dr Jenkinson's worth it', when in you walked, and she clammed up like a frog with a fly."

The possibility of me extricating myself from all this had long since disappeared. I was about to introduce myself properly, when the door opened again and Eustacia, my fiancée, walked in. Tall, slim, healthy-looking, and four years younger than me, she seemed to bring something of the simple sanity of youth. She bade Mrs Benge and Mr Smith good morning, then told me she had been looking for me. "I thought we had agreed to meet in Alma's," she said reproachfully. Her tone and bearing also suggested she was slightly wary of the stranger, and hoped either to be put on a better footing with him, or to leave in my company *post haste*; she did not particularly mind which.

"Eustacia Waller," I said, "this is Dr Elias Jenkinson..." And I went through each name in the shop in turn, twice, in the usual manner of introductions. I described myself as an architect, reluctantly confirmed Mrs Benge's assertion that I had followed Dr Jenkinson's career in the newspapers, and did my best to make it look as if I was fully familiar with the basis of his fame: lectures about how 'the mystical heart' of Christianity had been torn out by the Reformation, plus the occasional demonstration of 'real magic'.

While I was speaking, I was aware of a small crowd gathering outside. But it seemed to disperse of its own accord when Mr Smith glared at it.

"He's the good and famous Dr Jenkinson," Mrs Benge told Eustacia, when I had finished. And to crown her contribution of nothing whatsoever: "He's a celebrated lecturer on religion."

"Have you considered delivering a lecture here in the village, Dr Jenkinson?" Eustacia asked sweetly. "My father owns one of the largest houses in the whole road, and I feel sure I could persuade him to host you."

"That is too kind, madam," he said. He surprised her (and everyone, I think) by kissing her hand. "I have already reserved one of the show rooms at The Queen's Head, for a show which I hope you will attend?"

She turned hopefully to me. "William?"

"Certainly," I said. "Why not?"

"But I would be deeply honoured to give a talk at your home at any future time," he continued, addressing himself ardently to her. "God willing, we shall arrange a date and an hour." He turned to me, grabbed my hand and shook it a second time. "And thank you, Mr Jones, for your seal of approval. I foresee us becoming firm friends. If it's not too much of an inconvenience, I would be delighted if you could call on me at The Queen's Head."

"Er, well - "

"Tomorrow morning, ideally at around ten. But it can be any time at all - at your convenience! Not today, however. I need to settle in. A journeyman in a strange land needs a supporter, and you strike me as the ideal fellow. And of course, I can definitely find you useful work to do."

"Thank you," I said, trying to put as much gratitude into my tone as possible. Which was probably not very much at all.

"Now, Mr Smith," Jenkinson continued, "I wonder if you could tell me how much it would cost to post this advertisement where your customers can see it?"

"That would be free to you, sir," Jabez said. "And an absolute privilege."

II.

Eustacia and I had been engaged for six months now: long enough for me to distinguish when she was genuinely excited, from when she was just feigning excitement for politeness's sake. This was the former.

Ten minutes after emerging from the post office, as we looked through material for dresses at Alma Mott's, I learned there were two reasons. To begin with, she was enthusiastic on my account. She had completely swallowed Mr Smith and Mrs Benge's story about me being Dr Jenkinson's principal admirer. "Why didn't you tell me earlier, William?" she asked, in a hurt tone. "I don't like it when you keep things to yourself. If *you* are interested in him, then so am *I*." And so on, to which I protested hopelessly. The second reason was that she foresaw that her Tunbridge Wells friends, Catherine, Harriet and Jemima, would become envious. The fact that Dr Jenkinson had appeared in the newspapers, and was a minor *enfant terrible* (in *The Cornhill Magazine*'s words) gave him an aura of danger and therefore romance. "And he's here in Wadhurst," she said breathlessly. "*They'll* have to come to *me!* And they'll have to ask me about him, and I can become an expert on him, which they never can." She returned to her invitation for him to lecture at her house. "We could let him give *one* lecture in The Queen's Head, I suppose – especially now he's advertising it - but really, it seems just too awful for a man of his stature to be giving a talk in a draughty old *inn* with men drinking horrible *beer* all over the place! Our drawing room would be much more civilised and far more fitting."

It was therefore a huge disappointment when, four hours later, she broached the idea with her father over dinner, and he absolutely rejected it.

I should probably mention that, although I was staying in Wadhurst with a friend of my own age, Robert Farley (of whom more later), dinner at Eustacia's was a daily expectation. We always dressed for the occasion, and there were always six of us. Eustacia's father, Edward, was in his late fifties. He was straight-backed, bald and forthright in his views, having once held a governorship of some kind in India. Her mother, Edna, was ten years younger than him with soft features, a habitually morose disposition, and an aversion to novel ideas. Eustacia's sisters, Julia (sixteen) and Flora (seven), rarely spoke except when directly addressed, which meant they mainly recounted, on request, what they had done at school. The Wallers had two maidservants, one much younger than the other, and both were on duty every dinner time.

"The vicar is very keen that people should give Jenkinson the widest possible berth," Mr Waller said as he tackled his second lamb chop. "And it's not just us. The Baptists and the Methodists are entirely agreed. I'm not sure what the Roman Catholics think, but I'm open-minded about them: I like to think they're no less sane than us. I've a position to keep up in this village, and I'm certainly not about to jeopardise it for the sake of some second-rate conjuror with a trunkful of crackpot views."

Eustacia blushed and said nothing. However, anyone who knew anything about her could see she'd been quietly crushed.

A minute later, her father seemed to realise he'd misjudged the situation. He addressed her more gently, as if testing the waters anew. "So, what is your interest in this 'Dr Jenkinson', my dear? Where exactly did you hear about him?"

I'd passed the point of leaving her to his mercy. "We met him in the post office this morning," I said. "And I've followed his career in the newspapers for a while now. I must admit, I thought it would be entertaining to go and see him. He's a character, and definitely a conversation piece. He invited us personally to his lecture, and I accepted. I didn't know he had already aroused such strong opposition in the village."

Mr Waller believes that, since I was born and grew up in London, I must view all Wadhurstians (even perhaps Eustacia) as parochial bumpkins. He has never accused me of such a thing, and it is completely false, but I have noticed that he is often irrationally eager to prove himself The Perfect Cosmopolitan whenever we might be about to differ. The pair of us would go down well as a regular feature in *Punch* magazine.

"Yes, yes, I see what you mean," he told me. "Perhaps it *would* be rude to accept his invitation and then just not turn up." He turned to his eldest daughter. "That said, if you wish to accompany William, Eustacia, I've no real objection. I actually think it's *good* that you learn to think for yourself a bit. All I meant was that I draw the line at inviting him here. Especially to put on a talk. Look, the Reverend Codrington's a jolly good man, William, and I don't want him to think I've taken against him. He may not have been here long, but as far as I'm concerned, his word is law."

"I entirely understand," I said.

"And consider your own interests," he went on. "Given that we've arranged for you to get married in his lovely church, it's unwise to go upsetting him."

Eustacia and I exchanged looks. We hadn't thought of that.

Mr Waller sighed. "Of course, I'm sure I can mollify him in terms of your going to Jenkinson's 'lecture'. From the vicar's point of view, it's probably better that Jenkinson's 'lectures' – pretentious word for them, from what I've heard – fill up with intelligent sceptics like yourselves, rather than credulous nincompoops like the Battersbys or the Crones."

"Thank you, Father," Eustacia said. "I thought I might buy some tickets for Catherine, Harriet and Jemima too. I'm sure they would love to come."

"As a matter of fact, that's a very good idea," Mr Waller said. "Those three would actually lend an air of respectability to the whole thing. And of course, they're as sceptical as I don't know what. Cynical, some might say." He chuckled. "There, there, dear, only a joke. They could spend the day here, and even stay overnight. Where's it taking place, this 'lecture'?"

"The Queen's Head," she replied.

Mrs Waller emitted a not-quite-silent groan of disapproval, and sawed one of her roast potatoes in half.

"There's nothing wrong with The Queen's Head," her husband said. "I happen to be very fond of Robert Williams. If anyone can keep Jenkinson in order, it's him."

"Can I go with Eustacia?" Julia asked plaintively.

"Absolutely not," he replied. "You're far too young. I can get it past the vicar on the grounds that Eustacia's a grown woman with her own mind. But I'm still responsible for you and Flora. Besides, your sister will tell you all about it when she gets in. I'm willing to wager she'll have been bored witless, and she'll bore you in turn, then you'll realise you had a lucky escape. You'll thank me."

III.

Eustacia and I usually went for a short, leisurely walk just before eight o'clock, after which I would make my way back to Robert Farley's house in Buss's Green. We were normally chaperoned, at a distance of about twenty paces, by Mrs Waller and either Julia or Flora, who tended to bring a trug and pick flowers.

This evening, I could tell Eustacia was unusually anxious to speak to me alone. We set off along the main road at a quarter to the hour, intending to take our usual route around four fields and back via the long path bordering the labourers' allotments. We turned left at the Baptist chapel, then walked along the edge of a cornfield dotted at irregular intervals with mature oaks. Spring had almost completely given way to summer, the sky was darkening, but the day was still warm. Birds sang happily, and the air was full of the scent of flowers. As usual, we began by linking arms and telling one another how much in love we were. Then we revisited the minutiae of the day. Finally, I learned what was uppermost in her mind.

"Tomorrow, I want you to go and see Dr Jenkinson," she said. "Let him know my father's house is impossible. You can apologise to him for me. Tell him the truth. Just say the vicar disapproves."

"I don't suppose he'll be terribly pleased, but I'd imagine he's used to it."

"After I become Mrs Jones, it may be different. Until then, you can become his confidant, and then when Harriet, Jemima and Catherine come, I can speak about him with some authority. I can see what's going to happen, though. One of them will speak to *her* father, and he'll be all in favour of having Dr Jenkinson over to speak at his house. They might *all* speak to their fathers, and they might *all* want him. And then, he'll slip through my fingers, and it'll be entirely because I live in a tiny village, and I'm surrounded by people with cramped little minds. And obviously, they'll all laugh pityingly at me."

"I don't know why you're so worried about them," I said. "We're going to be married in just over a fortnight, then we'll move to Hampstead. You'll no longer be their 'little village girl'."

"I'll always be just that. Unless I start re-making myself. And this is the best time and place to do it: while they still think they've got the measure of me. Later on, when I've become a renowned society hostess, they'll look back and think, 'Actually, she began to change even before she'd left us.'"

"Why will it matter what they think? We may never see them again."

She laughed. "Of course we will! They're my friends!"

"But I'm still uncertain why their opinions count so much."

"Because I don't want them to imagine that all of the changes I'm about to make to myself – widening my horizons and so on - come from you, and from London! I want them to think I was someone capable of changing on my own!"

I told her she was already perfect, but it disturbed me when she spoke like this. Catherine, Harriet and Jemima were six years younger than her, and she'd met them – as I think she met nearly everyone until I came along – through her father, as fellow daughters of Freemasons. They'd been her only friends for the last three years, but of course they had much more in common with each other than they had with her. To make matters worse, I firmly believe they were disappointed when she met me. I think they hoped she would become a confirmed spinster. More than that: at twenty-seven with no potential suitors in sight, and a couple of indifferent parents looking after her interests, they thought they had her in the bag. I disliked them, and I disapproved of their influence on her.

She asked me to tell her more about Dr Jenkinson. I wasn't sure whether I would be able to oblige, but once I got talking, I found I knew far more than I realised. She listened intently as if it interested her: the triumphant lion, *prisca theologia,* Cornelius Agrippa, The Logos, theosophy, Egyptianism. My memory must have been far more retentive than I had ever given myself credit for: I couldn't remember ever having heard of half the things I was articulating. Even stranger, I suddenly realised Eustacia wasn't pretending. She was listening as if her life depended on it. Then, all at once, I had the disturbing feeling that *it was not me who was talking.*

In the meantime, thick dark clouds had blown in, apparently from nowhere, bringing nightfall with them. Rain looked inevitable. We quickened our pace, Eustacia held her bonnet with one hand and picked up her skirt at the front slightly with the other, I kept talking. In no time at all, we were hurrying along the narrow path behind the allotments. There wasn't space to walk side by side, and I always let Eustacia walk in front, because she preferred it.

She suddenly stopped and swivelled round, I assumed to tell me to be quiet (which I did), but instead she looked over my shoulder.

"Mother, *hurry!*" she called. "Keep talking, William."

She turned back round, then suddenly froze and let out a loud shriek.

I swiftly sidestepped her, putting myself in front to protect her from whatever it was – I guessed a cornered fox or a badger – and she swooned behind me so I had to twist round to catch her. My heart thumped. I sensed the same danger she had. I laid her hurriedly on the grass and turned back to face it.

Nothing. The path was clear. I could hear Mrs Waller and Flora running up from behind.

At that point, I heard something in the adjacent allotment. I turned to locate the source, and it took me a second to realise what I was seeing. Whatever it actually was, it left at speed, but since I am obliged to report the evidence of my eyes: it appeared brown, glutinous and leathery, and at least three feet long.

Something in it seemed to realise it had been spotted – even at this distance, I got a sense of cold intelligence – and it took flight. I do not know how, or even in what direction. It bolted as swiftly as if it had been a cat or a dog.

I think, if it had all ended there, I might even have persuaded myself it really was something along those lines. But then, the back door of one of the houses opened; presumably someone inside had heard Eustacia scream. An old man ran over. Mrs Waller and Flora were reviving her now.

"What the devil happened here?" he exclaimed.

It dawned on me that he was not talking about Eustacia, but about his allotment. It was half-decimated and covered in a thick film of translucent slime.

"I – I don't know," I said.

IV.

The thing I'd seen, whatever it may have been, was obviously cause for general alarm, and reporting its sighting should have far outweighed any supposedly mitigating personal loyalties. But I simply did not see it that way at the time. My concern was solely for Eustacia. My 'official' story was, and remained, that the thing in the allotment had been no more than a large cat.

In any case, I believe the thing itself was found, two days later, dead and shrivelled, about a mile away in Pell Green. It definitely caused a stir, but luckily, the agricultural community and the scientific one have never been particularly close: by the time the latter heard about it, the corpse was decomposed, and the alleged prior reality was dismissible as rural hyperbole. Received wisdom always swings closer to the urban rationalists than the country empiricists, and taking advantage of the general supercilious incredulity, I managed to keep Eustacia from learning anything more about it.

The result was that she rallied significantly at the outset, then quickly recovered. I stayed with her until half an hour after I would normally have left the Wallers' house, but at that point I think she was almost back to normal. She had been 'silly', it had been 'a morbid effect of the twilight' (both ideas which I think I put into her head), and no one need worry about her any more. Before we parted, however, she made a point of insisting I keep my appointment with Dr Jenkinson at ten the following morning. She would be waiting for me to tell her all about it. Presumably, I would be back to have dinner with the family as usual?

Mr Waller pressed me to stay the night, but I told him Robert Farley expected me, and was the kind of man to worry if I did not turn up. He lent me his horse and a rain cape.

Thirty minutes later, as I rode through the almost total blackness, I remembered how intently Eustacia had listened to me as I'd described the beliefs and opinions of Dr Jenkinson. Then I worried that she was becoming fixated on him.

But I worried about her a lot now. How to preserve her perfection, perhaps, against everything that seemed to threaten it: her friends' empty-headed crassness, the dubious charms of Elias Jenkinson, the lingering memory of the thing she'd seen in the allotment. She was so fragile, and I was so weak and inept.

The strange thing was, I couldn't remember a fifth of what I'd been telling her before we'd both spotted that … monster. It had all seemed perfectly coherent and highly cerebral at the time, but maybe I'd been spouting nonsense.

Perhaps I was the one I should be worrying about.

V.

Robert Farley was a thirty-five-year-old farmer with thick curly hair, a bushy beard and a genial personality. When he'd first arrived here ten years ago, he'd bought a rundown farmhouse with an under-cultivated patch of land on the north eastern parish boundary. Good luck and hard work had combined to make him moderately wealthy. I initially met him in my professional capacity in 1888, when I'd been in Wadhurst examining the church spire on behalf of Winston & Peckriss. He'd been sexton there for a year or two – I don't know how he got the post, because he wasn't at all pious - and had his own opinions on the matter. We quickly became friends, and when he discovered my interest in Eustacia Waller – I was introduced to her by the then vicar, John Foley, after the Sunday morning communion service - he was keen to bring us together. Our cause was helped by the fact that he and Mr Waller were longstanding friends.

After welcoming me back to his cottage that night, he gave me a glass of brandy and we sat in front of the fire in his parlour and talked. I did not tell him about the hideous creature in the allotment, but I told him all about Dr Jenkinson, and how I was supposed to meet him at ten in the morning. "I think he's likely to recognise me for a fraud," I concluded. "I really don't know very much about him at all."

"And yet you told Eustacia all about him."

I chuckled. "I honestly don't know how I did that. I must have imbibed a lot of information unconsciously."

"I'd be very careful of Dr Jenkinson if I were you. And I'm not speaking as the vicar's representative. I've followed him much more closely than you have, and I really believe he's insane. At the very least, I'm sure he's not spiritually wholesome."

"What do you mean by that?"

"He's one of those demented dolts who believes he can manipulate the natural world by means of charms and spells. Of course, obviously that's not possible, and anyone who believes it for long enough becomes incredibly frustrated or deranged. Usually both: the derangement helps ease the frustration."

I laughed. "Well, maybe I should talk to him about *that*. I wasn't looking forward to our meeting before. Thank you for reassuring me."

"I'd imagine he's pathologically vain. Those sorts of people always are. He'll talk about himself throughout, and all you'll have to do is listen. After thirty minutes, you'll fulfil Mrs Benge's unwitting prophecy: you'll become a world expert on him."

"And I'm sure that will do me a lot of good."

"Here's another prophecy. He and your future father-in-law are destined to become friends, or at least not-enemies, regardless of what the vicar thinks."

"Some chance! What makes you say that?"

"Freemasonry. It makes every crooked road straight, and all the rough ways smooth. Although I doubt if Edward Waller has the faintest idea what it really is. Like most members of his class, he probably considers it no more than a social advancement club."

"You believe Jenkinson's a Freemason?"

"I'd stake my life on it. And of course, Eustacia has obviously taken to him. In my experience, Edward Waller always falls in eventually with his wife and daughters. Anyway, speaking of Eustacia, I'd like to come with the two of you to this lecture of his. Especially now I know Catherine Henshaw is coming."

"I can easily get you a ticket. I didn't know Miss Henshaw had caught your eye."

He laughed. "I know you're not very keen on her. You think she's bad for your fiancée. But you're wrong. She's sophisticated and open minded. As are her two friends."

"I'm not sure she'd make a good farmer's wife."

"You might be surprised. Besides, you don't want to be alone with four women. And don't imagine Eustacia will take much notice of you. She'll be too busy trying to impress the Holy Trinity. And since they'll all be flirting with you – just to annoy her - it'll probably turn into a miserable evening for you both. This way, they can all flirt with me, and vice-versa, and everyone will go home happy."

I nodded. "Yes, I can see that's an excellent plan."

We spoke a little more of matters of interest to both of us, and ten minutes later, bade each other good night and went to bed.

It took me no time at all to get to sleep, but I had the strangest dream. Eustacia and Elias Jenkinson were walking hand in hand through a green meadow on a bright summer's day. The sun shone an unnatural shade of yellow, and there were angels somewhere in the background. I had no idea where I was; I figured in the dream solely as invisible eyes. Oddly, it did not seem to me that I was witnessing anything particularly outrageous, although the longer I watched, the more it became obvious the central couple were in love, had always been, and had no thought for me at all.

When I awoke, I couldn't make the slightest sense out of it. After a few moments I became stupidly indignant, then morbidly unhappy. My mind went back to the post office. I got the horrible impression Jenkinson's kiss had lingered on

Eustacia's hand a half-second too long, although I'd noticed nothing at the time.

It was still dark outside. It took me a long time to get to back to sleep. Outside my window, a storm raged.

VI.

When I awoke again, at eight o'clock, the sun shone as if it had never been away. I dressed, ate breakfast with Robert – I told him about my dream, but he seemed unusually withdrawn, muttering something about having had nightmares himself - and set off for 'town' (as the village centre was called round here) and my appointment with Dr Jenkinson.

Before entering the inn, I stopped at the Post Office to have a look at the advertising bill he'd given old Jabez. It featured a large ink-sketch of him, probably twenty years out of date, in between the following text.

The Show Room of
THE QUEEN'S HEAD WADHURST
Saturday 4 May 1889
To commence at NINE O'CLOCK
The Nationally Renowned Lecturer and Practitioner of Real Magic
DOCTOR ELIAS JENKINSON
Will talk for one hour and perform amazing magical feats!
Admission – Reserved seats 2s. All others, payment at the door 1s 6d.
Doors open at 8.30

I was bemused: Saturday was today. By tonight, he'd have been in the village a little over twenty-four hours. Far too little time to drum up a sizeable audience. And while I might be able to afford four shillings for Eustacia and I, a shilling and sixpence was far too much for most people in Wadhurst. It was almost exorbitant. Which meant he must be expecting people from farther afield. But how? At the very least they would need time to hear about it.

On the other hand, the show room at The Queen's Head was far from huge: perhaps this was merely the *hors d'oeuvres*; maybe he had something much more ambitious planned for next week. In that case, he'd need a marquee, but there would be no shortage of farmers willing to loan him a nearby field in return for a cut of the profits.

In any eventuality, it made me feel better that Robert Farley would be there. I could introduce him to Jenkinson - although Eustacia wouldn't be happy: Jenkinson was supposed to be exclusively mine and hers – in order to remove a little of the spotlight from myself.

I transferred Mr Waller's horse to Tim at the saddler's with instructions to return it to its owner. I walked across the road and entered The Queen's Head. The landlord gave no indication that I was expected, but neither did he look at me askance. Perhaps I was not Jenkinson's only visitor. Both in the saddler's and here, I sensed a general atmosphere of agitation.

A few seconds later, I knocked on the door. I heard a key turn within, then Jenkinson opened it aggressively and looked at me with a choleric expression. He wore a suit jacket, long johns and socks with holes. Then he seemed to recollect who I was and smiled. "William Jones! Come in, my good fellow, please! Ignore the disarray."

The room was small but homely, with faded yellow curtains and a pair of framed prints on the wall. The single bed against the far side looked too small for a man of Jenkinson's size, and its twisted bedsheets suggested he'd spent a restless night. An open trunk beside a ladderback chair had been partially unpacked, but most of its contents lay strewn across the floor: shirts, socks, a pair of boots, two bow-ties and a crumpled pair of trousers. In the middle of the room stood a large table topped with a bottle of *Bell's* whisky, what looked like a half-crumpled letter, a large crystal ball and a spread of Tarot cards. A single window at the rear looked out onto the woods and fields, and admitted a hard shaft of sunlight.

Jenkinson re-locked the door as soon as I was inside. He put the key in his jacket pocket. His genial demeanour faded. He unscrewed the whisky bottle, took a long draught, then sat on the bed with it. He looked morosely at his toes. "So, what do you know about me?" he asked.

"Very little," I said. "Only what I've read in the newspapers."

"In which case, you know nothing. Sit down. Sit on that chair."

My eye had been increasingly caught by the letter, where I thought I recognised Eustacia's handwriting. Obviously, that wasn't possible.

I broke the spell by reluctantly sitting down. To tell the truth, I was torn between that and leaving: after his initial mild enthusiasm, Jenkinson had made no attempt at hospitality, and seemed to regard my presence as an intrusion. Above all that, I got the uncanny impression that he had seen me gazing at the letter, and was as alarmed as I was.

I forced myself to recover. I had been charged with making a friend of him. Though his welcome left much to be desired, so far, he had done nothing seriously offensive.

"What made you come to Wadhurst?" I asked, by way of refreshing things.

"Clues in William Blake," he said gruffly. "Particularly, *Visions of the Daughters of Albion.* I am here for reasons you definitely won't approve of."

"Why do you say that?" Presumably, he thought I was allied with the vicar.

"I'll try to answer your question presently," he said. "I assume you want tickets to tonight's show. You can take that as a given. Your presence there is absolutely necessary. In fact, it's the reason I'm in the village at all."

"I thought you said it was clues in a poem."

"I have a single goal in life, Mr Jones. For over three decades now, I have striven to achieve it. William Blake told me where to go in order to finally be successful. And that is why I am here."

I was becoming irritated now. "And so, what part do the crystal ball and the Tarot cards play?"

He startled me by rushing to the centre of the room and sweeping everything off the table. I got involuntarily to my feet. He was drunk. Since he'd locked me in here, if he wanted to fight, a fight was probably inevitable. Comparing his size and energy against my sobriety, relative youth and the fact that I'd boxed a little at school, I considered the odds in my favour. But only marginally.

Yet he didn't attack me. He leaned on the table and wheezed. Then he stooped to pick up the letter and thrust it into his jacket pocket. "All rubbish," he said. "Forgive me. I had a disastrous night. I – I'm sorry. I'm here to take your Eustacia."

"What?"

"I'm not sure you've yet seen my machine." He gestured to a large metal contraption which, because it was in the corner nearest the door, and my attention had been elsewhere, I had not so far noticed. Scores of interlocking steel circles surmounting a baroque-looking brass stand, all decorated with what looked like hand-painted figures from the zodiac. He walked to it and beckoned me over. "Come and look."

I ignored him. "What do you mean, 'take your Eustacia'?"

"I meant that I am hopelessly drunk and I hope you both enjoy tonight's show," he said cantankerously. "Don't speak, just listen to me. Because I perceive you are becoming angry, my man, and we cannot have that, can we? Oh, I admit that, since you entered this room, my behaviour has been appalling by any conventional yardstick, but if you had suffered what I did last night, you would probably understand. But I am not ill. On the contrary, I have never felt in better health. No, no, no, I am talking about this machine. Have you ever heard of the Renaissance thinker, Giordano Bruno, Mr Jones? He postulated infinite worlds. Of course, most people think he meant outer space - whatever that meant in those days. However, I realised about twenty years ago that his true meaning was that there are innumerable worlds *actually alongside ours, right now*; worlds you could reach out and touch were it not for the fact that they are composed of a completely different type of 'stuff' to ours, utterly inaccessible to our five senses. Thankfully, they are as invisible to us as we are to them. Everything within each world is roughly related to everything in the others in the manner of *counterparts*. The inhabitants are in worlds which they must navigate just as we do ours: between apparently solid objects, that is, in some sort of temporal succession – which may not be at all the same as ours. In other words, there is an infinite number of different *types* of matter, but each world contains only mutually interactable parts, and nothing else. And no part of our world can interact with any part of the others. Do you follow?"

I didn't, but I nodded. In my defence, I was still thinking about that 'take your Eustacia', and my mind had gone back to Farley's claim that Jenkinson was insane. Insanity would definitely give him additional strength. I needed to be accommodating.

"Now, obviously, there must be some way of moving between these worlds," he went on. "They must all be visible, and accessible, to The Creator. And *quod est superius est sicut quod inferius, et quod inferius est sicut quod est superius*: as above, so below; in other words, what they are to the Creator, they ought, in principle, to be to us. Of course, the whole history of science is the bringing to visibility of things which would otherwise, 'naturally', be invisible."

"So that's what your machine does," I said, doing my best to keep up and play along. "It makes entities in these other worlds apparent to people in this one."

"Ah, but we could only see such entities as exist in *other* worlds by bringing them into *this* world. And that, in a nutshell, is what my machine does."

"How does it work?"

He hooted. "Only *I* know that! The machine is useless without me to operate it. Come, come over here. Have a closer look."

Getting physically closer to the thing brought no clarification, but I had not expected it would. It looked vaguely like an astrolabe. At the top, there was a small figure of a man looking down into a room with solid corners, but no walls or ceiling. Inside the room was a smaller man looking down into a smaller room. The whole thing was obviously meant to represent infinity, and for all I knew, may even have instantiated it.

"And you use this in your shows, I suppose?" I said.

"I don't give 'shows', Mr Jones. I give lectures, then I perform some real magic. Sometimes. If the audience is worthy. Otherwise, I palm them off with prestidigitation. In which case, I am not cheating them. Their minds are closed, and so they leave feeling entirely satisfied. To answer your question, no, I don't use it in my lectures, or afterwards."

"So, what are you saying? You use it in your own free time to travel between different worlds?"

He smiled sourly. "We are getting nowhere at all. Sit down again, Mr Jones. I will remove myself to the bed, for your imagined safety. I will also unlock the door, because you will almost certainly want to leave once I have told you everything. Consider this, though. When I divulge what I am about to, I am acting solely from compassion."

I sat down again. He unlocked the door as promised, then lay on the bed and took another long draught of whisky. "Last night, I managed to activate my machine, but I miscalculated the settings. One of the worlds 'next door' to ours, if you like, is a good world; but on the other side, there's the opposite. In a word, I unbolted the wrong door. Horrible things emerged – quite ghastly things! I console myself that they cannot survive here for long. How they can persist at all is a bit of a mystery, but, well, I don't claim to know everything. Tonight, I will open the door to the good world. Hopefully, good things will come through, and they will maybe transform this one - yours. But I won't be here to see it, nor will Eustacia."

"You keep mentioning my fiancée," I said testily. "You met her yesterday for the space of one minute. As far as I am concerned, therefore, you have no right whatsoever to speak her name. And if you are implying – as I think you must be – that you intend to kidnap her, then I think you had better pack that trunk of yours and leave, before you come to harm."

"I don't belong in this world," he continued, as if I had not spoken. "Nor does she. We both belong in that other world. Don't ask me how we got here. The laws of nature in the world we both come from are completely different to yours. We both know she was born and grew up in this world, but yes, she comes from elsewhere. A trillion, trillion miles away. Farther than you can possibly imagine, and yet – close enough to reach out and touch! Right here, now! No, when I take her back to where she belongs, she will have no memory of you, nor her father, nor anything pertaining to her life here. And nor will I."

I stood up. Things had reached such a pitch that I actually felt sorry for him. "I very much doubt we'll be coming to your 'lecture' now," I said. I picked up my hat, walked over and opened the door. "Thank you for the warning."

"Oh, you will come," he said. He got leisurely up and walked over. He took the crumpled letter from his pocket and handed it to me. "From your 'fiancée'."

I was on the landing now. He slammed the door on me, and I heard the key turn in the lock. I uncrumpled the letter, and my vision went momentarily black at the edges. It confirmed my wildest forebodings.

My Dearest, Dearest Elias! I am coming! Your Eustacia.

My God.

And if it wasn't her handwriting, it was an expert imitation.

VII.

There was nowhere to go now except the Wallers' house. I needed some sort of explanation, although as I walked up the drive, I thought I had one. Jenkinson was a conjuror: *of course* he could pull off a simple trick like imitating Eustacia's handwriting! And since he was quite clearly insane, he wouldn't even need a motive. He'd probably found a sample in one of the shops, possibly even in the Post Office. Which meant that he was a confidence trickster, and conceivably a thief into the bargain.

At the forecourt before the house, I was surprised to see what looked like Robert Farley's cart with a load of marl. I looked up at the house for signs that my coming had been noticed: often Julia or Flora saw me and notified the entire house, as if it was an event.

Mr Waller stood in the upstairs bedroom on the far left. He disappeared when our eyes met. I guessed, correctly, that he was on his way to see me.

He met me on the doorstep, and hauled me inside and into the study, closing the door furtively behind us. I sat on the armchair half-facing an empty grate, with him opposite. He looked drawn and angry.

"We've got Eustacia's three friends and their *entourage* here," he said. "They just turned up out of the blue! I know Eustacia said she was asking them, but they didn't wait for that. They heard Jenkinson was in town and they just invited themselves. They're staying the night, of course, but once again, that's on their own say-so. That blasted railway station has an awful lot to answer for, if you ask me. And they're as high as kites! I haven't seen them this excited since the Golden Jubilee! I don't know what on earth's got into them!"

"And Robert's here too, I see."

"Ah, yes, I was coming to that. I sent to his house for you, but I didn't need to. He was in town with his horse and cart. He could see he was needed, so he abandoned his plans for today – spreading marl on his land, apparently - and came here. You'd gone to see Jenkinson, I understand."

"We had a very confrontational conversation. Eustacia and I won't be going to see him tonight. He gave me this." I handed him the letter from my inside pocket.

He looked to be on the verge of saying something, but his eyes opened wide with astonishment. "Where did you – *Jenkinson* gave you this?"

"Why did you say Robert was 'needed'? And why did you try to send for me?"

He ignored me. "What did you see in the allotment yesterday? What caused her to faint?"

"I've told you, it was a cat."

He sighed. "And I believe you. Sorry, William, my nerves are completely shattered this morning, and so will yours be when you hear what I have to tell you. Firstly, there may be some sort of predator loose in the village. Fred Sykes lost nine sheep last night, and Ambrose Patterson three, and the signs are, they all died of *fright*. How big was this 'cat' of yours?"

"I – I couldn't see. It was nearly dark."

"Anyway, that's what the police are looking for: a big cat. And it's on your account. Better that than what Patterson claims he saw: a forty-foot-wide brown ghost with teeth." He laughed, despite himself. "My God, what's the world coming to? That's partly what I wanted to speak to you about – and why I sent out to Farley - but that's not the worst of it. Not by any means."

"Oh?"

"This letter: you say Jenkinson gave you it? Where did *he* get it?"

"I didn't get chance to ask. He handed it to me as a parting shot, then slammed the door on me."

He put the letter on the coffee table, and ran both hands across his head, as if unsure how to proceed. He went to the window, and stood with his back to me.

"We had quite a time with Eustacia last night," he said, "after you'd gone. I really wish you'd stayed, but I don't blame you. You couldn't have foreseen how things would turn out, and I don't suppose it would have made any difference."

"Is she – she *is* all right, isn't she?"

"She's still in one piece and singing songs, if that's what you mean. Smiling a bit too broadly for my liking. A bit of background might help you make sense of what I'm about to say. Eustacia and Julia used to both share a bedroom until Flora came along, but Eustacia's too old to be sharing now, and Flora needs watching; so, Julia does for Flora what Eustacia used to do for her. Last night, because Eustacia had such a scare, Julia moved back in with her, just for one night. At about one o'clock, she saw Eustacia get up. The way she moved, and the fact that she didn't answer Julia's queries, made it obvious she was sleepwalking. Julia came to rouse Edna and I. By this time, Eustacia had gone downstairs into the study. She sat at my desk, took a wad of letter paper from the drawer, and wrote. She wrote page after page, and discarded each one in turn. Of course, we couldn't disturb her. Wake up a sleepwalker, you're likely to cause them serious harm, possibly even a heart attack. We merely had to watch from a safe distance. And we couldn't remotely see what she was writing: we were too far away and it was too dark. Finally, she seemed to pen something she was satisfied with. She picked it up and strode purposefully out into the garden. Well, you may or may not have been asleep at one o'clock last night, but I can tell you, there was an almighty storm. She marched into the middle of the lawn, held this letter up above her head and released it. And then she woke up. Julia and Edna ran to her, of course, and brought her inside. In the meantime, I'd been examining what she'd been writing in the study." He handed me a wad of papers. "These."

I thumbed through them in horrified astonishment. Sixteen messages, all identical to the one I'd just handed Mr Waller.

"We got her back into bed," he continued. "She didn't know where she'd been or what she'd done, and with all the rain and cold, we were afraid she might come down with something. But no, she slept like a log after that, and this morning, she's as fit as a fiddle. We haven't told her anything about the letters, obviously. She doesn't know she wrote them, poor thing, and obviously I'm relying on you to keep it quiet too."

I returned the wad to him. He tore it into shreds and slotted the pieces into the tall coal hod for later burning.

"Have you told Robert any of this?" I asked.

"I had to. I couldn't very well bring him here and not take him into my confidence. And I know he's a good man: it'll stay between us."

"Did he venture an opinion?"

"He accepted mine."

I nodded. "I'd very much like to hear it, then I think we should ask him to come in. I need to tell you both about my interview with Dr Jenkinson."

"Of course, yes. Well, this is my theory, and I think you'll find it plausible. You know how Eustacia is. I love her dearly, but she's easily overawed: in her eyes, Tunbridge Wells is like Paris or St Petersburg; London's like Heaven: you only go there when you die shriven; and marriage is the very empyrean. Needless to say, last year, when *you* started showing an interest in her, she nearly died with excitement. And now we've got your wedding coming up, which would be rapture enough, but to cap it all, 'the world-famous Dr Jenkinson' arrives in town, kisses her hand, and apparently intimates that he'll favour her, above all others, with a visit to *my* house. Now, here's the crux: there's Jenkinson on the one hand, and there's the vicar and Eustacia's wedding on the other, and they don't quite harmonise. Inwardly, I think it's tearing her apart a little. She's at her wits' end, poor thing."

"It's a good theory," I said, "but it doesn't explain how Jenkinson ended up with one of those letters."

"Chance, obviously. It blew away, he picked it up much later, he saw it bore his name, he kept it, and now he's probably having all sorts of lurid fantasies about her." His expression darkened. "Fancy him using it as a weapon against you! My God, who does he think he *is?* I've a good idea to go down there - "

There was a loud knock. Then giggling. Mr Waller blinked slowly then got up with a bitter sigh. He threw the door open as roughly as Jenkinson had on me just over an hour ago.

Mrs Waller and Eustacia stood trembling with excitement. I could not tell from here whether it was the good or the bad variety. Eustacia had her hands clasped in supplication; her mother was in tears. They seemed equally speechless.

Eustacia was the first to break the spell. "William, Father, come quickly!"

Mrs Waller bobbed slightly. "Mr Farley - Mr Farley has just asked Catherine Henshaw to *marry* him! And she's just said *yes!*"

VIII.

We all had a break from thinking about Dr Jenkinson. The respite lasted about an hour, which I recall involved lots of excited young women running up and down stairs, men and boys trying to look solemn, Flora and her little friend, Thomas, in the garden sword-fighting with bamboo canes. The cook went to work making snacks and Mr Waller sent out to Newington's for fresh ingredients, and to Rowland Smith, the butcher, for four joints of meat. The happy couple stood together in the parlour looking slightly dazed, yet happier than I had ever seen either of them. Eustacia attached herself to my arm. She seemed equally delighted. I shook hands with Robert, told him good-humouredly I now understood why he'd seemed so preoccupied over breakfast, kissed Catherine, and said congratulations twice. The noise of conversation made hearing difficult, but no one seemed to mind if you shouted. Eventually, nearly everyone was shouting, and that brought more high-spirited laughter.

Mr Waller had earlier spoken of an 'entourage'. At the time I had not fully grasped his meaning. Eustacia's three friends had brought along their parents, their younger siblings, two governesses, and a grandmother in a black bonnet. All told – and not including myself and the Wallers - there were over twenty people in the house, most of whom had been improbably invited to stay the night. The others had put up in the village hotels. I later learned that The Greyhound, The White Hart, The Tunnell and The Hare and Hounds were all fully booked.

From the many conversations I had as Eustacia and I circumambulated the room, I learned that nearly everyone – children and governesses excluded - intended to go and see Dr Jenkinson that night. Such was the ostensible reason for their swoop on the Wallers, although I think at least some of them must have intuited a proposal was on the cards. Anyway, it cheered me. Mr Waller's words in the study increasingly struck me as correct: Eustacia was over-excited; Jenkinson had picked up her 'letter' by chance, and, upon it, had constructed a gargantuan edifice of fantastical nonsense. And it was this gibberish - nothing more - which he had expounded to me so passionately in The Queen's Head.

He was patently insane. But kept at a safe enough distance, he was probably harmless. In short, I could no longer see any reason to stop Eustacia attending his 'lecture' tonight. She would be with me, and both of us would be surrounded by a wall of protective friends. Thus safeguarded, the experience would probably serve to purge the entire poisonous thing from her constitution.

At one o'clock, Netty, the older of the two maidservants, announced lunch. An extra table had been brought into the dining room from I don't know where, and we ate cold ham, cheese, buttered bread, sliced onions and pickles. I think Mr Waller had forgotten about Jenkinson now: he was much more concerned with the day's expense, and probably indignant about being put upon. I saw him after lunch, in conference with two of the parents and Robert, and he looked happier. I believe they'd reached an arrangement to share the costs.

Everyone suddenly seemed to deflate. Excitement had fatigued them and the meal had made them drowsy. There weren't enough seats in the drawing room and the parlour, so they spread out around the house. The children became irritable. Catherine sat with Harriet and Jemima on a *chaise longue* and alternately laughed and cried while they stroked her back and rubbed her shoulders. They threw sidelong, suspicious glances at Eustacia, as if to warn her off sharing what little now remained of their longstanding intimacy, and I suddenly remembered why I disliked them. Robert sat alone in an armchair with his legs crossed and read Ovid's *Metamorphoses*.

There were still five hours until dinner. After a longish period of lethargy, everyone seemed simultaneously to decide on an outing, although the sky had clouded over. The Henshaws sent out for a carriage, and the whole family left with Robert for his farm. The governesses took the children, in a group, to a nearby field to play ball games. Everyone else went out 'exploring'. The result was that by three o'clock, the house was temporarily back to normal.

Eustacia and I waved goodbye to Robert and Catherine – she had loyally decided to accompany him on his cart, rather than go with her parents and brother in the carriage – then she led me into the study, closed the door and kissed me.

"What an exciting day!" she said.

I took her over to the chair I'd sat on earlier, made her sit down, knelt before her and took her hands. "I can't bear the way those three women treat you," I said passionately. "You're easily worth a million of each of them."

She laughed. "So, three million in all!"

"More than that. I really, really don't think we should see them any more after we're married. They're obviously under the impression that they're better than you. And they're radically mistaken. We'll forge our own life, and you can make new friends, people who will see you for who you really are.

You're The Ugly Duckling here. In a few weeks' time, in London, you'll be a swan!"

She smiled indulgently. "I only want to be a swan in your eyes, William. Besides, we'll find it difficult to cut ties with Catherine, now she's going to become Mrs Farley. Consider for a moment. We'll have to keep coming back to Wadhurst to see Mother and Father and Julia and Flora. We can't do that without visiting Robert and Catherine. It wouldn't be good of us, or polite."

I sighed. "No, I suppose not. Well, maybe not Catherine, then. But the other two: we don't have to see them."

She bit her lip and frowned. "You don't understand at all," she said. "They don't dislike me. On the contrary, they love me. They'd literally do anything for me! Oh, how can I explain it to you? I'm six years older than them. Think of Flora. When her friends come here, they occasionally huddle in a group when Julia walks by, and, to the unaccustomed eye, they might seem to be excluding her. But I know for a *fact* that not *one* of Flora's little companions doesn't worship the ground Julia walks on. I *know* it, do you hear? And it's the same with Catherine, Harriet, Jemima and me. I don't *expect* to be included in all their little conferences, and I know they'd be embarrassed sometimes if I overheard them. So, I maintain my distance. Like today. But they *do* love me. I'm not mistaken, William. I know them much better than you, and I'm utterly convinced that, if it became necessary, they would literally *die* for me: any one of them singly, or all together! As I would for them!"

It took a few moments for this to sink in, so complete a reversal was it of everything I'd hitherto believed. Then I laughed in surprise at my own reaction. I actually *believed* her. And it struck me as incredible!

Or maybe I simply *wanted* to believe her.

It didn't matter. I was prepared to give her the benefit of the doubt, and since I cared infinitely more for her than I did for my own assessment of her situation, I happily relinquished all my prejudices in a single inner act. All I wanted was for her to be loved by the world as I loved her. Nothing else mattered. Not even me being there to sit in judgement.

"I – I'm happy about that," I told her. "I'm sorry. I seem to have misjudged the situation." I laughed. "Thank God."

"I love you, William. I love you every bit as much as you love me, probably much more. Now, I've - "

"That's not possible."

She laughed contentedly. "Now, I've been dying all day – oh, that's an exaggeration: I wasn't expecting Robert and Catherine! – but I've been… well, *waiting* to ask you: how was your interview with Dr Jenkinson?"

I'd already made up my mind not to tell her about his horrid flights of fancy. But I couldn't tell her nothing. My intention was to reduce the whole thing to jocosity and leave it there. "Well," I said, "he seemed very taken with you! He's constructed a machine designed to take you away to another world!"

I don't believe I could have foreseen her reaction. Her face crumpled with concern. She backed into her father's desk. She clung to it and dug her fingernails in. I rose in alarm.

"You mustn't let me near it!" she exclaimed hoarsely.

But then she appeared to fully recover. She stood upright and laughed. I'd put my arms around her, anticipating another fall. I released her.

"Another world?" she said calmly.

"Yes."

"How eccentric! I wonder if he'll call me to the front tonight! I hope not. If he does, I won't go."

I remembered her father: *she's at her wits' end*. I needed to change the subject. "I hear you were sleepwalking last night?"

"Father's told you, has he? I wondered why he dragged you into the study! Yes, I think it had something to do with that cat we saw, and, of course, there were a lot of strange things in the village last night." She laughed. "I don't know whether you heard about the forty-foot-wide brown ghost with teeth?"

"Your father mentioned it, yes."

Her mood changed again. She sat down on the armchair with a dejected groan, put her elbows on her knees and ran her hands through her hair. "I had a very bad dream last night, William."

"Tell me about it then. Maybe we can work out what it means. That might make you feel better."

"I daren't. You might be angry."

"I promise I won't be."

She gathered her courage and looked at the floor. "Very well. It was about me and Dr Jenkinson. We were… holding hands." She looked at me to gauge my reaction. I stroked her face to reassure her. She continued: "And we were strolling through an endless green meadow on a summer's day. The sun was different somehow, and there were angels out of sight, all around us. I had the horrible sense – I mean, horrible when I woke up: it didn't seem so at the time – that I … I was in love with him. I knew nothing about you, or us, or Mother and Father, or anything else in this waking world. And I didn't love him in *anything* like the way I love you, I swear. It was more like something an ant or a bee might feel for its queen. I was utterly, utterly subordinate to him. And it was only when I woke up that I realised how … *awful* that was." She wiped her eyes.

I stood up and walked as calmly as I could to the window. Which probably sounds insensitive, only I was beginning to fear for my own emotional state now.

But of course, lovers often have similar dreams. The shared content means nothing; the point lies in the deeper sympathy, and that is a positive thing. *The two shall become one flesh*. The point now was not to alarm her.

I knelt in front of her again, took her hands and kissed them. "Perhaps, deep down, you're worried that you've become a little too taken with Dr Jenkinson," I said gently. "Remember how you said you wanted him all to yourself yesterday? How you didn't want to share him with Catherine, Harriet and Jemima? And how you wanted me to aid you in all that? Maybe this is your unconscious mind becoming unduly worried that you're forsaking your soon-to-be husband for someone far less devoted."

She reflected for a moment, then put her arms round me and emitted a spluttery laugh of relief. "What a clever man you are, William! You're right! Yes, it all makes sense now. Oh, I'm *so* glad I told you! It just proves how much in love we are, that we can talk, without recrimination, of such things! Some men would certainly have walked out and never come back! Let us never, ever have any secrets from one another, William, as long as we live!"

"Hear, hear!" I said. But then, when I thought of all the things I'd kept from her in the last twenty-four hours – the true appearance of the 'cat', the letters she'd written, what her father had told me, my own dream matching hers – I felt wretched. The feeling I'd had on the ride to Robert Farley's last night returned. I didn't deserve her.

"Everyone will be wondering where we are!" she said. "Come on, let's go and find the others! Let's go for a walk together!"

IX.

We left the house for the first time in several months without Mrs Waller following us at a discreet distance. But we were far from alone, and our 'walk' along the main road turned into a series of long conversational halts, first with Miss Watson the headmistress, then with one of the Tunbridge Wells governesses and her six charges, then Jemima and her mother, then Harriet and her younger brother, then Mr Fairbrother the Salvationist, then old Farmer Rabson and his wife. An hour passed in this way, and we'd progressed no farther than Sparrows Green. The moment I spotted Mrs Benge coming towards us from a distance, I suggested we make our way back across the fields. Eustacia readily agreed.

When we entered the house again, it was virtually unchanged except for the strong smell of cooking meat and vegetables. Everyone still looked morose or tired, and the absence of the happy couple meant there was no need to put on a show. Eustacia suggested a game in the garden. Mr Waller had been a badminton champion in India, and was instrumental in setting up the famous club in Folkestone, so there was never any shortage of racquets in the house. She took five people outside - Jemima's mother and father, the still mysterious grandmother, Julia, and Harriet's brother, a man about ten years younger than me – and they began passing the shuttlecock between themselves. In the meantime, I was ordered to stay indoors and 'cheer the others up'.

Jemima sat alone on the sofa reading the book Farley had left behind. She looked momentarily up at me and smiled thinly, but it was obvious she didn't want to be disturbed. Flora charged in from the hallway. "William, I need you to come and *help* us!" she exclaimed, as if I should have fallen in with her long ago, before creating the nuisance of having to be asked.

She took my hand and led me into the front room where six other children sat busily working at a table with the eldest of the two governesses, a woman in her late thirties with her hair in a bun, and a pleasant smile, apparently supervising. She turned to look at me. "They're making 'ghosts'," she said, half-apologetically. "It was their idea, but I could see we were headed for tears otherwise."

I chuckled. "Mr Waller has other things on his mind, and he's not the superstitious kind."

"That's a relief. One never knows - "

"*Help* us, William!" Flora demanded.

I sat down next to her and picked up a pencil. It suddenly struck me that all the ghosts under production were not of the usually willowy, white variety; they were made of brown parcel paper, much wider than high, supported by a pair of thin twigs at each end, and each sporting a set of sharp white teeth.

Mr Waller put his head round the door. He looked at me, then down at the table.

The governess blushed. "It was their idea," she said hurriedly. "I probably shouldn't have allowed it, but - "

"Whatever keeps them quiet on a day like today," he said wearily. "William, a quick word, if you wouldn't mind."

I followed him into the study for the second time. He closed the door behind us. "There's no need for us to sit down," he said. "It's just, you said earlier that you wouldn't be taking Eustacia to The Queen's Head tonight, not after your little *tête-à-tête* with Jenkinson this morning. Have you broken the bad news to her yet?"

"Not yet. I thought - "

"I really believe you should reconsider. She's thoroughly enjoyed today, and separating her from her only friends might spoil it. It might even humiliate her. They've never showed her anything but genuine affection before, but they're rather younger than her, they're considerably more citified, and they've got very different ideas in general. *Modern* ideas: John Stuart Mill, *The Subjection of Women,* that sort of thing. I'm not saying they're wrong, incidentally. Consider: if she does go – if you permit it - she'll be with her fiancé, and surrounded by well-wishers, so what harm can come to her? *But...* I understand your reservations, and as far as I'm concerned, it's your choice, so if you do decide against it, I'll support you."

"I'd reached much the same conclusion, but I'm glad we're of one mind. Will you be coming?"

He gave a relieved grin. "From what I've heard, it's sold out, but I wouldn't fancy it anyway. And as I said yesterday, I don't want to upset Codrington. I think it's wise that some us stay on the side of the angels. What exactly did Jenkinson say to you, anyway?"

"He believes Eustacia's going to abandon me and take off with him."

"My God! He's *my* age!" He seemed to realise we'd been through this already. Plus, I think he was wary of making me change my mind about taking her. He shook his head incredulously but calmly. "On the basis of that letter, I suppose. Well, he's clearly mad. Tonight should purge the entire thing from her system, then we can start discreetly pressuring him to leave. By that time, you two will be in London."

He opened the door for me and we parted in opposite directions. I went back into the drawing room and found it empty. I sat down on the sofa Jemima had vacated and picked up Ovid. She'd left a marker in at Book Three, the story of Actaeon. I knew it vaguely. Actaeon, the hunter, accidentally sees the goddess Diana naked. By way of punishment, Diana transforms him into a stag, and shortly afterwards, he's torn limb from limb by his own hounds.

When now the fleetest of the pack, that pressed
Close at his heels, and sprung before the rest,
Had fastened on him, straight another pair,
Hung on his wounded haunch, and held him there,
'Till all the pack came up, and every hound

Tore the sad huntsman grovelling on the ground,
Who now appeared but one continued wound.
With dropping tears his bitter fate he moans,
And fills the mountain with his dying groans.

I closed the book and laid it aside. I was beginning to feel as gloomy as everyone else in the house, and Ovid certainly wasn't likely to help. I looked at the clock. Half past five. Another two and a half hours, but dinner would help pass some of the time. Robert and Catherine would be back soon, and they would be certain to be animated, and things would begin to look cheery again.

Jemima ran in from the garden and sat down next to me. "Hello, William."

At that moment, Flora and two of her friends entered, holding their 'ghosts' aloft and running haphazardly with a whoo-ing noise. They zig-zagged for a minute then left the way they'd come in.

"Farmer Patterson's forty-foot-long brown ghost," I said. "I assume you've heard all about it? It's rather a morbid subject for a game."

"I think it's good that they learn to laugh at it," she replied breezily. "That way, when they see the real thing, they won't be so frightened. Let's hope they're not looking out of their bedroom windows tonight."

I laughed. "I've been reading your book."

"How did you know it was mine? I assumed you'd think it was Robert's. You saw him reading it before you saw me, and Ovid's a man's poet, isn't he?"

I laughed again. She was trying to catch me out. "I didn't know it belonged to either of you. I thought it had come from the study."

"What do you think about Actaeon? Do you think he deserved to die?"

"Of course not. He didn't mean to see Diana. And to be torn apart - "

"He was a huntsman. He only received what he'd gladly inflicted on every stag he'd ever come across. Perhaps that was what Diana was really thinking: 'He's a butcher of the worst kind, and, to cap it all, now he's seen me naked. Well, that's the straw that breaks the camel's back! Time for him to get a taste of his own medicine!'"

"But Diana was a huntress. She must also have killed a few stags in her time."

"Yes, but she was perfect. Her first shot always went straight through the heart. Death was instantaneous."

"Well, I suppose that's one way of looking at it."

"And she always ate everything afterwards. And the stag came back to Earth as another stag, at some future time. Anyway, I think it's a wonderful story. And Addison does such a good job of translating it. *Who now appeared but one continued wound:* I think that's my favourite line."

Perhaps it was time to change the subject. "Are you looking forward to this evening?"

"I understand Dr Jenkinson has a machine. Where is it?"

"What? Did Eustacia tell you about that?"

"How else could I have found out? Just answer my question, William, and I won't pester you anymore."

"You're not 'pestering' me." I let out a deep breath. "Very well, if you must know, it's upstairs, in his room, just behind the door. That's where it was last time I saw it, anyway. It probably won't be there tonight, because he's going to wind it up and set it working, and it's going to suck Eustacia into another world where he and she can be together forever. It will probably be on the stage, in the centre."

She moved forward and twisted her torso, so her face was right in front of mine. She looked me directly in the eyes. "Best not to jest," she said.

She stood up and ran back into the garden.

It seemed a shame. A very brief encounter, but I'd actually begun to like her. Then it struck me that, in her eyes, I was probably an old man, and even more outdated than Eustacia. And that, for all her affected urbanity, she was really little more than a child. We were best off keeping each other at arm's length.

Mr Waller entered. "Farley and the Henshaws are on their way back," he told me unenthusiastically, as if it was his duty. "Netty intercepted them outside The Hare and Hounds, about to go in and order dinner. She told them in no uncertain terms that we were expecting them. I know they're only trying to save me expense, but it's unnecessary." He sat next to me on the sofa. "So, they're on their way. End of announcement. The sooner this day comes to an end, William, the better, although there's still the almighty fuss of church to come, tomorrow morning. They'll all want to present themselves fully dressed, and thoroughly devout, before Codrington, if only to show him they don't need exorcising. Which, even without taking Jenkinson's wretched lantern show into account, is probably premature." He laughed at his own joke. I joined him.

X.

Dinner had the opposite effect to lunch. It reinvigorated us, especially now Catherine and Robert were back. Necessity is the mother of invention, and since we *had* to be cheerful, we really were. Mr Waller brought out a tonic wine and some ale, which probably helped. Everyone ate the host's roast beef, Yorkshire puddings and several vegetables, then went to get changed.

We set off for The Queen's Head at quarter to nine, having been reassured by Harriet that "All the tickets have been sold! We can turn up whenever we like!" We walked down the main road in pairs. The sun set, and I noticed, without feeling any pleasure in it, that we formed a moving carnival of fabulous dresses, smart suits, hats, attractive faces, and dignified gaits. Eustacia and I occupied the middle. Harriet, Jemima, Catherine and Robert took up the rear. The parents – although obviously not Eustacia's – were in the vanguard. As we passed Wace House, someone pointed to the sky and let out an exclamation of delight.

At a considerable distance directly overhead, a brown shape, like a colossal kite, emitted a quiet moan as it slowly drifted eastwards in the wind. It was just possible to make out a row of misshapen 'teeth' at its centre. I'd have put its width at closer to four hundred feet than forty, but since its precise height was impossible to gauge, I might have been wildly mistaken. In any case, it was clearly a clever illusion; a spectacular foretaste of the show, designed to create an expectation of awe.

... Because, really, what else *could* it have been? Since we'd all been laughing at Farmer Patterson throughout the day, we had no choice but to keep laughing now.

What I will say, however, is that the first whoop of delight was also the last. I'm sure I wasn't the only one to experience a shiver of unease: common sense should probably have told us that what we were seeing was vastly too clever for any mere sleight of hand.

We entered The Queen's Head steadily without having to queue. The show room was on the ground floor and large enough for forty wooden seats, arranged in ascending tiers towards the back, and a makeshift stage. The walls had been hung with expensive-looking patterned fabric, and the lighting was a gloomy mixture of oil lamps and candles. A couple of incense burners on a box filled the air with a pale smoke and a sickly odour. A narrow aisle led along one side of the room to the exit. At the opposite side, right at the front, two chairs had been placed beside each other at a ninety-degree angle to the rest of the audience. When Eustacia and I entered, we tried to sit two rows back in the middle, but four people stopped us, one after the other.

"Your places are over there!" Harriet's brother said, laughing. "At the front! You can't sit here! You'll be in trouble!"

My view of what he was pointing to – the two foremost seats - was temporarily obscured by people trying to establish themselves, swapping places, standing for belated introductions.

Partly out of a morbid curiosity however, partly from a growing sense of other people's frustration with us, Eustacia and I edged reluctantly forward to get to where we'd been directed. We found ourselves confronted by two chairs, each with a 'Reserved' notice: one marked 'Eustacia Waller', the other 'William Jones'. With virtually all the other seats now filled, and everyone snugly established and waiting, we had no choice but to sit down.

Suddenly, we were as much a spectacle as Jenkinson was about to be. In the absence of anything much else at the front, we became most people's focus of attention, Silence fell. My heart sank. I wanted to retreat to the back row, which, for some reason, was still empty, but I wasn't sure I could get Eustacia to accompany me. Not given the looks it would elicit.

A smart middle-aged man with wiry red hair walked briskly down the aisle and mounted the stage. "Ladies and gentlemen!" he exclaimed, "welcome to the show room of The Queen's Head inn!" His voice rose. "*Now, behold!* One of the most *influential* and *thought-provoking* thinkers of the *modern age! A spiritualist! A thinker! A radical theologian!* An *expert* on the poetry of *William Blake!* An *inventor* and a *magician!* Ladies and gentlemen, I present for your edification and delight: *DOCTOR! ELIAS! JEN-KIN-SON!"*

The audience clapped politely, though it sounded rather too much like a music-hall introduction to me. Not in any way offensive, obviously, but the wrong tone for what was supposedly a lecture. Dr Jenkinson entered the room from the back. He paused just after he'd squeezed past the exiting compere, then waved his hands theatrically above his head and yelled: *"The four winds!"*

Suddenly, the entire room filled with what felt like a hurricane. Women held their hats and squealed. Men yelled. The younger people laughed excitedly and nudged each other. Without breaking his stride, Jenkinson kept waving his hands until he was on the stage. He cast a lurid glance at Eustacia, then turned back to his audience. *"Creatures of the underworld!"*

A woman in the third row gave a full-throated screech. She stared wide-eyed at the floor. She tried to back away, and she was not the only one. Those around her leapt to their feet and for a second, it looked as if a full-scale panic might be about to erupt.

"The spirits who command repose!" he shrieked.

The upturned chairs seemed to right themselves and the people who had risen to their feet sat back down on them, as brutally as if they'd been set there by a robust pair of invisible hands.

There should have been an indignant uproar; at least a few people should have rushed angrily to the exit; but suddenly, there was total stillness. Jenkinson stood on stage, still gesturing, his eyes glaring wildly. *"The silence of the grave!"* he yelled.

I turned to Eustacia, expecting her to be as petrified as everyone else. But she seemed to be enjoying it. She leaned forward enthusiastically and burst out laughing.

Suddenly, the sound of her mirth was accompanied by a different noise: a gentle throbbing from the floor directly above, as of an engine puffing. His machine? It had to be. I wanted to stand up, but I couldn't move. Jenkinson looked at the ceiling and closed his eyes as if he was in ecstasy. He mumbled to himself. The sound from above got louder.

I don't think anyone knew what to expect next, and I could see most people were terrified. But then something occurred that transformed the atmosphere, and, as it turned out, the whole evening.

What happened was simply that four latecomers entered. Robert, Catherine, Harriet, and Jemima came into the room in the same way everyone else had, ten minutes earlier. They edged along the back row, sat down in a line and looked directly at Dr Jenkinson. They seemed completely unaffected by the spell he'd apparently cast, and there was something intensely hostile in the way the three women regarded him.

He noticed their entry immediately and I got a distinct sense of him losing a significant part of his confidence. He stopped waving his hands, and looked about him as if he couldn't quite believe what had just happened. He suddenly looked apologetic. For a few seconds, the room felt as if a vestige of normality was on the verge of restoration.

"And of course, I – I am here to give a *lecture,*" he said. "My subject tonight. The subject is – my – *yes*, I would like to talk to you for the space of about *thirty minutes* on the - on the, yes, *difference* between good and bad magic!"

Catherine, Harriet and Jemima had noticed the noise coming from the ceiling. They engaged in a short, whispered conference. Jemima got up and slipped through the exit.

Dr Jenkinson stood with his hands behind his back and began his talk. He started to sweat. He stuttered and scratched his head. I found it hard to follow what he was saying because there were so many long pauses, but the gist seemed to be that 'the exact counterbalance of magic' in the universe had to be preserved, and that meant that good magic was easy to perform – since there was so little good in the world already –

and bad 'or black' magic was difficult, because the world was already so evil. His audience listened as attentively as if they'd forgotten everything they'd been subjected to earlier. It was easily the strangest event I had ever attended.

When he reached the point of explaining the many impediments to performing bad magic, there was a commotion upstairs. It began with a bang, like a chest of drawers being knocked over, then continued rhythmically as if someone was violently but methodically hammering something. Everyone looked at the ceiling as if they expected it to cave in. Jenkinson shivered, put his hands distraughtly on his face, and regarded the exit as if it was his last remaining hope.

Suddenly, he ran. Before anyone knew what was happening, he had left the room.

People got cantankerously to their feet and erupted with terror and anger. At least one woman swooned. Before that, I saw Catherine and Harriet leave. Robert looked across at me with an expression of complete bemusement, and went after them.

XI.

I got Eustacia to her feet – if I didn't know better, I could have sworn she'd been drugged – and helped her outside with the help of Harriet's brother, the man with whom she'd played badminton that afternoon.

We were among the first to leave, and the fresh air was unbelievably bracing. My only thought now was to get her home as quickly as possible, but I couldn't help noticing Robert Farley standing some forty yards off in the middle of the road in the Ticehurst direction. He trotted over when he saw me. "I need help," he said breathlessly. He gestured for me to leave Eustacia in the care of Harriet's brother, so we could talk frankly. I stepped a few paces away from her, but I was not prepared to let her out of my sight.

"Do *you* know what's happening?" I asked. "Where are Catherine and Harriet?"

"I – I don't know." I could see he wanted to tell me more, but knew it wouldn't make sense. His need for help won out. "I came outside to find Dr Jenkinson staggering away about a hundred yards further on from where you just found me. He looked petrified!"

"Of what? Of Catherine and Harriet?"

"And – and Jemima. I know this sounds outlandish, but the three of them – they'd – *they were in a state of semi-undress*. You mustn't tell anyone, do you hear? This is just between us."

I had to get Eustacia home. But I wavered between that, and my strong desire to help my friend. "What do you mean?"

"They'd torn – their *skirts* off. Their legs were *completely naked! They were bare-footed!*" He took a deep breath. "But, my God, that's not even all! They looked like they were *stalking Jenkinson!* Wide-apart positions - to prevent him double-backing!"

I laughed hollowly. "Sorry, it *can't* have been what it looked like."

"And to cap it all, they were carrying long knives. *Really* long knives, like they meant to skewer him. My God." He put his hand on his head and laughed. "No, no, of course. I've just realised. You're right! *Obviously,* you *are* right! Jenkinson clearly released some sort of hallucination-producing gas in The Queen's Head! Of *course*. Why didn't I see that before? It's undeniable! I'm still under the influence, I suppose. Please, William: forget everything I just told you. And, er, like I said: don't tell anyone."

"But where are they?"

"I only know what I saw. Which obviously can't be right. As I just said, ignore me."

"What did you see?"

He sighed as if he might as well indulge me. "Jenkinson suddenly took off at a speed much too fast for a human to run. And they went after him at the same velocity. Look, I'm still suffering the after-effects. We probably all are. The police need to know about this. *Magic, my foot!* Poisoning people's brains, that's all it was! Look, you get Eustacia home. You can leave her in the care of her father and one of the other men. But we need to find Catherine and her friends! They could be in trouble! I need your help now like I've never needed it before!"

"I can get a search party together."

"No! ... I mean, what if it's true? What if they really are unclothed?"

I re-joined Eustacia and Harriet's brother. "I'll be back as soon as I can," I told Robert from a distance. "Give me fifteen minutes."

"I'll be searching – although, frankly, I've no idea where to begin."

We both heard a quiet roar. We turned to look. The brown thing we'd seen earlier was still visible, in the far distance.

"I'm free, William!" Eustacia declared when I got back to her. She looked overjoyed. She clasped me. "I'm free! *I'm free!"*

Harriet's brother chuckled. "Something dubious in the incense, I think!"

XII.

I left Eustacia with her parents and set off on what I knew in advance would be a hopeless quest to find Robert and the women. Duty always trumps rational common sense with me. I wandered through the woods and across the fields for four hours until I became hopelessly lost. At sunrise, however, I finally got my bearings and headed for Buss's Green, hoping to find some sort of resolution there. I knew Eustacia and her family would be worried about me, but I had to find Robert first.

I don't know what time it was when I finally knocked on his front door, only that I was at the end of my strength. He bade me come in, sat me beside the fire and gave me a plate of devilled kidneys, two slices of toast and a large cup of tea.

After half an hour, when my strength was returning, he took me into the kitchen. Harriet, Jemima and Catherine sat at the table wearing trousers and consuming brandy and toffees ('The Wadhurst breakfast', Harriet called it). Jemima actually had her feet up on a stool, like a man. How and where Robert had found them, or how they'd located him and each other, I never asked and no one explained. "On no account must you tell anyone about this," he instructed me… yet again. I was too tired to care.

He had borrowed five horses from a neighbouring farm and we rode back to Wadhurst. At the Wallers' house there were tearful reunions, disjointed explanations, incredulous laughs, relieved sighs, affectionate recriminations, kisses. Ten minutes later, the three women had changed out of their borrowed trousers into new dresses. They looked very similar to when they'd arrived yesterday afternoon.

I never found out what had happened to Dr Jenkinson. For three days, I half suspected the women might actually have killed him – more in the manner of precipitating a heart attack than directly - but then his clothes were found, unsullied, in the woods near Ticehurst. Questioned by the police regarding his character, several people said they considered him insane. This led to speculation that he had stripped naked, but after that, even the most imaginative theorists ran out of suggestions. No grave was ever discovered, and no dead body.

In the continuing absence of a satisfactory explanation, I choose to believe he will turn up some day, having received the fright of his life and retired into seclusion. I doubt the world has seen the last of him.

As to why he chose to lay such comprehensive waste to his room at The Queen's Head, there are a number of theories. Since none are remotely satisfactory, I will not bother listing them here. Suffice it to say that Jemima Clarkson cannot have been involved, as one or two silly people initially suggested. No mere woman possesses the strength to inflict that degree of damage. It gave me great pleasure to learn that the 'machine' came in for particular punishment, having been demolished not just beyond any possibility of repair, but also of recognition.

Eustacia and I were married in Saint Peter and Saint Paul, as planned, a fortnight after the events I have described above. Robert and Catherine tied the knot a month later. In the peculiar manner we British have of disregarding our surroundings, Eustacia and I moved to London and became countrified traditionalists; Robert and Catherine set up home in rural Wadhurst and gained a reputation as citified radicals. Jemima and Harriet married Tunbridge Wells worthies, within a month of each other, a year afterwards, and subsequently became leading lights in the women's suffrage movement. I strongly suspect that at least one of them was behind the 1913 arson attack on Tunbridge Wells cricket pavilion. But of course, I may be wrong.

Roddy Samhain

I.

It's so difficult to know where to start. I mean, how do you begin to make sense of someone like Roddy Samhain? (Which almost certainly wasn't his real name, by the way, although we still don't have any other.)

You've got to remember that all this happened recently. I'm not going to revisit the coronavirus 'debate' here – how effective the repeated lockdowns were, whether the general level of fear was justified, etc. – because it's irrelevant. The fact is, a lot of people *were* scared. Some were terrified. And, of course, apart from that, the so-called Holocene extinction had become impossible to ignore. We were slowly strangling everything in existence. More pandemics were definitely on their way, and some of them would be worse. Young people started taking to the open road, having finally despaired of their parents' injunctions to get qualified, get a good job, get yourself a foot on the property ladder. Millenarianism gradually became fashionable again. In short, Roddy Samhain appeared at exactly the right moment. In some ways, he personified his time.

I can describe him, certainly. He looked to be in his early forties, although I was never able to ascertain his exact age. He claimed to have been born in Wadhurst, which I don't necessarily consider impossible (though no one there remembers him). I think he was probably the child of New Age Travellers - or hippies, as they may have called themselves then - and that, somewhere along the line, his parents simply vanished from the equation, in the tragic way radical outsiders sometimes do. He had an unkempt beard, a ruddy, rather choleric-looking face, a slight paunch, a genuine personal hygiene problem – not only did he smell, but he also looked like he needed a wash – and he always wore a grubby medieval jester's costume. Red, blue and yellow, like The Fool in the Swiss 1JJ Tarot, with a dangly-bell coxcomb. He was exceptionally taciturn. Actions, not words, were his forte.

Even so, that doesn't give you the half of him. Yes, by now you've probably gathered that he was highly bizarre. But that bit's always easiest to explain. The difficulty comes in persuading people just how *dangerous* he was. I should know. I was in charge of the CID team assigned to watch him. Interpol definitely believed he was a criminal of the worst kind. By that, I mean they thought he wasn't motivated by personal gain. No, he broke laws, flouted conventions and transgressed moral norms almost incidentally, as a function of *who he was,* and he seemed always likely to get worse.

But I still haven't begun to tell you what he was really like.

This is what I'll do. I'll re-introduce him by means of a thought experiment.

Imagine you are born with powers that enable you do things supposed to be scientifically impossible: read people's minds, for example, or levitate. Let's say you make this amazing self-discovery when you're still quite young, about eighteen. Now, imagine you're mature enough to make fully rational choices about where to go next. My firm conviction is that the very *last* thing you'll do is publicly announce you've got supernatural powers, and, hey, you can *prove* it, just watch! In this day and age, you'd have people queuing up by the hundreds to 'debunk' you. You'd never get rid of them. And even apart from that, no one would ever believe you: they'd just think the experts hadn't rumbled you yet. They'd bitterly resent you for not coming clean. Finally, to the extent that you believed in yourself, you'd be viewed as an obnoxious crank. All things considered, you'd end up living a pretty miserable life.

No, by far your best bet would be to set yourself up as a professional 'magician'. The kind of show-person who, fifty or sixty years ago, would have pulled rabbits from top hats, made playing cards disappear, and sawed attractive young women in half. Genuinely apply your supernatural powers, get paid for it, and keep schtum about the real metaphysical foundations. More than that: actively pretend it's all sleight of hand. That way, you'd stay in the company of the sane – because that's all 'sanity' is, really: a socially approved way of relating to others - *and* you'd make lots of money, *and* you wouldn't creep out your friends. Heck, you'd actually *have* friends, which you probably wouldn't in the former scenario! And if you were sensitive enough to fret about the deception involved (because even harmless deception, as all sensible people know, incurs costs), you could give some of your money to charity. At a pinch, you could even *heal* a few people. But not too many. You wouldn't want to attract that petty-minded line of debunkers I just mentioned.

I never used to think Roddy Samhain belonged in the latter class. I used to think he was just very skilled at his craft. But I don't think that any more. In any case, if I'm to help you make sense of him, I need to add a few things to my generic biography, because Samhain would never have given money to charity. And he certainly wasn't disposed to heal, or even help, people. So, if there actually *was* a eureka moment in his life at which he discovered he had magic powers – and I admit, I'm assuming the reality of such things here, but bear with me – he quickly became embittered by the knowledge that the world would never, ever permit him to use them without pretending they were spurious. He very reluctantly agreed to the only possible contract on the table – very well, do your magic, but make out it's trickery – yet he determined to extract revenge indiscriminately at every opportunity.

Now that I've told you all that, I can perhaps be a little more specific about him. Obviously, he must have realised that he couldn't be the kind of magician who appeared in theatres and on television: he would put too many backs up. No, he set his sights on becoming a street magician – or more accurately, a 'guerrilla' magician - someone who wanders through towns and villages, picking on people and performing conjuring tricks for them, right under their very noses. You probably know the sort of thing I mean. David Blaine, or Derren Brown, or Dynamo.

Those aren't random names, incidentally. I really think Samhain must have considered them early in his career. If so, it's instructive for us to do likewise. Because they all have their 'personas', you see, their public faces. Every TV personality does. David Blaine: he's a charismatic loner; Derren Brown's an ex-Christian intellectual; Dynamo's a friendly-faced guy-next-door. Basically, however, they're all relatively amiable.

In short, there was definitely what is sometimes called a 'gap in the market' (though I doubt Samhain thought of it in those terms). What was missing was a *malefactor:* a genuinely vindictive figure whose magic would scare people out of their wits, and sometimes even unite them against him. Being run out of town was excellent publicity, and since he was never accompanied anywhere by his own camera crew, or anything like it, it was always his preferred endgame.

Central to his new persona: he only ever appeared at 'Hallowtide', that complex of festivals connected with the transition from autumn to winter and life to death. He was never seen after the end of November, nor before the first of October. You'd think a ten-month furlough would have dimmed his appeal, but in fact it added to it, in the way that rarity often does. And it allowed time for rumours, half-truths and well-meaning fictions to become accepted as facts.

Of course, Halloween tricks were his speciality. He made people see their own bones through their hands, or he instructed them to take a long blink and when they re-opened their eyes, his were just two black holes. Then there was his cartomancy – never entirely innocuous – culminating in Death or The Hanged Man, or the ace of spades. People reported seeing him emerge, at dawn or twilight, from beneath the surface of a field, like a zombie. Once, he supposedly 'infected' an entire village in Hertfordshire with an imaginary disease: the victims experienced small growths of moss on their bodies, which vanished whenever anyone else was called to examine them. I have even heard it said (though I've been unable to confirm it) that, whenever he was in an area for any length of time, the death rate always rose; dead birds appeared with greater frequency; ponds became inexplicably stagnant. After he left, many people – especially his victims - experienced nightmares. But all of this was par for the course. Perverse as it may sound, it only increased people's thirst for more.

Meanwhile, you might be wondering what brought him to the attention of the police. Well, I believe he spent most of his early adulthood on the continent, to all intents and purposes preparing for his mission. The report compiled for Interpol by the German *Bundespolizei,* which I read shortly after I was assigned to watch him, suggests that he crossed swords with a few thriving criminal cartels in Prague, Berlin, Paris and Rome. More particularly, he provoked some sort of furious dispute, then waited for them to approach him on bended knee. For that to have borne fruit – which it undoubtedly did – he must have had to inflict catastrophic damage somewhere along the line, and his victims must have become utterly convinced of their own relative impotence. In this instance, I cannot be any more specific. I don't know what he did to them.

I do know that when he finally arrived back in this country, his reputation preceded him. The British underworld already knew him as someone to be reckoned with and preferably avoided. Yet strangely, as far as I have been able to tell, although he liked to be in close physical proximity to criminals, he had no interest whatsoever in becoming one – at least, not in any sense they'd recognise. Rather, he seemed to enjoy imbibing something of their… essence? I am talking about pimps, human traffickers, modern slavers, drug barons, arms dealers, contract torturers. Nothing supposedly 'victimless'. No Robin Hoods.

If this makes it sound as if the general public regarded him with widespread revulsion, nothing could be further from the truth. In the strange manner of our times, people actually idolised him, especially the young and disaffected. He was clearly beholden to no one. And he had no interest whatsoever in money. Because he hardly ever spoke, he could be anything you wanted him to be. So, he was an anti-establishment, anti-phoney, anti-capitalist figurehead. Religious people were divided: most disapproved, a few saw him as the Antichrist, a small handful considered him God's servant (I'm not joking: 'God sometimes uses miscreants to fulfil his purposes!'). In any case, he was one of the enduring beneficiaries of the so-called Trump Effect: he did bad things - sometimes really bad things - but because 'he was who he was', he escaped the consequences. In most people's eyes, inauthenticity had become the only real crime.

Inevitably, he became a star on social media, although, of course, he had no direct hand in that. At one point, there were over a hundred Facebook pages devoted to him in the UK alone. Several TikTok, Twitter and Instagram accounts did nothing but document his movements. Some people undoubtedly made a fortune out of him.

Above all, he had physical followers: New Age Travellers or 'Tribulationists' (as they called themselves), who followed him devotedly from place to place, filling the air with their medieval dance music. Some of them became almost as famous as he was: 'Herbert Foghmhar the Great' with his drum and magic wand, 'Lady Gemred' with her red face and ivy headdress, 'Mildred Lughnasadh' with her lute. They shared a predilection for the music of Steeleye Span, Musica calamus and Fairport Convention: 'Come All Ye' was their anthem, and when they appeared in Wadhurst, you could always hear a different version of it on every street corner. They expected the imminent end of the world, which they saw as a cause for great celebration. Samhain was the exact point at which their salvation would begin, so it was necessary to keep him as close as possible. To say the least, there was an odd disjunction between the carnival atmosphere they evinced, and the black hole that lay at their centre.

In the real world, it reached the point where every major talent agency in London, New York and Hollywood wanted to hire Roddy Samhain. All thought they could probably control him, but that, in any eventuality, there was enough money to be made in the short-term to make his longer-term volatility irrelevant.

Finally, one of them – 'City of London Parts' – decided it could plausibly make him an irresistible offer. For obvious reasons, it never released the specifics. But it felt confident enough to despatch one of its representatives to Wadhurst – where Samhain always appeared first – at the beginning of October.

Which is when I met 'Stephanie Forsythe'.

II.

It happened in the same way every year, always on the morning of the first day of the tenth month. People would be going about their daily business in the Wadhurst High Street - shopping, strolling, dog-walking – when suddenly, apparently out of nowhere, Roddy Samhain would appear in the form of a 'living statue'.

I'm not sure whether you're familiar with that notion, but, either way, it's self-explanatory. It simply involves a person, in a public space, adopting a rigid posture for a prolonged period of time. You see them a lot in cities; they're rare in villages. In Samhain's case, the performance could last as long as two days (which seems inconceivable but, well, we've been through that).

His specific pose was always the same. Right knee raised to the waist, standing on the ball of the left foot, upper arms outstretched, forearms drooping, and a manic grin. Even more singular was his manner of appearing, because people insisted he just *materialised* from thin air. St James Square, or the corner of Washwell Lane, or on the green in Watts Close, or outside the fire station, or next to the bus stop in Sparrows Green: the location differed every year. On the first two occasions, I believe he was harassed by schoolchildren and late-night drunkards. But that stopped after what local hearsay described as 'nightmares and terrible accidents.' If the *Bundespolizei* report was true, Samhain had taken on Camorristi and Hell's Angels; a few village scallywags weren't likely to tax him. Anyway, a few years later, his 'fans' started appearing in the village, and they mounted unasked-for vigils. One year, after they'd guarded him reverently all through one drizzly night, a sudden gale blew up just as the sun rose. Roddy Samhain crashed to the ground. Or rather, a plastic model did. The reality was nowhere to be found, and never appeared anywhere again until the following October.

The year I first met Stephanie Forsythe, Samhain posed in the churchyard for thirty-one hours. We both went to see him on the first morning, at different times. Already, he was surrounded by flowers, candles, sticks of incense, 'The Fool' Tarot cards, pentacles, corn dollies. A cardboard notice read, 'DO NOT STEP ON THE CANDLES THANK YOU'. People crowded round and took photos. It should have been entertaining, but as usual, there was a moribund atmosphere. And no birds sang.

I left wondering what the vicar thought. After all, this was supposed to be consecrated ground. Then I heard that a journalist was on her way to ask him, presumably on the optimistic pretext that nothing makes good copy like an outraged Christian. I hoped he wouldn't see her.

I crossed the road to The White Hart which, as usual on this day, was full to bursting, almost entirely with out-of-towners. After twenty minutes, I managed to get a coffee, though most people seemed to be ordering pints and cocktails.

This was my sixth year in Wadhurst for the purpose of watching Samhain, and every October, the crowds got bigger. The travellers' clapped-out vans, Vardo wagons, lorries and buses increasingly clogged the car parks and grass verges. But even apart from that, it had become some people's annual pilgrimage. While all this was going on, the actual villagers nearly all stayed at home. They hadn't invited Samhain, and mostly, they didn't want him here. His appearance always brought trouble. The best that could be said was that you'd probably avoid it if you stayed completely out of his way.

I'd noticed Stephanie Forsythe in the churchyard. Tall, black, with long dark hair, a thin nose, wide set eyes, probably in her mid-thirties, and dressed in a smart raincoat and high-heeled boots. I'd been struck by her seeming detachment. She examined Samhain with barely concealed disapproval and shuddered. I noticed her again in The White Hart. We exchanged smiles, although hers appeared first.

I'm never under any illusions where that sort of thing is concerned. When a complete stranger makes affable eye-contact with me, it's always because they know what I do for a living, and they believe I can be useful to them. Depending on how eager they are, they might decide to follow up by buying me a drink. However, small talk is cheaper, and usually no less effective.

I left the pub with my coffee. I went to sit on a bench at the side of Washwell Lane, and waited for her to turn up. After a few seconds, I was joined by a man and a woman in their early twenties with painted faces and occult tattoos. I prepared to keep myself firmly to myself, but to my surprise, they turned to me and struck up a conversation about the weather, then how difficult it had been to get here this year, and where they thought 'Roddy' would go next. They seemed to have no hidden agenda whatsoever, and when they got up and left, wishing me a 'happy rest of the day', I felt ashamed of my bigotry.

Thankfully, I didn't have time to brood because Stephanie Forsythe sat down in the space they'd vacated. She held an empty glass with a straw and a chocolate stick in.

She noted my cup and saucer. "Coffee?" she said. "You're obviously well behaved!" After I chuckled, she offered a handshake. "Stephanie Forsythe. Nice to meet another tourist, albeit a teetotaller."

I noticed she had a faint accent. Italian. "I'm just very fond of caffeine," I said jocosely. "What was yours?"

"A Roddy Samhain. My own invention. Basically, a tequila sunrise topped with blue curaçao. The chocolate stick represents the grime," she added, taking a bite out of it. "It's a work in progress. I think the barman was quite pleased. After I left, I heard someone else order one."

"You ought to patent it."

She pulled a face. "With *his* name attached? You must be joking!"

"Other people make a profit from him and he doesn't seem to resent it. The T-shirt sellers will be out soon, and the key-ring sellers, and the postcard sellers, and - "

"I understand you're with the police."

I smiled. As I've just mentioned, I'd seen it coming. "Plain clothes, obviously. Why? Are you in trouble?"

"This isn't my first drink. I'd already had two when I saw you in the churchyard. I'm pretty much – what's the word - ?"

"*Completamente ubriaco,*" I said. "Completely plastered."

She drew her chin back incredulously. For a split second, she seemed horribly offended, and I prepared to make a grovelling apology. Then she laughed. "How much do you know about me?"

"Enough," I lied. Then it dawned on me. Her command of English was too good for her not to know the term 'drunk'. She'd been testing me. "Enough to know your real name's not Stephanie Forsythe," I went on, hazarding yet another guess. Gosh, how I loved to live dangerously.

"So, what *is* my real name?"

"I don't know. But the fact that you're going under a false one sets alarm bells ringing. Obviously, it won't be long before I find out."

She blinked slowly and nodded. "I'm sealing my own doom! Just as I did in the dream!" She laughed manically. "What possessed me to *ask* you if you were with the police? I *knew* you were with the police! What made me even *follow you down here?* Oh, I know what you're going to say: the fact that I was 'completely plastered'. But that doesn't solve anything! I told myself to keep away from you. I arrived with every intention of avoiding *any* contact with you whatsoever. And now *this!"*

"You, er, sealing your own doom?" I said. She'd overwhelmed me slightly, but I'd snapped fully into policeman mode.

She put her elbows on her knees and covered her face with her hands. "Okay, I… I believe I am in trouble, yes. I think Roddy Samhain's out to get me. I would leave the village, but I can't."

I hmm-ed. "Okay, well that's not going to get us very far. Why are you here to begin with?"

"Before I answer that question, let me just say that I know all about you. What little there is, I mean. I probably need a guardian angel, that's all. If I'm killed – which I could be, though it won't be anything anyone can tie to him – I at least want it added to a list of 'people he had reason to hate and who then died in unusual circumstances.' There must *be* such a list, and you must be able to edit it: add things, change them, remove them."

"With respect, you're not making much of a request. Most people who think they're going to be killed ask for some level of protection."

"That would be ideal. But I doubt you could provide it. My biggest hope is that we might become friends, and you might come to feel some sort of personal attachment to me; such that you'll come to my aid if I'm in trouble."

"That's also my *job*."

"Of course," she said bitterly. "Ring the police, they'll always get straight out to you. They'll 'bend over backwards' to send a cop car over at the speed of light. Sorry, no: that's useless. If that's all you can offer, I might as well hire a private detective."

We sat in silence for a few seconds. Eventually, I said, "Well, if we're going to be friends, I need to know something about you."

"What choice have I got?" she replied wretchedly. "You're pretty much my only hope at this point. Okay, then, here goes. I used to run a Twitter fan club for Roddy Samhain. One of six in Calabria, where I was born. Mine was the biggest and most successful, and it won me a fabulous job offer. Specifically, the job I'm doing – or failing to do – right now. My real name doesn't matter, but if it helps, since you know I'm Italian, you can call me 'Violetta'. Officially, I was sent here by a London Theatrical agency called CLP – short for 'City of London Parts' – to get Roddy Samhain to sign an employment contract. That's right, CLP wants him to work for them. They'll take the usual ten per cent, and he'll become rich. There's only one problem with that. As everyone knows, he doesn't give a damn about money. And it's not as if this would be the first offer he's ever received. People are promising to turn him into Croesus all the time. And that's why CLP's no ordinary theatrical agency.

"Which brings us to the unofficial part," she went on. "It's a front for – well, let's say Sicilian gangsters. Men who believe they've 'got something' on Roddy Samhain that could easily put him in jail for twenty years, and possibly the rest of his life. I've never met these men. That was deliberate on their part. Why? Because they genuinely think Roddy Samhain could *get inside my head and 'see' them;* my mental impression of them; my memories. Then they believe he could kill them, even at the distance southern Italy is from where we're sitting now! Superstitious guys, or so I thought. More than that: paranoid. I've been offered an awful lot of money to put their offer to Roddy Samhain. Obviously, he might turn on me. But I do have a safety mechanism. I'm supposed to tell him that if he kills the messenger, he's effectively condemning himself. All

I've got to do is get his signature – duly witnessed, of course – and I'm wealthy beyond my wildest dreams."

"And you actually trust these men not to double-cross you?"

She smiled patiently. "They've already given me half. It's in a numbered bank account where they can't touch it anymore, and it's enough to make me rich on its own, even if they renege on the second instalment. Which I don't think they will. Honour means a lot to them, albeit of the warped kind that involves gruesome murders, torture, extortion and fraud."

"Wow."

"That's right," she said. "'Wow'."

"In other circumstances, I'd offer you some sort of witness protection; but it could only be on the basis of going after these 'men' of yours. The problem is, you haven't met them. And to compound matters, I'm not sure we could begin to *prove* they've done anything wrong. Even their attempt to blackmail Samhain's a matter of your word against theirs."

"Roddy Samhain's already inside my head. And weirdly, I've been given a horrible glimpse of the inside of his. I'm doomed. He doesn't care about them or what they've got. He can kill them without accessing my memories. But he'll probably kill me first, and it won't be nice."

"I must admit I'm a Roddy Samhain sceptic. And I'm pretty sure I'm in the majority. He's just a trickster."

"But that's the whole point. He's never claimed to be anything *else!* It's his followers that make the grandiose claims! And his victims!" She took a deep breath and expelled it. "Which now includes me."

"What we need to do, then, is to make you more sceptical."

"I don't really care what you think the solution is, so long as we stick together. Are you married? How old are you?"

"I'm forty-seven. And I was married, yes. It didn't work out. Listen, we may, or may not, become friends – though I admit, so far, I've enjoyed your company – but I try to keep a firm boundary between work-related things and non-work-related things. One of the reasons my marriage collapsed is, I ignored the dividing line."

"And you see me as the former?"

"It's not about 'seeing you' that way. You came to me in my capacity as a police officer, and asked for my help. The friendship offer came later and, as far as I'm concerned, it was purely incidental."

"Could I stay with you overnight? I mean, on a friends-only basis?"

"If you think it's necessary. I'm staying in an Airbnb on Balaclava Lane, about a mile away. You'd have to sleep on the sofa. And I'd have to include that in my report."

"I'd need to sleep in the same room as you. Even if that's on the floor. Let's exchange numbers."

We got our phones out. "How do you see all this ending?" I asked. "I mean, you're involved with gangsters, you think Samhain knows about you, you think *he* might kill you, or *they* might. That's pretty serious trouble. You must have a plan. Other than just sticking to me for the rest of your life."

"I'm hoping 'sticking' to you will give me time to think of a plan. And two heads are better than one."

We sat in silence for a moment. She scrolled through her messages and laughed.

"What's so funny?" I said.

"Just looking at hashtag-Roddy-Samhain. The vicar's just taken him a slice of cake and a few biscuits on a plate, under some cellophane. Then he read him a bit of the Bible. 'And there was a great company of publicans and others that sat down with them. But the scribes and Pharisees murmured against his disciples, saying, Why do you eat and drink with publicans and sinners? And Jesus answered, They that are whole need not a physician; but those that are sick. I came not to call the righteous, but sinners to repentance.'"

"It's a courageous gesture," I said. "I don't expect Samhain appreciated it."

"If only there was some way we could find out what he wants."

I scoffed. "Samhain? Presumably, fame-stroke-adulation. The prestige of being the undisputed leader of a modern counter-culture."

"Yes, that's what CLP thinks. It thinks most of his followers believe he's essentially a good guy; that the nasty bits are just directed at boring conventionalists. And that he's latched on to that, and he's playing to the gallery."

"Assuming his followers are totally deluded, that sounds reasonably plausible."

"Really? It would be very rare. Think of just about any counter-cultural hero you've ever come across. They're always accumulating tons of cash in the background. Alternatively, if they're genuinely not interested in money – and I admit, such people do exist – they're idealists. They never shut up about their vision for the world."

"Yes, I see your point, I suppose."

"Roddy Samhain doesn't fit either model. He's definitely not making money. He sleeps in ditches, he rarely washes, he probably doesn't even wipe his bottom, and he's got no interest whatsoever in telling politicians how to run the world, or even other people how to live. Sorry, fame can't be his motive."

"Your belief, then – let me get this straight - is that, if you could find out what he wants, you could provide it, and maybe he'd leave you alone?"

"Lame, I know, but you've got to admit it's the *beginning* of a 'plan'."

"You mentioned him being 'inside your head'. What exactly has he done to you?"

"It sounds trivial to say 'bad dreams', but I'm scared to go to sleep tonight. Or ever again. And I've got the creepy feeling he's standing right beside us now, listening to everything we're saying."

"Okay, well, in the absence of fame and money, *I've* no idea what he wants. Or *could* want."

"I believe he's been sent by God."

I hooted. "I'm not religious, but I'm prepared to go out on a limb and say I can't see a loving deity sending us someone like Roddy Samhain!"

"Can you find ten righteous men in the city of Sodom anymore? I doubt it. Even the nicest of us is pretty self-centred when the cameras are turned off. I don't think God hates us. But I think we've reached a point where he thinks it might be a good idea to give us a taste of our own medicine."

"Sorry, you've lost me now. I'm an atheist and, as I said earlier, I'm a Roddy Samhain sceptic. He may not be making bold metaphysical claims on his own behalf, but I'm sure that's because his followers are doing that for him. And don't tell me he's not directing them - "

"He isn't."

I frowned. "You sound pretty certain!"

"What do you think will happen to the vicar? You called him 'pretty courageous' earlier."

"I won't tempt fate by speculating. Something bad."

"Do you honestly think this is the first time Roddy Samhain's ever posed in a churchyard? Or the first time a priest's ever seen that as a pretext to show him a little kindness and do a bit of preaching? Nothing's ever happened to any of them before. And he's got no interest in Satanism or the Golden Dawn or Wicca or any of that."

"He's certainly shown no interest in *Christianity!* You're surely not suggesting that you'll be safe from his whatever-they-are – magic powers? – if you become a *Christian?*"

"I'm a practising member of The Ethiopian Orthodox Tewahedo Church, thank you, and no, that's not what I'm saying. Not at all." She laughed. "Because that's my whole *point,* dummy: maybe he's been sent by God."

The conversation had long since taken a crazy turn and I'd run out of things to contribute. "Your English is very good," I told her, for want of a better pronouncement.

"Thank you. I learned it from YouTube."

We fell into a glum silence. She'd already invited herself to stay with me. It suddenly struck me that I might find myself looking after her for the rest of her life. She'd explained her predicament clearly enough to suggest it didn't admit of a quick solution. She definitely didn't know what to do about it.

Yet I couldn't abandon her. I needed to think, hard.

Okay, so she was obviously obsessed with Roddy Samhain, and she was frightened of him. The best way to help her was perhaps to –

"You've had an idea," she told me. "It's a good one."

"How did you know?"

"I've been watching your face. Go on."

"I'm trying to see things from your point of view here, so I'm temporarily suspending my 'Roddy Samhain scepticism' for pragmatic reasons. So, you need to go to him in the churchyard, bow down to him, and publicly ask his forgiveness. Then you need to give the gangsters back their money. Then you need to send them a message explaining the situation, then you need to go into hiding for a while. I can stay on the scene as your spokesman, in case they want to send you some sort of message."

"You mean, like a horse's head."

"Something like that."

"Or *your* head."

"I'm a policeman. They'll be inviting trouble if they come after me."

She shrugged. "I'm not as scared of them as I am of Roddy Samhain."

"The goal would be to extricate yourself from all your obligations and any conceivable possibility of blame. The question is whether Samhain's generous enough to forgive you, even if you beg. My feeling is, it's a long shot. From what I know about him, he's pitiless. More so than any mere gangster."

She sat up. "Yet it *could* work, couldn't it? Yes, it's worth a try. I'll need to go and see him on my own, and I'll need another drink. Or two. I can't afford for him to see you. If he *can't* look inside my head – although I'm sure he *can* – then we need to keep you out of sight. Especially since I'm staying at yours every night for the next two months."

"Er, hang on..."

"Or less, if this works. Don't forget, he hibernates from December to the end of September. No one knows where he goes. We'd need to team up in twelve months' time, same time and place. And every future year. Until he dies, maybe."

"I don't *live* in Wadhurst," I said. "I mean, I'm not a resident. I just stay here while Samhain's around. Then I follow him. The longest he's ever been here in the past is four days. There's never any telling where he'll go next. You don't really want to be following him around, do you? Not if – best case scenario – he's forgiven you."

"Don't forget, the gangsters might come after me. And that's the last place they'll think of looking: wherever Roddy Samhain is. And you said you'd protect me from them. I need to be with you."

I don't know how we'd reached this point. It seemed both outrageous and completely natural that here I was, having a conversation with someone I'd never met before about how we were going to spend the indefinite future together; not even in a romantic way: as a police officer and a fugitive. What was happening to me?

She waved her hand in front of my eyes. "Are you all right?"

"I think you should go and ask Roddy Samhain's forgiveness first," I said, "though I can't believe those words have just come out of my mouth. Buy a candle, if there are any to be had. What am I saying? There are always candles to be had, once he's here."

"Okay, I need you to come with me to the pub. I'll buy you a drink there. Afterwards, I'll buy you lunch, if we can find a table. Or we can get something from a van. A burger, maybe, or a pizza. Or both, if you're hungry."

She'd obviously pegged me as the classy type. We crossed back over to The White Hart. She insisted I join her in something alcoholic, so I had a whisky and soda. We made arrangements to meet at the bus stop by The Greyhound in half an hour's time. She went off to buy a candle.

I ordered another coffee. As soon as I was alone, it struck me again just how offbeat all this was. Like someone was setting me up for something. She hadn't seemed like a villain, but they never did, and in one sense, she actually was a villain: she'd teamed up with a bunch of gangsters to blackmail someone. Even more weirdly, I didn't even know her real name.

Oddly enough, it was that last detail that calmed my nerves. The first thing a con artist does is give you a plausible name. It's one of the most important ingredients in building trust. I don't know why she'd thought 'Stephanie Forsythe' would be any good. Or why she still hadn't supplied her real name, or even pretended to. If she really was a con artist, she wasn't a very good one.

Maybe she was just one of the many oddballs that turned up in Wadhurst when Roddy Samhain was around. If so, there was a good chance I might never see her again. No deep loss, although, as I think I've already intimated, I'd enjoyed her company. I'd chalk it up to experience and get back to the grim business of shadowing.

I finished my coffee with an increased feeling of heaviness. Somehow, whether or not we ever clapped eyes on each other again, I already knew she hadn't been successful. Considered rationally, how *could* she be, with Roddy Samhain presumably committed to complete motionlessness for the foreseeable? I'd been looking at the whole thing through the prism of her – mental instability? Should I call it that?

I walked the hundred or so yards to our arranged meeting place outside The Greyhound. I'd give her an hour. Best to err on the side of caution.

Ten minutes later, I spotted her as she emerged from Church Street into St James Square. Her face already told me everything I needed to know. Unequivocal failure. I got up and crossed the road briskly to meet her.

She linked arms with me. We began to walk away from the village centre along the Lower High Street. She didn't speak, but I could tell she was shaken.

Finally, when we'd covered about two hundred yards, she stopped, put both hands on her knees and took four deep breaths.

"He's utterly determined to destroy me," she said. "It's just a matter of time."

III.

We spent the rest of that day together, hardly speaking. We ate lunch, or I did: for obvious reasons, she wasn't feeling hungry. We didn't see Roddy Samhain again. I heard that he was still in the churchyard. We went back to the house I was staying in at 5.30, having spent a miserable day mainly traipsing back and forth from one end of the village to the other. I sat her on my sofa and made a speech about rationality and self-fulfilling prophecies, the gist of which was that she had nothing whatsoever to fear from Samhain; her worst enemy was herself. "He can't get in and hurt you," I told her. "But he can make you ill with worry. He could even make you inflict harm on yourself." It was only as I said these words that I realised I was the wrong person to be talking to her. She needed a psychologist.

"I know what he *is* now," she said quietly, as if she was telling herself. "He's a living ghost."

"A what? Sorry, ghosts are dead people. How can they be living? It's a contradiction in terms. Quite apart from the fact that they don't exist."

She smiled like she felt sorry for me. "A normal ghost is a bit like a flickering lightbulb. It's a slowly collapsing remnant of a person's consciousness. A living ghost is fully conscious."

"Only, dead."

"Not dead, no. They've never been alive, and they can't ever become alive. At least, not in the sense you or I are. Apart from that, I don't know what they are. Or how many of them there are. Or where they come from. That's all I know."

"It's tosh. Where on earth did you even get it? I assume it's some internet theory."

"You can try looking for it online, but I doubt you'll find it. No, I got it from him, today. As I told you, he's inside my head." She chuckled. "I'm resigned to my fate now. You and I should go out and enjoy our remaining time together. Or stay in, with a big bottle of brandy. I'd like to be oblivious when the axe falls."

"You're quite the drinker."

"I know. Wouldn't you be?"

"No, because I pride myself on not believing in nonsense."

"On the bright side," she said miserably, "I don't have to drink anyone's blood. I don't think I could face that, although I suppose everyone says that at the beginning. Joke. I'm joking. I know there are no such things as vampires: I'm not that stupid. No, I'm just going to be killed, that's all. And I'm a believer, and I haven't ever really hurt anyone, so I'll probably go to Heaven and live in glory with Jesus Christ. At the very worst, I'll spend a few hundred years in Purgatory, assuming the Catholics are right. What's a few hundred years, really? I can't see me going to Hell. I don't think that's very likely at all."

"You're rambling. You're not going to die. He can't get you."

"He already has."

I suddenly felt incredibly sorry for her. As well as seriously out of my depth. I stroked her hair and took her hand. It felt like trying to comfort a child. "You need to talk to a mental health professional. We'll find one for you tomorrow."

She laughed.

I managed to dissuade her from her bottle of brandy, although I briefly considered conceding on that front. Not because I thought it would be a good idea for either of us to get blotto, but because I thought alcohol might calm her, and possibly even help her get a good night's sleep.

I wrote my report, describing my meeting with her, and logged it into the system at Scotland Yard. We went to bed at 10pm after watching five episodes of a comedy on Netflix. I couldn't let her sleep on the floor, and the third bedroom had a double bed, so we slept in there. I didn't want to complicate matters even further, although I was beginning, as I later realised, to care for her in a more than professional way, so I discreetly laid out the 'ground rules' – effectively, a make-believe bundling board - without implying (I hope) that I considered her some sort of sex maniac. She seemed more than happy.

At two am, I awoke to the sound of her crying. I switched on the light and tried to rouse her with the reassurance that it was just a bad dream.

But I couldn't get her to wake up. I tried putting the pillow behind her and pulling her up into a sitting position, but her head lolled and she continued groaning. Tears spluttered from her eyes like they were being forcibly ejected. She started to call out in distress, and ten minutes later, she was yelling. I still couldn't rouse her, and I knew it was only a matter of time till the neighbours knocked on the front door (I would have), wanting to know what was going on. I dialled 999 and asked for an ambulance.

Ten minutes later, the neighbours knocked. I told them what was happening. Their annoyance turned to concern and they came inside, but they couldn't help either.

Fifteen minutes after that, the ambulance arrived. I followed in my car. We went to Pembury hospital and separated at the entrance, when they wheeled her away into the Emergency section. I went to wait in reception. When the receptionist asked me how I was related to her, I said, 'partner'. An hour later, they discharged her. They'd done all the relevant tests and they couldn't find anything wrong. She hugged and kissed me and cried, and we went back to my car.

On the way back to Wadhurst, I called into a 24/7 and bought a big bottle of brandy. We drank it in the kitchen. After three drinks, she relaxed, then she became emboldened.

"You don't blend in enough," she told me. "Before very long, people will get to know you by sight. The New Age Travellers, I mean. Then they'll twig you're a cop."

"I've got a cover story. I'm an academic. I'm following Roddy Samhain with a view to writing a paper about him for *Sociology Today*."

She laughed. "That's lame. Besides which, why do you think it's going to endear you to anyone?"

"Well, it's better than 'cop'. What's your suggestion?"

"It's not a suggestion. It's a done deal. I've got lots of money, remember? I've bought us a van."

I chuckled nervously. "Er, wait a minute. A *van?* How?"

"Online, of course. While I was in hospital. I won't go into details. With the money I got from the gangsters. It's all settled."

"Oh, my God. That's not money you should be using, is it?"

"We can pick it up tomorrow." She laughed as if she'd only just noticed how hilarious it was. "Don't worry. Chief Inspector Havisham will understand. That *is* his name, isn't it? Your boss?"

"How did you know that? I mean, it's completely beside the point, but - "

"We need to sleep. *You* need to sleep. Let me take charge from here."

I was too drunk to care what she meant. We went back upstairs, lay down apart in our former positions on the bed, and probably passed out more than fell asleep. I had a dream in which all that screaming earlier had imbued her with a magical power which also deposited her somewhere on the wrong side of sanity. I kept repeating, "A *van?* You've bought us a *van?*" She tried to ignore me for a while, then she looked deep into my brain and said, "Roddy sent me to seduce you. I'm not real. I'm just one of his servants."

I jerked awake. Daylight. I rubbed my eyes. Her side of the bed was vacant, with nothing to suggest it had ever been occupied. For a second, in the hinterland between sleep and reality, I wasn't sure she even existed.

Then I remembered: the obligation to look after her, the screaming, the hospital, the van she'd supposedly bought, the full bottle of brandy we'd drunk.

A complete mess, on one interpretation. And yet ... it could have been a lot worse. It could have been someone I didn't like.

Strange thought.

My head throbbed, my stomach felt like a small furry animal had climbed in there, and to aggravate matters, I had the depressing feeling it probably wouldn't be my last bottle of brandy this week.

I made the bed with an effort, and went downstairs.

But she was nowhere to be found. A handwritten note lay on the kitchen unit.

> *Thank you for everything you've done. You can't save me. The best possible outcome now is that my end comes quickly. Roddy's calling me to be with him, and if I do as he requires, I can get off easily. Quick, not slow and painful. In case you don't believe me, I'm going to Great Ayton in North Yorkshire. I am only telling you because I know you've been briefed to follow Roddy, and so you'll soon be there anyway. If we catch sight of each other, please ignore me. I wish we could have been together. I was really, really getting to like you. Don't be sad. See you in Purgatory. Yours, V.*
>
> *PS. £20 for the brandy. And thank you again for everything.*

There was a twenty-pound note on the table.

I went to look out of the front window. My car was still on the drive, although she could easily have stolen it: the keys were hardly in a vault: they were on the very visible hook where I always left them.

I got my laptop out and went to Facebook, then Twitter, then the Roddy Samhain live cam.

He was still in Wadhurst churchyard. He certainly hadn't relocated to 'Great Ayton', wherever that was. I checked my list of his past locations. He'd never appeared in a 'Great Ayton' before, although Google Maps confirmed its existence. North Yorkshire.

Last night's eruption probably meant she was mentally ill. She needed help. God knows what had put Great bloody Ayton into her head.

I called her mobile. It went straight to voicemail, as I half-expected. I told her she wasn't safe, we had an agreement, to which I was now fully committed, she needed to ring me back as soon as she got this, I *wanted* to help, etc.

After I'd hung up, I went into the living room and plonked myself disconsolately on the sofa. I'd been left alone with nothing to do. The last twenty-four hours had been unbelievably intense. Those two things, combined, had created a situation highly conducive to obsessive brooding. And perhaps that wasn't accidental: *Roddy sent me to seduce you.*

It suddenly struck me that she was attractive. Or had I merely been *told* that by the nightmare? Or should I use the term 'dream' instead? Would it have *become* a dream if I'd stopped going on about the van, and succumbed to her powers of seduction?

Or was *I* really the one who wanted to seduce *her?* Well, disturbingly, maybe, yes: your unconscious reveals things in dreams that you're otherwise reluctant to admit to yourself, doesn't it? Or that's one theory. And she hadn't given me the slightest reason to believe she *was* a seductress, so the best interpretation was that part of me *wanted* her to be one.

I was lurching about from idea to idea more perversely than if I'd still been drunk. On the one hand, I was Mr Rationalism, so of course, she wasn't a succubus: how the hell could anyone be something that didn't exist? On the other hand, Wadhurst was full of New Age crazies whose influence I'd never felt before, but which seemed to have succeeded in reaching me through stealth; through her. Insanely, I found myself wondering if she could have slipped a 'love philtre' into my brandy last night, so I'd wake up besotted with her. And if, in running off coquettishly to 'Great Ayton', she'd somehow activated it.

In the end, Mr Rationalism won. He was bound to: you can't change the habits of a lifetime. When I stripped away all the superstitious garbage, however, one thing remained: for some reason, I'd begun to feel emotionally attached to her.

But of course, even at this point, I can't have been *fully* Mr Rationalism. Not as fully as I'd always been before, because I didn't consider cutting my losses and focussing on the job. I was probably a quarter in love with her now, if that makes any sense. But I also felt morally obligated, and I was fixating. A heady mix, guaranteed to intensify my involvement.

My job required me to keep a close eye on Roddy Samhain, and he was definitely in Wadhurst churchyard right now. However, 'Violetta' was clearly having some sort of breakdown, and surely she'd realise, once she got to North Yorkshire, that there was no Roddy Samhain there? If I could persuade her to see sense, I could quickly bring her back. Then we could get psychiatric treatment for her. I could help her convalesce. Given her, *I wish we could have been together, I was really, really getting to like you,* which fully mirrored my own sentiments, anything was possible. My mind was racing. I felt feverish, and perhaps thanks to that, strong enough to do anything.

It took me less than an hour to make up my mind. It perhaps shows how far my emotions were becoming captive that, by this time, Violetta (I might as well call her that) meant more to me than shadowing Roddy Samhain, and, really, what did I expect Roddy Samhain to do anyway?

And I needn't be acting unprofessionally. Violetta would obviously interest Interpol. She was arguably our strongest ever lead to the dark heart of the enigma that was Samhain.

But I'd protect her even from them if I had to. I honestly didn't know what was happening to me, and the more time passed, the less I cared. Looking back, I think I'd always been a fairly bloodless type. Now, suddenly, I'd been shot by Eros. And since I wasn't used to it (he shoots some people on a frequent basis, I believe), my reaction was off the scale. But still well within the bounds of normality for that sort of thing. Nothing supernatural. No love philtre, succubus, 'Roddy's servant'. Nothing unprecedented in human history. Just a dead man – me - who didn't even know he was dead, coming alive again at speed. It probably happens all the time.

I got in my car and set off. As usual, there was an inexplicable hour-long queue on the M25. On the M1, I stopped at Watford Gap services for a cup of tea and a baguette. It was three o'clock when I got back into my car. I went to Facebook and Twitter, since they were always the most reliable means of keeping tabs on Samhain.

It turned out he'd disappeared. No one knew where he'd turn up next. It might even be somewhere else in Wadhurst: he'd done that before. But the travellers were tentatively packing their things, and they'd been right nine times out of ten in the past.

I pulled off at every single service station after that and went straight to my newsfeed. At five o'clock, the 'first sightings' started appearing. Hesitant at first, as usual, then more confident, then certain. The travellers left Wadhurst beeping their horns and leaning out to wave goodbye.

They were heading three hundred miles north. Destination Great Ayton.

IV.

Admittedly, when I heard where it was, I had to do a rethink. Maybe she wasn't so mad after all. The policeman in me resurfaced. Surely, there was only one place she *could* have got it: Roddy Samhain. Which meant the two of them were working together. So maybe I *was* being set up for something, after all!

On the other hand, why even mention Great Ayton? Why thereby *alert* me to the fact that they were working together? Added to which, by the time I arrived, it would be common knowledge anyway. What advantage could they conceivably get from briefing me in advance?

In short, the policeman in me gracefully shrugged his shoulders and lay back down. As far as I could tell, the central dilemma hadn't altered. She needed saving. When I'd first met her, she'd needed saving from Samhain; then she'd needed saving from herself (or so I'd reasoned); now she needed saving from Samhain again.

Because yes, he had to have told her. And if it wasn't psychically (as she seemed to think), but literally, in the churchyard when she'd been to see him (as was really the only rational possibility), the problem's kernel was identical. He was manipulating her, and she needed an ally. All things considered, that was easily the soundest hypothesis.

Obviously, I arrived in Great Ayton well in advance of the travellers, but not in advance of hundreds of his more respectable fans. I managed to park on a grass verge, about a mile from the village, on the long road to Captain Cook's monument. Samhain was doing his living statue on the green opposite the parade of shops. How he could have travelled three hundred miles between one o'clock in the afternoon and when I arrived, at six, and still found the energy to strike a physically demanding pose, no one seemed to have asked.

And that 'no one' included me. Honestly, I couldn't have cared less about Samhain: my only concern was to find Violetta. About half an hour after I'd arrived, I learned that he'd abruptly abandoned his performance. He'd repaired to a pub about a mile further down the road.

And it was there that the first of several catastrophes struck.

V.

The next few days passed without me tracking her down. Every time I arrived on the scene, I was half an hour too late. I got several garbled versions of what was going on, from a variety of different individuals, but no fully coherent account. She quickly got a reputation as a 'nutjob'. She did crazy, but not very interesting, things: what more did I want to know?

Some people were more helpful than others, but no one, in the whole time I was there, had more than a fragment of the whole picture. What follows is what I've been able to piece together.

She arrived in Great Ayton two hours before Samhain – she probably came up by train, then bus – and rushed to see him when she heard he'd appeared on the green. There, she begged his forgiveness again. But this time she didn't stop. She became increasingly effusive, and, predictably, the crowds began to find her more entertaining than him.

Eventually, she stopped being funny. She was jeered. Samhain cut his performance short with obvious irritation. He went to a local pub. He sat down with a group of local 'troublemakers' (my witness's word, not mine) who plied him with drinks and nervously pretended to be his friends.

Violetta appeared an hour later. She tried to carry on where she'd left off on the green. Samhain – or someone with him - attacked her 'savagely' when she came too close. A fight nearly broke out when two women, otherwise unconnected to events, tried to come to her rescue.

The landlord called the police and an ambulance. Samhain was arrested; Violetta was taken to hospital, although I think she must have been more shocked than injured. The paramedics sedated her to control her heartbeat. Forty minutes later, the doctors announced that they could find no physical evidence of assault (despite the supposed 'savagery' of the attack), and Samhain, who was sitting impassively in a police station without a lawyer, was released without charge at 9pm.

Violetta recovered from the sedative and discharged herself from hospital without telling anyone. I arrived there thirty minutes after she'd gone.

I lost track of her until three days later, and once more, the news came too late. After she left the hospital, she made her way back to Great Ayton. According to what I've heard, she'd taken to dancing everywhere, which cemented her reputation as a crackpot. It should have made her easier for me to find. It didn't.

Within a day, she'd managed to ingratiate herself with a small band of New Age Travellers. From their point of view, she had as much reverence for Samhain as they did (they'd undoubtedly heard about her performance on the green), and, to make things even better, she was obviously 'mad'. You've got to understand that the 'mad' have an inbuilt credibility in certain radical circles, probably the drip-feed influence of tomes like *The Divided Self* and *Madness and Civilisation*. They painted her face green, put laurels in her hair, cooked meals for her, gave her their clothes to wear, and a warm, dry place to sleep. I can't fault them. I know they worshipped Samhain, but, speaking with the benefit of hindsight, never was a nicer group of people more misguided in its loyalties.

Inevitably, she found her way to Samhain again. This was the morning of 7th October, about 10.30. The sun shone and a warm breeze stroked the grass. He was performing another of his living statues on the green. Possibly, since she'd interrupted the first one, he hadn't got it out of his system.

The moment she arrived, the crowds parted to let her through. They seemed to recall the woman who'd put on such an entertaining show four days ago (or perhaps they just felt sorry for her). I don't know how they recognised her, or whether Samhain did, because she looked completely different at this point: apart from all the makeup and greenery, she wore a peasant's smock and she was barefooted.

A few people said they noticed Samhain flinch when she first entered his field of vision. She was quietly singing a very old English folk song. Fourteenth century, I believe.

There's all for thee, and none for me
And though this age now ends,
We'll hang ye up from the old oak tree
And that way make amends, my friend,
We'll gladly make amends.

This time, she didn't get down on her knees. She drew a twelve-inch kitchen knife and rammed it into Samhain's ribcage. According to the post mortem report, he died instantly.

VI.

The assassination of Roddy Samhain created headlines everywhere. For an entire day, the world went into a news-gobbling frenzy. Everyone wanted to know how and why he'd died and, much more than that, who was responsible. Obviously, his self-appointed representatives on social media – those who'd loved him most, although perhaps chiefly for the money he'd helped them make – did their best to whip the outrage to a peak. Mainstream Social and Cultural Affairs Commentators spoke diplomatically about his profound influence on certain classes of people: radical environmentalists, New Age Travellers, the rebellious young, inveterate outsiders.

As so often happens when a celebrity dies unexpectedly, he became much more in death than he'd been in life. Obviously, a dead person can't turn around and bite your hand off, which is why critics often discover how 'truly great' an individual is only after he or she is definitively out of the way. And obviously, they want to assimilate themselves to the person in question. It takes a genius to recognise one: that's often the hidden subtext.

But two days later, much of the excitement had died down. It turned out Samhain – though a hugely 'influential performer' – had never been as popular as some people thought. By definition, disaffected classes and outsiders find it difficult to sustain the solidarity necessary to keep a controversial evaluation afloat, and taking advantage of that, more conventional, common-sensical opinions gradually rise to the surface and eventually come to dominate. Samhain had been a bit of a nuisance, and, in the broader scheme of things, his death was no real loss.

Obviously, Violetta was arrested and charged. As soon as she'd rammed the knife home, a group of valiant bystanders wrestled her to the ground and kept her pinned there till the police arrived. She made no attempt to struggle and she declined to speak. A legal aid team was brought in at short notice, and advised her to do what she was already doing. But she wouldn't speak to them, either.

By this time, I was hard at work marshalling evidence to prove I was her partner. I'd been seen with her in Wadhurst; I'd filed an official police report mentioning her; my Airbnb neighbours could testify that she'd spent the night with me; I'd accompanied her to Pembury hospital and described myself as her 'partner' there; she'd written me an affectionate farewell note; I'd sent her several texts telling her I was looking for her in Great Ayton. No one else seemed to want her, and it didn't take long for the authorities to rubber stamp my claim.

I dismissed her legal aid team – not because they were incompetent, but because I wanted to control the situation - and hired my own. I told them nearly (but not quite) everything I knew about her.

Her Italian Twitter account, though now defunct, yielded her real name: Violetta Abate. She really was called Violetta! And her birthplace: Reggio Calabria, in southern Italy. And her age: forty-one. Her parents had moved to Ethiopia ten years ago, and couldn't be traced. She had no siblings. Lots more information surfaced, none of it detrimental. She'd studied at Exeter University, twenty years ago, and she'd spent ten years working as a PR consultant in Plymouth before returning to Italy. Like me, she'd been married. Like me, it hadn't worked out. Her former husband had married again, and no longer wanted anything to do with her. Most importantly, she had no priors.

I didn't tell the lawyers about her agreement with the gangsters. Instead, I called the offices of City of London Parts. I told them who I was. I subtly indicated that I knew all about the money, and that if they wanted it back, I was the person they'd have to deal with. They made contact two days later via a solicitor. I obtained the number of the Swiss bank account from Violetta. I provided CLP with assurances, through their representative, that she would never tell anyone else about her deal with them. Without once appearing in person, they expressed regret that things had turned out the way they had. My lawyers arranged for the repayment (without needing to know what it was for), and City of London Parts shut up shop for good two weeks' later.

However, despite my best efforts, I was pretty sure that wasn't the end of it. I'd bought us some time, that was all. They were gangsters. Revenge was their speciality. In the long run, they'd do everything in their power to extract it, and if (or when) it came, it wouldn't be pretty.

The trial date quickly arrived. Violetta pleaded guilty, as, obviously, she had to. What surprised me was that, on the day she was sentenced, a group of New Age Travellers turned up outside the courtroom, and played their olde worlde music as she was escorted from the prison van to the door. They even gave her a little cheer. Weirdly, they seemed to have forgiven her. I've already said they struck me as good people, a little piece of Chaucer's Harry Bailly in the modern day. It may have helped – though obviously it could hardly have been decisive - that she still insisted on dressing like them whenever she could.

Sadly, they may have been the only ones in the entire world who felt well-disposed towards her. The internet was bulging with practical tips on how to kill her. She received a daily sack full of death threats through the post. I took care to vet them, just in case there was anything compassionate or encouraging, but I always ended up putting the whole lot in the bin.

Thanks to her lack of previous convictions, and the expert testimony concerning her mental health, the judge sentenced her to just five years. Because she wasn't considered dangerous - and I think partly (though no one ever said as much) as a consequence of prison overcrowding – the Ministry of Justice agreed that she could serve her sentence at a secure private hospital in Devon. My offer to meet part of the costs may have helped. But I was aware that my money was limited. I couldn't see it lasting five years.

While this was going on, there was a parallel court case concerning Samhain's dead body. In the complete absence of traceable parents, siblings or relations, a small group of his New Age followers, including Mildred Lughnasadh and Jennifer the Anabaptist, claimed it as theirs. A GoFundMe page raised them two hundred thousand pounds for lawyers. On the opposing side, the authorities claimed there was a good chance that, should the travellers get their way, they would dispose of the corpse illegally. After all, they'd already declared their intention to bury it in the woods outside Wadhurst, and they refused to budge.

Yet in the end, a very reluctant compromise was reached: Samhain's body was transferred to a certified crematorium for immediate incineration; the travellers got his ashes to deposit in the woods. His 'funeral' – the scattering, accompanied by prayers to all sorts of gods, goddesses and demons, but oddly replete with Christian motifs – attracted over twenty thousand people and temporarily blocked the roads around Wadhurst for about seven miles.

My life's goal became nursing Violetta back to health. Strange how such a fleeting acquaintance – we'd only been together for a day before the murder – could have brought me to this point. But it had. Strange as it might sound – or maybe it doesn't - I was in love with her. The emotional bonds had all been expertly forged; all that remained now was to consider the practicalities.

I couldn't afford to resign from my job, and I was too young to retire. My colleagues mostly didn't like the fact that I'd attached myself to a convicted murderer (however much they might have despised Samhain), so my workplace relations were difficult. I took a desk job and a demotion in return for a relocation to Devon and more free time. I moved into a caravan so I could free up funds and be closer to the hospital. A typical day involved me nine to five-ing, then getting a takeaway, then going to see her.

The doctors were open-minded and caring enough to appreciate that my visits would probably have a positive effect on her. In exchange for the occasional 'intelligence briefing' (only when it was in her interests, they assured me), they agreed to extend my visiting hours. I usually sat with her from six till nine, although even that wasn't set in stone. I won't go into precisely how we got there, except to say it was a surprisingly smooth journey, but by this time, we regularly talked about how much in love we were. She did a lot of reading, but in the evening, she was usually worn out, and so I would read aloud to her. Her favourite text was *The Imitation of Christ*, especially that long chapter entitled, 'Of the King's Highway of the Holy Cross'. *Thou art deceived, thou art deceived if thou seek any other thing than to suffer tribulations; for this whole life is full of miseries and signed on every side with crosses.* A lot of that sort of thing. And for some reason, she also loved *Sir Gawain and the Green Knight*. Two months into her sentence, in December, we were married by a prison chaplain.

The hospital regime was designed to maximise the service users' (that being the approved term for patients) prospects of recovery. She got a job tending the vegetable garden, which she normally did, with four others, in the mornings from eight till midday. Lunch lasted sixty minutes. Counselling sessions took up the next two hours, then 'hobbies', which could be anything at all within reason (she chose drawing), then meditation. There were twenty service users in all with a range of different disorders. Some occasionally became angry and had to be restrained. Others sometimes threatened to kill themselves. But strangely, they all seemed to find Violetta calming. Because she was so 'helpful', the managers allowed her the indulgence of painting her face occasionally, and putting foliage in her hair. I don't know why that gave her any pleasure, but it did.

Another month went by, and the doctors told her she was obviously recovering. Nevertheless, on the outside, she still had truckloads of enemies. Two women broke in one night, armed with hunting knives. They were apprehended only when they were almost on her doorstep. The next day, the *Daily Express* published a two-page account of the incident. The hospital's senior administrator had already announced a security review, but it was accelerated to minimise the PR damage. Someone on the inside had obviously leaked information about where to find Violetta. Four days later, the culprit – a middle-aged woman with a penchant for Snakes and Ladders – confessed and was transferred to another institution.

Meanwhile, the failed assassins told their high court judge that, so long as they lived, Violetta Abate's days were numbered, and if they didn't get her, others would. For a while, Her Majesty's Prison and Probation Service debated whether to move her to another institution. The eventual verdict - though no one ever put it in these terms - was that she'd probably be no safer elsewhere.

By February, I think she'd mainly recovered from whatever she'd been suffering from in Great Ayton. I say 'mainly' because there were still grey areas: beliefs she held that weren't quite consistent with a clean bill of mental health. For example, when she heard about the two armed intruders, she claimed she'd never been in the slightest danger: she couldn't be killed, at least not by any of Roddy Samhain's followers. Secondly, whenever we talked about the few days leading up to her attack on Samhain, she insisted that he had actually given her *clues* as to his whereabouts that day; that she was the 'good' to his 'evil'. Most egregious of all, however, was her claim that Samhain wasn't actually dead. Since he was a living ghost, he could only disappear.

In terms of me gainsaying all this, it didn't help that she still had a trump card: well in advance of even his most ardent followers, she'd actually known he was in Great Ayton. How could I explain that? Well, I couldn't. I'd long since given up thinking he might have told her. Why would he have? And, really... how?

Anyway, that's why I said, above, that she'd 'mainly' recovered. Is 'mainly' a colossal exaggeration? That's probably not for me to say. It was a leap year that year, so the twenty-ninth gave me an entire unwanted extra day to think about it, but, in fact, all I did that whole month was go round in circles. I'll let the reader decide.

By March, my funds were more or less exhausted. I tried in vain to get NHS England to cover more of the costs of her treatment through its 'special commissioning budget'. The doctors backed me, but without success. I attempted, and failed, to secure a bank loan.

I had to prepare Violetta, so I broached the subject as gently as I could one windy evening at the beginning of April. When I'd finished explaining, she seemed much less concerned than I thought she'd be. She kissed my hand. "So long as we've got each other," she said.

But by this point, something even more ominous was beginning to trouble me. Sooner or later, she'd be released. She'd probably be sent back to Italy, and I'd have to follow her. Or at least try, depending on the vicissitudes of EU immigration. Even with a visa, I'd be a foreigner, with uncertain rights to remain. The gangsters would resurface, but obviously they wouldn't be the only ones out to kill her. At the bare minimum, we'd need to go into hiding. At worst, we'd have to keep moving. That sort of thing isn't easy, and it's far more expensive than it sounds. Even with the best luck in the world, we'd probably get cornered eventually.

Alongside all this, the incursion of her two would-be killers had had the unintended effect of publicly announcing her whereabouts. That might sound like a bad thing, but actually, it turned out to be the opposite. You may remember that, on the day of her trial, she was greeted by a band of New Agers with music and a cheer. I still couldn't get my head round that, but it turned out it wasn't a one-off. After the *Daily Express* report, which laid everything bare, a whole lot more of them set up camp outside the hospital gates.

The Chief Administrator initially threatened to disperse them with a court order, but in the end, I persuaded him their presence might not be a bad thing. I'd learned from a journalist friend that, for reasons which struck us both as obscure, they regarded Violetta as Samhain's successor. (Possibly, she'd announced herself as such in Great Ayton?) In any case, they were here for her protection. They began lighting candles, burning incense and leaving Tarot cards for her: 'The Empress'. Violetta seemed to know all about them without being officially told. But perhaps that's not surprising. There are hundreds of ways news can travel, even in somewhere as apparently well-regulated as a prison.

Perhaps thanks to all this, however, I began to have dreams in which she was slowly *turning into* Roddy Samhain. When I awoke, they always seemed less risible than I'd have liked. Had I believed in magic, they might even have appeared vaguely reasonable.

Her mood fluctuated. Some days, she seemed very depressed, at other times, elated. Shortly after I spoke to her about our financial worries, I won a large sum of money on the back of some premium bonds I didn't know I had. I was euphoric for about six hours, then disturbed. I wondered whether she might actually have magical powers, after all. I still couldn't explain how she'd known Samhain was in Great Ayton. When I broke the news to her, she said she wanted me to buy a house in Wadhurst, because that was where we were going to live when she came out.

At that point, I wished to God I'd never spoken. But afterwards, Wadhurst became a fixation, and talking about it, the only thing that seemed to cheer her up. She wanted to get married again in Saint Peter and Saint Paul; she wanted to go for long walks to Bewl Water, to Ticehurst, to Mark Cross. She wanted to eat at The White Hart, The Greyhound, The Piccolo café. In the end, I had to play along. She still had four and a bit years of her sentence to run. We'd tackle the appalling subject of deportation later.

After April, the doctors decided we could walk together in the garden. Daffodils and wood anemones gave way to ragwort and willow-herb as spring became summer. Summer reached its zenith in blue skies, warm breezes, and twenty kinds of birdsong, and then dwindled. September was all drizzle. On the first of October, Wadhurst played host to about two thousand hardcore Samhainians, there to 'pay their respects'. It rained hard all that day. Bunches of flowers were laid in the places he'd appeared. Dedicated men and women trudged the streets and the public footpaths carrying covered candles and looking solemn. Such was the deeper indifference, however, that the next day, they'd all gone: people and flowers.

The seventh day of the month – the anniversary of his murder – was next. No one really expected much from that. The fan club had made its point and got cold, wet and tired for its efforts. The general prognosis now was that he would fade further and further in the collective memory.

I booked a holiday for that day. I wanted to be with Violetta in case she had some kind of relapse. I mentally rehearsed the possible scenarios as I drove to the hospital: the newspaper reminder, the TV reminder, the personal reminder, the self-accusation: how each might appear to her on a sliding scale of viciousness. I must admit, I was nervous. I didn't ever enjoy talking to her about our impossible future in Wadhurst, but I thought I might have to deploy it, just for this one day. I got there at nine. We sat alone in the lounge with a pot of tea between us, and a cream scone each, and talked about world affairs and the weather.

At ten-thirty, she took a sip of her tea, smiled at me, and said: "It was exactly a year ago today – to the very second – that I stabbed Roddy."

I'd already decided to play it philosophically. "Things have changed a lot since then."

"A few things. Not the important things. The seasons come and go. People are born and they die. All things pass. He's forgiven me, you know. Roddy, I mean. I couldn't possibly be sitting here, otherwise. Remember, that's how you and I met. You advised me to go and tell him I was sorry. And you were right. Just as you're right now: a lot *has* changed since then. I'm totally safe now."

I smiled noncommittally. She obviously had no conception of the problems that lay in wait for both of us. But at least she wasn't having a relapse. And the way she kept referring to Samhain by his first name, as if he was a friend? Yet maybe that's what he was becoming now: her imaginary comrade. I wasn't sure I'd be able to compete. But we'd got through a lot of problems over the last twelve months. This was the least of them.

We talked for another hour and a half. I was only permitted to remain on the premises for three hours each day, and, just after twelve, one of the orderlies came to escort her away. I kissed her lips lightly.

She squeezed my hand. She beamed. "It's finished," she told me. "Everything's about to come to an end. We're going to be all right."

"I hope so," I said, expressing the opposite of what I really thought. As far as I knew, there were no really good outcomes to our situation.

But at least she felt optimistic, and we were parting on a positive note. Visiting hours were over, anyway. There wasn't any more I could do today, no matter what. I put my coat on and walked to the exit.

Then disaster struck.

VII.

A mellow male voice: "Excuse me, could I have word before you leave?"

I turned around. The Clinical Director himself, Doctor Laghari. Tall, about fifty, with deep set eyes and a stubbly beard. He wasn't smiling. "While you're here, could I have a word?" he repeated. "It's very important."

I could already tell it wasn't good news. 'A word', said unsmilingly, usually means someone's going to pour a bucket of excrement over you.

I followed him into his office, a small room with two filing cabinets, a utilitarian bookcase, and a view of the grounds. He went behind his desk and tersely asked me to sit down.

I hoped he'd get straight to the point. He did. "How would you react if I was to tell you we've decided to release Violetta?"

Bloody hell. In the few seconds between the corridor and here, I'd tried to guess what he might want, but I hadn't anticipated this. For a second, I wasn't even sure whether it was good news.

Then the penny dropped: it definitely wasn't. "She's only done a fifth of her sentence," was all I could manage.

"The doctors here believe she's now cured. The probation service believes she poses no danger to the public. Taking those two things into account, the Ministry of Justice has decided to release her on the condition - which obviously isn't up to her - that she goes straight from here to Heathrow airport and leaves the country. The Italians have agreed to take her back. They'll meet her at their end, in Turin."

"Hang on, this sounds like a done deal."

"She'll be leaving in a week. That should give you time to make preparations."

I laughed bitterly. "What about those women who broke in here and told her they'd kill her?"

"It might interest you to know that they're both dead. They died within a week of each other in circumstances that, however suspicious it might look that they died separately in quick succession, don't seem to require an actual murderer. Accidental deaths. *Freak* accidental deaths. I believe she may also have had a few enemies in Italy. They're dead too. I'm talking about high level gangsters here. Do you know anything about that?"

"Of course not. What makes you think she might have anything to do with gangsters in Italy?"

"Only that, about two months ago, we received a large envelope from Messina in Sicily. It contained a collection of photographs – of the now dead individuals, as it turned out - and a message: 'please tell Signora Abate that everything relating to Roddy Samhain has now been completely destroyed'. The police questioned her about it at the time, but she claimed to know nothing. She may or may not have told you. If you know anything about it, you should probably tell the police."

"Why didn't the police question me themselves?"

He scoffed. "Not even the Italian police care that a bunch of Mafioso have died in a series of freak accidents, however interesting such events might appear to someone of a philosophical bent, someone intrinsically interested in matters of chance, coincidence, contingency, etcetera. The British police care ten times less. In my opinion, when they questioned Violetta, they were merely going through the motions. And even that, very reluctantly. However, as I just said, if you know anything, you should probably contact them."

"What's going to happen to her when she gets to Italy?"

He shrugged. "As I believe I mentioned a few moments ago, she'll be met at the airport. The police might well decide to tag her, just for a while. That's up to them."

"Will I be allowed to accompany her?"

"On the plane itself? I very much doubt it. But there's nothing to stop you going to Italy, and being there when she arrives. Since you're married, and it's obviously not a marriage of convenience – I can, and will, vouch for that, by the way, if necessary – it might even be possible for you to bring her back to live over here. Given her criminal record, however, and the way the government feels about immigrants generally, I wouldn't be too optimistic about that. You could go and live over there, but ..."

He tailed off. A bunch of people were shouting, outside, in the grounds.

Because I was facing the window, I caught sight of the whole thing while he was still in mid-flow. Five or six New Age Travellers – all young women, as far as I could tell - had broken into the garden, and were attempting to storm the main building. The security guards had arrived, but they were having difficulty catching them, let alone restraining them.

No, my mistake: two women had been wrestled to the ground now. One other was being accompanied somewhere with both arms twisted behind her back.

But more were flooding in. They were all yelling something at the tops of their voices.

Doctor Laghari got to his feet. "Excuse me," he said wearily. He twisted round and threw the window open. I don't know precisely what he intended to do, because we never got that far.

For the first time, we could hear what all the commotion was about.

"He's alive!" the nearest woman bellowed at him. *"Get Violetta! GET VIOLETTA! TELL HER HE'S ALIVE!"*

For the first time, I saw that none of them were angry. They were all yelling the same thing. And they were ecstatic.

VIII.

At seven o'clock that morning, a man and a woman in their late sixties were hiking in a mature pine wood just outside Wadhurst. Both wore anoraks and stout shoes, and carried trekking poles. A light mist had fallen overnight, and they were walking briskly because they were cold. They came to a fork in the way. To the right, the path led up a gentle incline; straight ahead, it descended a little. In between stood a huge pile of old, apparently neglected logs, each about eight feet long, blackened by the weather and dotted in places with fungus. The couple already knew which way they wanted to go because they'd followed this route several times before.

Suddenly, there was a loud creaking, of the sort a tree might make as it collapses. They looked up and nearly died with fright as a man appeared on top of the log pile.

Yet it wasn't merely his sudden appearance that struck terror into them, but its manner. It was as if he was entirely solid, and he'd been raised into an upright position by an invisible cord.

It took them a second, no more, to realise what they were seeing. The living statue of Roddy Samhain. That grubby jester's costume, that beard, that parody-of-a-cross posture, that manic grin.

Because he'd risen so artificially, both assumed it must be a trick, although they were badly shaken. In any case, if it *was* a trick, where was the perpetrator? The presence of an invisible, completely silent, prankster was no less frightening than the too-horrific possibility that it was exactly what it appeared to be. They took a few hasty photos to prove later that they weren't hallucinating, then frantically rang a friend. Ten minutes later they were on the main road. Their emergency contact picked them up and drove them safely back into the village.

The news that someone had erected a life-size model of Roddy Samhain in the woods quickly spread, and was greeted with rolled eyes and sighs. Inevitably, however, people came out to investigate. A consensus quickly formed that culprit was an expert craftsman: whatever one might think about the morality of scaring an elderly couple like that, the effigy was undeniably Roddy Samhain's double.

Then someone climbed up the log pile and announced that, actually, oh my God, it was a *real person*.

And suddenly, the whole world was interested. The performer, whoever he was, remained completely motionless for two days. The crowds maintained a respectable distance, but someone (I don't know who, or how) finally got hold of something that permitted the experts to do a DNA test. And which - after several days, but a lot of people had made up their minds long before that - proved conclusively that the man on the log pile really was Roddy Samhain.

All things considered, it was an even more amazing feat than Houdini's burial alive in California, in 1915. No one could begin to guess how he'd pulled it off. His body had lain in a morgue for six days while the authorities wrangled with a bunch of New Age Travellers for its possession. It had been 'cremated'. Yet all smoke and mirrors, apparently.

Obviously, an innocent woman had spent a year in prison, but equally clearly, she was his accomplice - 'The Empress' - and so she had to have been complicit in her own incarceration. Either way, she'd definitely needed psychiatric treatment, which she'd received *pro bono*. In short, no harm had been done, and she probably didn't have any legally valid grounds to sue.

A day later, Violetta Abate was released unconditionally. She'd received a few death threats in the past twelve months, but no one wanted to kill her now. No one would have dared.

I picked her up on the morning of her discharge and took her straight to Wadhurst. We were just in time to see Roddy Samhain before he left for some other location. He kissed her on the forehead. Afterwards, he went to St James Square and temporarily blinded a group of teenagers.

IX.

A lot of this story has dealt in radical uncertainties. I still don't know who Roddy Samhain was, or is. I don't know how Violetta knew he was in Great Ayton. I don't know how he apparently came back from the dead. I don't know about all the deaths of bad people along the way, although I'm genuinely sorry they *are* dead.

What I can say is that it ends more happily than one might expect. Today, Violetta and I live in Wadhurst. We married again in Saint Peter and Saint Paul, just as she wanted; and we frequently go on long walks to Bewl Water, Ticehurst, and

Mark Cross. We try to make the most of our remaining time together.

Because the world's end *is* coming. Despite all the uncertainties, everyone knows that now. The jester, the harlequin, the pierrot: they'll survive; others may not. Meanwhile, the sky darkens, the wind picks up, crows gather anxiously on high rooftops. The crunch could come at any time. Any time at all.

Who knows where we'll all be then?

Acknowledgements

This book would not have been possible without two outstanding others:

Victorian Wadhurst: Glimpses of Our Past, Wadhurst History Society (The Ink Pot, 2005);

Wadhurst: Town of the High Weald, Alan Savidge & Oliver Mason (Meresborough Books, 1988).

As regards place-names in and around Wadhurst, where there are two alternatives, I have tried to pick one and stick with it. For example, Savidge & Mason, above, have "Wood's Green", as does Google, but other authorities – most estate agents, some online maps, and much local signage, as far as I can tell, have "Woods Green", without the apostrophe.

I would like to thank my wife for proofreading the first draft, and for her helpful suggestions. I would also like to thank Lynn Hallbrooks for her final, very meticulous proofread.

Read More by James Ward in Cool Millennium!

The Bright Fish

Something's not right aboard the cruise ship *Aurora*. Yet that's probably what you would think when you're with the girl you love and everyone else is about fifty years your senior. You're three thousand miles from home, young, and high on emotion. Maybe it just ratchets up the sense of adventure.

And yet perhaps something really is wrong. There's the passenger everyone thought was dead, but who reappears one evening in the lounge without comment or explanation.

And eighty-year-old Celia Soper who reads Tarot cards, but only for 'the history of the world' … whatever that means.

And then, of course, the disappearances. Which, apparently, only you two have noticed.

Above all, there are the bright fish, creatures the size of dolphins that materialise unexpectedly, at intervals, alongside the hull, glowing with indescribable colours. And which never seem to inspire the sort of delight one might expect.

The Bright Fish deals with the meaning of love, and life, and ultimately, death. Are we always essentially alone, or is true interdependency possible? Is death our beginning or end? Or both?

Conversely, is the truth stranger than we can possibly imagine?

The House of Charles Swinter

Charles Swinter is eighty. When his estranged wife dies, he decides to go to Thailand and find a bride. He's not ready to die yet. Not by any means.

Edward Grant, his best friend, is young enough to be his grandson. When the old man goes missing, Edward travels halfway across the world to find him.

Yet what happens next is not so straightforward. The demands of conscience, murder, mental disturbances, reports of ghosts, a sham marriage, wrongful imprisonment, a slew of irreversibly changed lives.

The House of Charles Swinter is an epic romance. It concerns human dignity, the relationship between the sexes, goodness and beauty, poverty and wealth, globalisation, tradition and modernity.

And one man and woman.

The Kramski Case

When someone starts assassinating paparazzi in three countries, MI7 sits up. Apparently, the killer is none other than Dmitri Vassyli Kramski, retired SVR field-operative and former Kremlin protégé. True, the Cold War is long finished, but everyone knows Vladimir Putin is as unhappy for Russia to play second fiddle on the international stage as even the most strident of his Communist predecessors. In 2010 therefore, East-West relations remain as tortuous as ever.

Kramski's trail leads deep into London's émigré community, forcing his pursuers into conflict with an unknown organisation bent on protecting him. Bit by bit, he begins to look less like a professional assassin and more like someone plotting to scupper the foundations of Western democracy itself. To compound matters, the Russians are as baffled by him as anyone.

The Eastern Ukraine Question

A cabal of Russian oligarchs instigates unrest in the far east of Russia as the first stage of an attempt to unseat Vladimir Putin. Britain offers covert support in the form of five MI7 agents. The disturbances mirror those in Eastern Ukraine and, if pushed far enough, might persuade the Kremlin to retract its territorial interests in Donetsk, Luhansk and Zaporizhia.

However, once the five operatives are shipped east, events take an unexpected turn. One by one, they begin to disappear.

Enter Grey Department's John Mordred, by grudging consensus, MI7's best agent. Young, idiosyncratic and a linguistic genius, Mordred prefers diplomacy to battle, doing the right thing to defending the realm.

Yet he won't necessarily duck a confrontation. Especially when the lives of his co-agents are at stake.

Which – given the job description - they usually are …

Hannah and Soraya's Fully Magic Generation-Y *Snowflake* Road Trip across America

Hannah and Soraya are in the business of making rock music with a social conscience. The way Britain currently works, that means they're 'snowflakes', 'social justice warriors', 'virtue signallers'. They've learned to live with the mudslinging, but not happily. Worse than that. It's starting to overwhelm them.

Then, out of the blue, they suffer a string of personal and professional crises.

Their solution? A change of scene designed to keep the lid on a looming family cataclysm and draw artistic inspiration from the pre-musical roots of rock (but without the Beats' misogyny, plus in an eco-friendly car).

Books by James Ward

General Fiction

The House of Charles Swinter
The Weird Problem of Good
The Bright Fish
*Hannah and Soraya's Fully Magic Generation-Y *Snowflake* Road Trip across America*

The Original Tales of MI7

Our Woman in Jamaica
The Kramski Case
The Girl from Kandahar
The Vengeance of San Gennaro

The John Mordred Tales of MI7 books

The Eastern Ukraine Question
The Social Magus
Encounter with ISIS
World War O
The New Europeans
Libya Story
Little War in London
The Square Mile Murder
The Ultimate Londoner
Death in a Half Foreign Country
The BBC Hunters
The Seductive Scent of Empire
Humankind 2.0
Ruby Parker's Last Orders

Poetry

The Latest Noel
Metals of the Future

Short Stories

An Evening at the Beach
Wadhurst Ghost Stories

Philosophy

21st Century Philosophy
A New Theory of Justice and Other Essays

Lightning Source UK Ltd.
Milton Keynes UK
UKHW010216091022
410145UK00007B/408

9 781913 851545